BITTERSWEET REVENGE

A DARK MAFIA SERIES

AGOSTINO CRIME FAMILY BOOK FIVE

DAHLIA REIGN

Copyright © 2024 Dahlia Reign, LLC

This book is a work of fiction. Names and characters are the product of the author's imagination and any resemblance to actual persons, living or dead, is entirely coincidental.

All Rights Reserved. No part of this publication may be reproduced, stored in a retrieval system, or transmitted, in any form or in any means–by electronic, mechanical, photocopying, recording or otherwise–without prior written permission.

Cover Image: Rights reserved for Dahlia Reign, LLC

Editing: Pagan Proofreading and Editing

Formatting Images: Shutterstock.com Rights Reserved

Cover Creator: 3Crows Author Services

https://www.instagram.com/3crows.author.services/

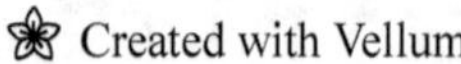 Created with Vellum

DEAR READERS,

DARK ROMANCE IS MY SPECIALTY. THEREFORE, TRIGGERS LIE WITHIN THIS BOOK. YOU HAVE BEEN WARNED. XOXO, DR.

About the Book

Daddy painted her up like his little doll. Polished and pretty, she smiled as she waved at onlookers from her protective shelf. The public face of the Agostino Crime Family was made to appear innocent and pure. She was their weakest link and the pawn I'd use to enact my revenge.

The saying went "an eye for an eye" but that family had taken everything from me. When the west came to the east, it was our turn to leave blood on the streets. And I had a feeling her blood would leave the darkest trail.

I wanted to see the real woman who lay beneath that painted veneer. The woman who would be the catalyst to end the Agostino Crime Family. A monster, a beast, had her in his dangerous grip, and I couldn't wait to see how much she could take… before she cracked.

DEDICATION

Samandafer... Cheers to you bitches. In my twenties, I came alive. I was both my best and worst self—at the same time. To the booze, the bad decisions, and the epic chaos fueled by past trauma... We. Fucking. Thrived.

PROLOGUE
OCTAVIA AGOSTINO: PRESENT

When you got a tattoo, the needle punctured the skin between fifty and three thousand times per minute. Unlike a hypodermic needle, however, the tattoo needle didn't inject liquid when it sank into the vein. Instead, it released ink into the dermis, the outer layer of your skin.

The tattoo gun itself was an intricate tool that used a coil to make a "hammer" tap rapidly at the top of the needle. It attacked the flesh, marking it with what you hoped would be a beautiful design. It only went one to two millimeters into the skin, whereas a cut could be as deep as a simple laceration or as far as amputation.

This knife, presently afflicting the pain tearing through my body, wasn't intending to amputate. Its only intention was to cause pain and leave behind a permanent reminder that they'd marked me. One after another, he'd sliced through my skin. His deep, cathartic moans as the layers separated told me how much he loved hurting me.

One man to hold me down. The other to taint my olive skin. They said Octavia Agostino was her family's weakest link. Yet, if I survived, my silence would show my strength. I refused to be the catalyst for this war.

And I wouldn't be responsible for ruining my family.

"Your screams are turning me on."

My arms were pinned above my head, near his erection, as the other man sat on my hips, carving something terrible into my skin. The more I screamed, the more his hands shook.

"Please, stop!" I cried out, though I wasn't sure why.

They wanted my pain; they wanted my screams. Their only intention was destroying the Agostinos' most prized possession. They wanted to use my torture, my scars, to send a message to my father.

I shied away from the life of a mafia daughter, preferring books and my own company. The world—my family included—took my need for self-care as fragility. When in turn, the violence and blood that surrounded *il famiglia* created someone I couldn't control.

A monster. A fiend. Bloodthirsty and maddening.

Savagery gnawing just under the surface as my metallic life force dripped across the bedding. It was a scent you never forgot. A scent that lingered, no matter how many showers I took—much like the scars they left behind. With every drop, a creature that was cruel and twisted reared its dangerous head.

Let her loose. Let her tear her teeth through their flesh.

As the knife was dragged across my skin, I clenched my fists, wanting my attacker to feel the same pain he inflicted on me. My eyes rolled to the back of my head just as a voice that should've protected me now hounded me awake.

"Wake up!" he sneered. "Scream, bitch."

My natural reaction was to scratch at his face, the mask slipping. The man smirked down at me as realization fell between us.

One of my assailants was once a trusted friend while the other remained unknown.

"If you open that plush little mouth, flash those pretty little scars, I will dismantle *il famiglia*." His expression was stern, relentless. "One fucking word and I'll make you watch your father bleed out."

My father, Mario Agostino, was the head of the east coast branch of the mafia. He controlled everything from his throne in New York, though his empire was stretching farther and farther west. But even the New York *capo* wasn't invincible.

How had I never seen the evil lurking behind this man's eyes?

"Or I'll make you watch as your mother becomes my whore." My captor laughed as I cried. "Sell your sister to the highest bidder."

The strokes of the knife had slowed. The unknown man was sitting on my waist, seemingly entranced as my flayed skin continued to soak through the mattress. He didn't speak, just followed commands. I focused all my attention on him. I needed him to stop. My eyes penetrated through him—I wasn't above begging for my life—and his hand froze at my navel. The cold blade sat against my flesh while his eyes were a mixture of things that terrified me.

One part lust. One part emptiness.

"N-no more." My fight was draining rapidly.

"Shut up, bitch," the traitor barked. "Such a pretty red." His fingers ran through an open wound, eliciting a ragged scream from the depths of my lungs. My blood coated his skin as he wiped it across my cheek. I just wanted to sleep, let go of reality and beg for sweet relief.

Until he spoke once more.

"Enough. Now, take her."

My eyes flew open, flicking back and forth between the two men. My unknown captor pulled down my panties and a renewed fight took over as I kicked wildly.

The traitor's fist connected with my chin. "Fuck. Almost knocked her out." He laughed as my entire body lay limp.

The second man licked his lips, his lustful eyes lighting up as he pulled himself from his pants.

Let her loose.

"Please. Don't." It was barely a whisper, but his millisecond of pause gave me hope.

"Make her bleed *more*." The traitor slapped his counterpart's back.

And then he took another part of me.

The shriek that filled the air did little to stave the agony as he ripped through my innocence. My muscles cramped as he pulled out only to thrust back in, without concern as I begged him to stop, while I drifted in and out of consciousness and he kept up his assault.

The man taking my virtue *owned me* now. I was his toy, his possession. These two men had taken pieces of me I'd never get back. They wanted my screams, so I bit my lip to silence myself. They wanted to ruin my father, so I vowed to tell no one.

"Mario thinks the world of his precious little girl. Well, now, Daddy doesn't own you, princess. He does." The traitor slapped his cohort's shoulder. "See, son. Nothing is out of your reach. Bastard or not. She belongs to you now."

Son? No one ever told me he had a son?

That made my rapist thrust harder, faster. He punished me, sending a message. A deep growl tore from his throat as my pained body was pushed until he finished and tore himself free again. My insides felt like sandpaper. My brain finally shutdown and I was given a short reprieve. Only coming to randomly as I was moved around.

Bathed and bandaged. Like nothing happened.

Their treatment of the wounds was never meant to stop the scarring. No. They wanted me to remember what they'd done. Every day I'd see the marks they'd given me as payment for being my father's daughter.

He'd commanded me to keep quiet, but a part of me knew he wanted the war. This was done to send a message and the only gratification for the sender was when that message was received.

And I refused to allow that to happen.

The rapist's parting comments made my fractured mind officially crumble. "Every time you look down at your beautifully scarred body, think of me. Because you're all I think about." And then they were gone.

However, this… this was my secret.

This was my cross to bear for my family's sins. If they knew what had happened to me, it would just confirm I was as weak as they always assumed me to be. I'd show my tormentors that they were wrong for choosing me. My silence would prove they'd lost.

The wounds would heal, but they'd never go away. Nor would the nightmares as I waited for them to come back. The monster under my skin now had places it could seep out—begging to escape through the tattered remains of flesh.

I'd often felt something bubbling under my skin, a dark and disturbed presence. The story was told using the word "and" to break up the two characters… but what if beauty *was* the beast?

If these cowards wanted to take down my father, they needed to find another way. As much as they suffocated me, I'd die before I let someone hurt my family.

The Agostinos would continue to be untouchable even if my silence slowly killed me instead.

CHAPTER 1
OCTAVIA AGOSTINO: PAST

"What the fuck did you just say?" my older sister seethed as she stared down my bully.

Tatianna had grown up around us because of her father's political influence. Often attending the same schools and parties because of *our* father's power and wealth. Yet her family couldn't hold a candle to ours. She and her little minions, the typical mean girls in school, loved to prey on the weak. And that was me, how they saw me. Weak. My father raised my siblings and me with love; we had plenty of opportunity at our fingertips. He wanted to ensure we could handle *the life* our last name set out for us.

My brother, Lucky, took his position as eldest son as an honor and made it look easy, while Sienna was the female, outspoken version of him. Had she been born a boy, we all knew she'd have killed our brother for his place in *il famiglia*. Marco was the youngest and the most immature of us all. Where I shied away from attention, my little brother thrived in the spotlight—in his debauchery.

"Did I stutter?" Tatianna practically snarled in response to my sister.

We were forced to attend this birthday party. My dad and Lucky were off talking business with the birthday girl's father. Dad's best friend was standing beside them. We'd been raised with Riccardo always in the mix. Our Uncle Rick, as we called him, was practically family.

And then there was Sienna, one step in front of me, forever my protector. She knew I hated altercations, despised being the center of attention, and now several people were watching the commotion.

"Couldn't understand you past those fillers, *cagna!*" Sienna spit back while throwing out some exaggerated hand gestures.

Tatianna crossed her arms over her inflated chest, baffled and clearly at a loss for words. She wasn't the brightest; one could even say that her brain had been eaten away by plastic impurities that were slowly consuming her entire body.

"What now?" Apollo stepped to the group, staring at Sienna's aggressive stance. He glanced down at me, assessing my face with his cold stare. The enforcer was also my older brother's best friend, his number two. My father pulled him off the streets and he worked his way up in *il famiglia*. Besides that, he was my sister's unhealthy addiction.

As if hearing his approach and knowing her clock was ticking, Sienna moved. My sister gripped Tatianna by the arm and leaned forward to meet the girl's haunted gaze. "Go anywhere near her again and I'll knock your fucking teeth down your throat, bitch."

"Sienna, let her go." Apollo's order fell on deaf ears as Sienna raised her fist. "Sienna!" He caught her arm.

"*Fino alla prossima volta.*" Sienna snarled in Tatianna's face as Apollo pulled my sister back. *Until Next time.*

Tatianna licked her lips as she eyed the object of my sister's obsession. This bitch had a death wish. "Hey, Apollo."

Yup, the girl was begging to be murdered.

I clenched my hands into fists, my breaths coming out as soft pants. Seeing the flash of pain across my sister's face made me angry. Apollo was Sienna's weakness. He couldn't grasp her need for him and she didn't know how to let it go. Something stirred in my stomach as my blood simmered to life.

Violent. Angry. Needing to be set free.

Apollo moved between them. "Leave. Before she kills you." Sienna smirked at Apollo's quick dismissal of his would-be admirer. "And I will let her."

Al and Peiro, two of my father's men and my brother's confidants, stepped into the circle. They were loyal friends, tasked with protecting me and Sienna. Their arms were crossed over their chests, their silent threats looming in the air, as Tatianna batted her eyes at them before flouncing away.

"Fucking whore," Sienna muttered, making Al laugh. "Let's dance." Then she tugged me towards the center of the room, ignoring my obvious reluctance.

"Sienna." My skin burned bright red as all male attention turned on us.

"Come on! I've seen you in the studio. You can move! So, let's go."

Al and Peiro blocked us in, halting any outside advancements. My throat was dry and my limbs frozen in place. I'd often found reprieve at the studio, dancing away as the world around me became no more than a blur. I had no interest in taking ballet professionally, but I found it to be physically challenging.

Books and music. They were my thing. Constantly surrounded by noise and chaos, I found myself unable to breathe—choking on the all-consuming environment that was my life. I preferred dreamy men, whose passions unfolded within the spine of my books. Music and dance drowned out the noise from outside the pages. My mind was always active, but ballet helped to exhaust my body. Helped calm the storm within me.

As usual, I gave in to Sienna's demands. There wasn't a time I could remember that I didn't look to appease my sister. My body's natural rhythm swayed to the music and I ignored the world. When the song ended, only then did I open my eyes. And shelved my calm. The entire crowd watched in stunned silence. Mixed expressions spread throughout the room, and I wanted to die from the attention.

"My sissy is amazing," Sienna boasted before slugging Al's shoulder. He and Peiro nodded along, a smile plastered on each of their faces. One of a proud brother, the other with something I didn't want to press. This wasn't the first time I'd caught Peiro giving me *that* look.

People were still staring, whispering amongst themselves. That same feeling in the pit of my stomach returned, drifting up to my chest. My heart thrummed and something dark, sinister, yearned to make itself known.

I loved Sienna, but she never listened. She always got her way and it was *always* at my expense. I was nothing more than a pretty doll everyone liked to proudly display on a shelf—away from the real world. As if I'd break if you got too close.

"I-I'm thirsty," I mumbled before practically running from the dance floor while each curious gaze felt like a thousand knives piercing my skin.

"Here."

I looked up into Peiro's face and smiled abashedly before taking the proffered bottle of water he clutched in one hand.

"Thank you." Snapping the lid off, I practically chugged the contents in one gulp.

"You're so talented. Shouldn't be ashamed of it." Peiro's words held such conviction, but I couldn't agree less.

"I'm n-not ashamed," I whispered, reclaiming my seat at the family table. "I just prefer to dance alone."

Peiro nodded, standing behind my chair like a silent menace as we each eyed the room. People were curious creatures. While my family remained the center of attention, I sat in the shadows—

watching and listening. People didn't think before they spoke or acted. It was almost as if they were in a trance, feeding off the energy that spilled around them.

Movement caught my eye as I noticed Apollo and Lucky positioned at the edge of the dance floor. I laughed at the ridiculousness of these terrifying men in expensive suits standing amongst glittery pink decorations. The birthday girl opted for a theme befitting an adolescent Barbie doll even though she was long past the stage of playing with toys.

Slapping a hand over my mouth, I couldn't stop the cathartic laughter that loosened my nerves. My family mixed with the politicians and CEOs' daughters like our money wasn't drenched in blood. All thanks to my mother. She milled about the room smiling, shaking hands, and rubbing elbows with the elite. An enigma. Her background in the mafia went back several generations. Yet she moved gracefully and with purpose. My parents' beginnings were wealthy, but we sat as prominently as we did because of her. I envied the way she did it. It came so naturally. People flocked to the woman. They were enthralled by her every word, every move, every passion.

"She smiles." My father pulled out a chair, swatting away the pink confetti before taking a seat. "You move with the grace of a professional dancer when you let go."

I wanted to ask him: *Let go of what?* But I stayed silent.

My father, Mario, was a perplexity wrapped up in a designer suit, coiffed dark brown hair, and blue eyes that matched my own. He'd handed down his "cold steel-blue eyes" to each one of his children, making it impossible to deny his offspring. But the figure described on the streets as a calculated, murdering businessman wasn't the same one who had raised me.

I knew that side of him lurked under the fine threads of the Armani suit, but he never showed it to his daughters. He was a strong, hardworking, and loving father who wanted to hand me the world. At times, even smother me with it.

My father glanced down at the dress he'd handpicked for me to wear tonight. "You look beautiful. Are you having fun?" He smirked when I glanced away.

Let her loose. My fists clenched as my nails dug into my palms. *Breathe. In. And out. Smile pretty.*

"I know how much you hate these things. But I appreciate you being here. For me." He glanced over his shoulder, smiling adoringly at his wife. "And for your mother."

"I-I'm sorry."

My dad raised a hand to stop another apology. Only I wasn't going to apologize. Not really. I'd caved to my father's every demand and I hated it. I loved him more than anything—loved them all. But at what cost would I continue to allow them to shelter me? To quiet the woman I was on the inside?

"We all do things we hate to appease someone else. I'm here because of Samantha's father and our business arrangements. And you're here because you're my daughter. Bound by oath, but that does little to tamp down our wills." He patted my hand.

"Sara," I said, and his brows pinched in confusion. "Her name is Sara, not Samantha."

"Yeah. Her." My father laughed, looking at the girl in question, who had joined in on the gaggle of simpering halfwits surrounding Lucky. "Anyway, I wanted to say thank you for blessing us with your incredible grace."

"Wait." I grabbed his arm, when he rose from his chair, and swept a palm over his rear as a handful of glittery pink confetti fell to the floor.

"Christ. Isn't she older than you are?" he hissed, and I started to laugh as he aggressively brushed the glitter from his suit.

"It's a good color on you, Pops." Sienna grinned, joining the table with her usual bodyguard following closely behind her.

"Older than both of you?" Dad pressed. We nodded, and he shook his head. "Damn, I love you girls. Thank God you are both angels who aren't predisposed to pink… *madness*."

Our next bout of laughter drew the attention of my brother and mother. "What's so funny?" She floated towards us, wrapping an arm around me.

Have you ever felt like you were standing in the middle of a crowd, thousands of people surrounding you while you screamed at the top of your lungs, only to realize that no one had even spared you a glance? That was exactly how I felt around my family.

"Pink is your color, Pops." Lucky chuckled as our father flipped my brother off behind his back. Then, with an arm draped over our mother's shoulder, Dad guided her across the room to join the growing horde.

"This is… *something*." My uncle Rick approached the table a few moments later.

"Not your scene?" Lucky asked our uncle.

"I need a fucking drink." He stared at me for a moment, a strange expression on his face, before turning and walking off. Uncle Rick had always been… well… himself. A silent, brooding man, who had been glued to my father's side for as long as I can remember.

"Is this shit over yet?" Sienna growled, aggressively rubbing her temples.

"Wanna dance?" A guy I remembered from school approached the table with his hand out towards my sister.

"Mhmm," she replied while giving him what I liked to call her *shark* smile. Whatever she was up to, it wasn't good.

"She has a death wish," I muttered while glancing at Apollo's rigid form.

He remained at my side, his eyes focused on Sienna as her corpse of a partner swept her around the dance floor. Apollo didn't blink, his knuckles cracking as he more than likely envisioned what he wanted to do to the man who had his hands on my sister. He'd never mention this aloud—nor admit it to himself—but my brother's best friend was in love with our sister. Or whatever a man like Apollo could call *love*.

I looked out to the dance floor and saw her step closer to the boy who now had a target on his back. Then she looked over to the table, staring directly at Apollo. *That* smile was a challenge. Their push and pull was fun to watch from a distance, but it was a game neither of them would win. He was practically vibrating with anger, shaking his fingers loose at his sides.

"You could ask her to dance." He looked startled, almost as if he'd forgotten I was here. "If *il mietitore* is even capable of *asking*," I urged.

His normally stoic demeanor broke as he smirked down at me. It was rare, but Apollo's smile brought a human element to the man known as the *Italian Grim Reaper*.

"What're you doing?" Lucky stepped up to us, breaking me from my thoughts. "Under that quiet, peaceful facade is a devil worse than Sienna."

"There is one *diavolo* in this family and it's not *me*." I smiled shyly.

My older brother was known as *il diavolo*, the Italian devil. People were terrified of him. It was a persona he'd fought hard to create for himself. A statement that told the world he'd show no mercy when he took over for our father. He may have been the Agostino's prodigal son, but his ownership of the city was cultivated because of the man he was, and not because of the name he was born with.

"I need to talk to you about the Ragetti issue." My father motioned my brother to follow him.

"Fucking John Paul Ragetti," Lucky groaned before doing as he was told.

The Ragettis were creating chaos in California. The patriarch was insane and my dad was concerned that he'd turn his attention onto the east. So my family was keeping a close eye on their rivals. Apparently the lunatic had three sons Lucky wasn't too keen on.

"If that bastard tripped me one more time, *maldestro!*" Sienna flopped back into her seat and waved at a waiter, tapping her wine-glass with one of her perfectly manicured nails. "Thankfully, he held my waist *extra tight*." My sister winked at me, ignoring Apollo's presence at her back.

"*Lui e morto,*" he growled. Stepping around Sienna's chair, he stormed to the dance floor. I hopped up from my seat and snatched his hand before he made it to his intended target.

"Will you dance with me?" I asked, softly. His murderous brown eyes were filled with fire until he looked down at me, his expression immediately softening to nothingness.

Taking my hand, Apollo sighed before glancing over his shoulder one more time. "Your heart is too big to be an Agostino," he said, and I frowned. "Never lose it."

"I wish I could be stronger. I know what everyone says about me." I watched my family move about behind us.

"I've been on the other end of your left hook, Octavia. You have strength. You just use yours for good unlike the rest of us." He spun me out and brought me back against his chest again.

"We're only as strong as our weakest family member." Which was me.

Perché non possono aprire gli occhi? Their eyes were sealed shut to the truth. If they looked deeper… If they watched… If they understood… Maybe then they'd realize they were underestimating me.

"Your silence is only confused as weakness. We find our place amongst people who resemble the parts of us we are missing." Apollo glanced around the room.

"Sienna is the calm to your calamity. If you'd let her be," I muttered, my attempt at playing coy.

"Changing the topic, very psychological of you." Apollo spun me once more. "I'm sure you're familiar with the saying *a wolf in sheep's clothing*. Don't let the monster lay dormant for *too* long, Octavia."

My body went rigid. *Did he know?*

His mouth twitched as the song ended. "Now, I have someone to kill."

Before I could reach out for him a second time, Apollo disappeared into the crowd. If Sienna's dance partner had any self-preservation, he'd have fled already.

I headed back to the table, quietly taking my chair and listening to my family banter back and forth. Even in their worst moments, I loved each of them so much. And yet… They were suffocating me with their *protection*.

"You looked ravishing on that dance floor." Uncle Rick caught me off guard, standing at my back with Peiro at his side.

I smiled in return, too embarrassed to respond. "Excuse me."

When I stood from the table, the men rose with me. Just a few moments of peace. That was all I needed. These gatherings were too much for me, too loud, too busy. The solace I sought was separation from my familial obligations, my solitude. Constantly being around my family was sensory overload. Yes, they were loud, boisterous. But it was the attention they put on me—the demure, proper daughter of the illustrious *famiglia*—that was truly overwhelming.

The restroom door opened and Tatianna sauntered in with her usual flair. "Fucking tacky." Not even a second later, she was at my back, her minions blocking the door.

I did my best to ignore her as I dried my hands on a paper towel. Apollo's words were at the forefront of my mind. *Don't let the monster lay dormant.* Breathing slow and even, I stood taller and stared at myself in the mirror.

They're all so wrong about you…

"It's really a shame that your invitation was out of pity. Because of your daddy." Tatianna smirked, her puppets erupting into laughter. "No one wants you here, crybaby."

Let her loose.

"Then let me leave." My fists clenched as I cocked my head, stepping into Tatianna's space.

One. More. Word. That's it. Just one. Then I'd show them.

Our fronts were about to touch as I inched closer.

"Your sister isn't here to save you now, bitch." Her normal confidence suddenly lacked merit.

And I smiled. "What're you going to do about it?"

The flinch was subtle, but I caught it. My hands shook, clenching into fists at my side. My siblings were violent and outspoken. Under my silent façade, *she* was champing at the bit. Begging to gnarl her teeth, sink the sharp fangs into their flesh.

Anger swirled in the pit of my stomach. My chest felt tight and I was screaming on the inside. My teeth ground together and my control slipped away, shattering into a million pieces on the tile floor.

It was time they all learned who I was.

All the pain and anger that rattled deep within my chest came to the surface. A single, threatening glance had her eyes widening with fear. Girls like Tatianna just needed one good punch to send them tumbling off their pedestals.

Closed fist, cock, and release.

The audible crunch of bone against bone made me want to howl in satisfaction. Tatianna's head snapped back, and her pained cry was music to my ears. I grabbed at her collar and tugged her towards me, my fist raised and ready to strike again.

"You fucking whore!" The bathroom door swung open and my sister pushed past Tatianna's pack of lackeys.

And *she* returned to her cage the moment my hand dropped.

Tatianna was on the floor in a mess of bloody blonde hair and torn clothes. My sister sat on top of her, a tight grip on my bully's head as my sister screamed in both English and Italian.

The small space was suddenly filled with *made men* looking to take control of the scene. Apollo gripped up Sienna before barking for Peiro to tend to me, and Lucky was picking Tatianna up from the floor. My dad rushed into the room, demanding to know what happened.

"Take Octavia straight home," he ordered Peiro.

My anger didn't dwindle. If anything, it rapidly increased. My entire family looked at Sienna, seemingly amused by her assumed outburst, as well as with one thing I'd wanted more than anything— pride. Lucky and Apollo were men, so when they came home bloodied and bruised, the family was proud. Whereas if the chaos within me was unleashed, they'd lock me up. Label me certifiable. They had no clue about the madness I kept locked away.

It'd begged to be unleashed. To allow my hands and body to be coated in the blood of our enemies. The savagery I'd impose would startle them. Oh, how I looked forward to that day. The day I stepped out from the shadows and showed the world *who* I really was.

Lucky stepped out of the bathroom with a bleeding Tatianna under his arm. A broken nose, but otherwise she was fine. Yet she milked the moment by clinging to my brother like her life depended on it.

"Don't fucking help her, Lucky." Sienna, now rejuvenated, thrashed against Apollo's hold. "The bitch wanted to hurt Octavia."

"What happened?" Tatianna's father walked up to us, but his daughter wouldn't let go of Lucky. My dad ushered the politician to the side. The two stared between the three of us, their conversation short and angry.

"You just cost me a small fortune tonight, Sienna," Dad said, his authoritative tone a mixture of laughter and something else—no doubt it was pride over the fact that one of his daughters was tough.

"I'll happily write you a check because it was worth pummeling manners into that bitch." Sienna smirked at him, causing our tight circle to share a collective chuckle.

Sienna ran a successful software company that focused on surveillance, creating apps, building super computers, and developing insane technology that she patented, then sold to the highest bidder. She didn't hurt for family money, nor her own.

"Time to get you home. To rest." My father beckoned for me to follow Peiro.

As if I were so shocked by seeing my sister get into a fight—the damsel that I was—that I would need a nap. This wasn't *Gone with the Wind*. I didn't need a break from the party. My chest felt tight, like an elephant was sitting on it. My hands locked as I fought to flex them. Tunnel vision filled me as I struggled to breathe through the building anxiety.

Peiro placed a hand to my back. His aura of protection should've made me feel better. Instead, it tied him to the shackles of my familial obligations. Unable to do what I wanted, when I wanted.

The soldier was taller than my five-five frame while large muscles pulled his black suit jacket tight. He had dark-brown hair and matching dark eyes. He was always on alert and his ever-present attention annoyed me. He didn't stare at Sienna the way he eyed me. It was unnerving, like I was a mystery he couldn't solve.

I followed everyone outside, my chin practically resting against my clavicle. I was ashamed of the way I was treated and how I constantly tolerated it. My family passed around hugs and kisses as my car idled at the curb.

Their concern felt like heavy bindings, restricting my wings from taking flight. A knot of anger roared in my belly and I wanted to lash out. As we pulled away, I refused to look back. They thought they could protect me. But like every good mafia story, the next threat was just around the corner. Or, more precisely, two cars back.

"We have a tail," the driver stated. "Black Cadillac." He slammed his foot on the gas and we propelled forward, my body forced into my seat.

Peiro ordered me to get down, but I no longer cared if I lived or died. He rolled down the window, leaning out while firing shot after shot. My teeth were grinding, ready to break. They'd sent me home *to protect me* when all it did was paint a target on my back.

Bullets flew and the cars raced between lanes. The center of New York City traffic would bring us to a deadly standoff if we didn't end this now. Our opponent made the first move as their car connected with ours.

"Octavia, brace!" The SUV lurched forward, followed by the sound of crunching metal as we bounced in the air when the opposing vehicle collided with our rear. My driver was scrambling to maintain control, but it was a lost cause. Jerking the wheel to the right, he overcorrected, and we tipped onto our side.

The heat from the scraping metal warmed my cold soul. I'd never put on my seat belt and that was a big mistake. By the time we came to an abrupt stop, I was pressed up against the dashboard, barely conscious. As pain erupted across my entire body, I was consumed by anger. This shouldn't have happened. I shouldn't have been sent home.

Men moved around outside the car, and all I could think about was how I wanted to rip them all apart.

Peiro and the driver were both silent and bleeding. A piece of metal glinted at Peiro's side and I pulled the knife free as feet stomped closer. Climbing through the broken windshield, a large man blocked the sun above me while the blade remained tight in my grasp.

Show them your teeth are sharper than theirs.

And then everything went black.

CHAPTER 2

OCTAVIA AGOSTINO: PAST

"It was like she blacked out. I couldn't see what was happening, but I heard the shouting, the body dropped within seconds, and the fucker was bleeding from the neck." Peiro's voice sounded a million miles away.

"She did that?" My father seemed shocked.

"Had to be her. When she climbed back through the windshield, she was covered in blood and collapsed against me."

"I told you." My mother spoke barely above a whisper. And then there was silence.

Fluttering open my lashes, I yawned past the brutal headache pounding behind my eyes. I'd been returned to my room, where my family lurked in every corner. Their concern was misplaced and not appreciated. I'd gotten hurt because *they* sent me away.

"There she is. Hello, gorgeous." Sienna's smile was strained, forced.

My entire family was watching me with the same broken expressions on their faces. A mixture of concern, wariness, and—I glanced at a bruised Peiro—guilt.

Great. Just great. I could tell there was something I was missing, some detail I wasn't privy to.

"Tell me," I insisted, and they glanced at each other, waiting to see who would drop the imperial bomb. "Damn it! Stop acting like every little thing will make me shatter."

My father appeared apologetic, but he remained tight-lipped.

"We're going on lockdown." Lucky crossed his arms over his chest—my brother's word was meant to be law. Maybe to his men and the other members of *il famiglia*, but I was done being their puppet.

The Russians. The west. Rival families. Our list of enemies never came to an end.

"We or me?"

Instead of responding, my sister looked to the others for help. Their lack of answer confirmed what I already knew. The *lockdown* was exclusive to me. Sheltered and battered. The weak little girl, the most fragile Agostino…

I hated it.

No matter what was asked of me, I did it. They dressed me up, paraded me in front of cameras. I smiled and was courteous at every event my mother hosted. Happily stood on the arm of my father, the formidable mob boss. *Oh, but look at how sweet his daughter is!* I was the ruse that kept our secrets hidden behind closed doors.

My family started talking amongst themselves, almost as if I weren't there. As if I never had been. Sitting up in bed, I decided I was done being their pet sheep, constantly herded around blindly. The doll prominently posed and placed.

I pictured their stunned faces when they finally saw the chaos I could create. The words that had filtered into my subconscious stopped me.

She was covered in blood.

Was the *she* me? I thought I had dreamed up cutting those men into pieces…

I could feel their eyes on me. My mother almost looked proud—yet wary. My father was trying to act indifferent, but I saw the same wariness beneath his facade. Lucky had perfected his stoic expression, so he gave nothing away. It was Apollo who confirmed it.

I pushed to my feet, approaching him as he smirked in my direction. "Told you not to let her lay dormant for too long," he muttered under his breath, and that stopped the chatter as the rest of the room turned to glare at us.

My palms itched. My heart raced. I felt the pressure releasing from my chest as the urge to let loose loomed in the back of my psyche.

Show them. Now.

Instead, I slammed my bathroom door shut behind me and stared at myself in the mirror, only to be shocked at what I saw. Cuts and bruises marred every inch of my face but that wasn't what left me aghast. It was the blood. So much blood.

It was clear my family tried to wipe me down, but the aftermath was harrowing. How…

And like a flash of light, I saw it. Saw everything that happened after I blacked out and let *her* take the reins.

"Take her." A large shadow stood over me, while a deep voice barked at his back.

"Don't," I muttered, the knife tight in my hand.

"Come with me, now," the shadow ordered.

My pulse raced, my eyes remained focused, and I could taste his death. My jowls salivated and I was ready to tear through his flesh. Two steps and my hand swiped between us. A fine mist permeated the air, coating my face. The knife sliced through his throat and he dropped.

The man behind him had already turned and was walking away. More voices shouted as tires screeched in the distance, and I saw my father's men darting towards us. As if on autopilot, I climbed back into the car and everything went dark again.

I'd done it. I'd let her loose. And I felt lighter. Thrilled. Breathed easier.

Far too many years had passed since I've felt so at ease with myself. This house—this family—it was tainted. They'd barely spared me a glance as the walls crumbled around us. All because they didn't see me. The real me.

Once I was showered and dressed, I left my room and headed downstairs, but Peiro was quick to block my path. "I'd never forgive myself if something happened to you, and I didn't try…" He reached out a hand before dropping it again. "Octavia, I-I…" He shook his head.

"Relax. I'm fine."

The man had been following me like a lost puppy, while my attempt at reducing his guilt came out sounding agitated.

"I'm glad."

I smiled tightly. "Will you take me to the studio?"

He nodded, gently cupping my face. And then he was gone.

What was going on with him?

I walked into the kitchen and the conversation ceased. "Where are you going?" my brother asked me.

Silence was my answer before I turned on my heel and left. My sudden dismissal threw them all for a loop. I could hear them mumbling behind me.

Smiling at Peiro, I climbed into the back seat of the SUV. He closed me inside and made it to the passenger seat before his phone started ringing. As he went to place it to his ear, I snatched it out of his hand and disconnected the call.

"Drive. You can have it once we get to the studio."

The driver exited the compound through the gates, while Peiro was completely turned in his seat, staring at me with a mixed expression on his face. Lucky for me, his fast reflexes were hindered by his odd position, which meant that when he lunged for his phone, he missed it… again.

"Next time, it'll go out the window." I waved the device towards the open glass. It rang once more and this time I answered it. Lucky was none too thrilled when I told him what he could do with his orders. Damn, did this *new Octavia* feel good.

"Even sexier," Peiro muttered to himself, while I did my best to ignore him and the rest of the world.

With each mile placed between my family's overprotectiveness and me, my smile widened.

The studio was empty this late on the weekends. Everyone was usually here extremely early in the morning and out by the afternoon. By the time I dressed and stretched, I was the only one left in the building. Besides my brother's men of course.

My driver waited outside while Peiro guarded the door. Today, however, I noticed he stood just over the threshold. Trying to block him out, I began working on a new routine I was choreographing. I didn't dance for other people. I danced for myself. Several instructors over the years had begged me to join their schools, but it wasn't what I wanted. My goal was to learn how to dance ballet correctly to avoid hurting myself, then to just enjoy it.

My muscles shook and moved as I got lost in the music. The sweat dripping down my back spurred me on, pushing me harder. The song came to an end and I turned towards my towel draped across the bench.

Peiro handed me my water. "Your brother… he's… uh…"

"A controlling asshole?" My bluntness appeared to stall Peiro in his tracks.

He laughed before adding, "You surprise me every day."

I finished the water and wiped down my face.

"I like days like this," he said, breaking the silence.

"Days like what?"

"Where I have you to myself. It's nice to see you be… you." He stepped closer, lowering his mouth to whisper in my ear, "Like I get to see a part of you no one else sees."

"Huh…" I stared off into the distance for a moment. "Guess you really do. No one else has cared enough to come here. But this is your job."

"Lucky's been talking to me about being a captain." He shrugged. This was news to me. It was also a big deal. "Start my own crew."

"Congrats."

"I told him I'd be ready soon. I need more time with you."

"What? You… you told him that?"

No way did he say that… No way would my brother have actually listened…

"No, just that I had a few things going on. It could wait a bit." Someone had gone against my brother's wishes. For me. "My crew is coming together and waiting for me to step in."

I didn't know how to feel about that.

"You know I'll always protect you, right? Even if I get my crew, I'll still be there for you," Peiro said. I didn't respond.

The music switched to a slow waltz as Peiro tucked a loose strand of hair behind my ear. Reaching out, I accepted his hand as he pulled me against him. My point shoes made a slow sway difficult and uncomfortable. I resisted the urge to pull away, instead placing my head on his chest.

It was exhausting, constantly building up walls to keep people out.

For one singular moment, I felt… normal. Just a girl, dancing with a man. I wasn't the mob boss's daughter, and he wasn't a made man sent to protect me. We were just… ordinary.

And then his phone rang. It was loud enough to break the spell that this innocent silence caused. Peiro looked conflicted, but before he could speak, I headed back to the floor. We'd had a moment, but it was done now. If I allowed another, he'd get the wrong idea. He was handsome and kind, but not the man for me.

As the days quickly turned to weeks, I buried myself in work. No one spoke of my defiance, but I did notice they all looked at me differently. Or maybe I was just imagining it.

Either way, it felt damn good.

Until that night. The night those two men took everything from me. Everything in the name of their revenge.

And nothing. Would ever. Be the same.

CHAPTER 3

OCTAVIA AGOSTINO: PRESENT

"I can't believe he's engaged," Sienna said as she aggressively typed on her keyboard.

I was in my sister's office as she multi-tasked between gossip, work, and eating lunch with me. So much had happened to the family—to me—it almost seemed surreal.

Lucky was getting married to a rival family's daughter and our big brother appeared head over heels for the girl in the short time they'd known each other.

"I like her," I replied while picturing the mafia princess, who was the perfect pairing for my overbearing brother.

"Just because she's a book nerd." Sienna chuckled, not taking her eyes off her computer screen. "And you totally have the hot librarian look going on today."

My black silk blouse was tucked into my matching high-waist pencil skirt, while my red-bottom shoes were simple with a strap around my ankle and a tall spiked heel. My brown hair was wrapped into a high professional bun. I'd woken up late, so I was rocking my black-framed glasses instead of my usual contacts.

"Sir, wait a minute!"

My sister and I turned towards the sound of shouting, both rising to our feet as the door burst open.

They were here… They'd come for me…

It was the first thought to come to mind as the scars across my stomach burned to life. I glanced down, driven to check that the wounds weren't seeping through my shirt. They'd long since healed, but the terror seizing my lungs made me second-guess *everything*.

A large figure loomed in the doorway. *Him.* A beast of a man standing well over six feet. He was impossibly wide with muscles far too large to fit comfortably through the door.

"Carmine," I muttered as Sienna glanced at me questioningly.

We'd seen each other before. Met at random. A simple passing-by. Yet, for some reason, my sudden unease seemed to calm. As I stood a lamb in front of the lion, unsuspecting and naïve. The memories of our first exchange hit me like a tidal wave and I welcomed them to the surface.

I really didn't want to come, but if I didn't show, my sister would have been ticked off. Sienna was especially entitled on her birthday.

She was downstairs table dancing and passing out shots. I opted to forego those antics and hang out in our brother's VIP suite that overlooked the entire club.

"Why won't you let me help you?" Lucky asked while sipping his glass of dark liquor.

"Because I want to do it on my own."

My brother wanted to be my silent partner, to finance my new idea. It was a sweet gesture but no one in my family seemed to understand that I wanted something that was mine and mine alone.

He stared at me for several long seconds. My same blue eyes assessing me from my brother's face. "I can respect that. Just know the offer stands if you ever change your mind."

This was us, thick as thieves. And it was during moments such as these that I struggled with keeping my secret to myself. Their pain would be too much if I told them, and I refused to let those bastards win. They wanted my family broken. I wouldn't give that to them.

I watched my sister shaking her ass on an elevated stage, near the DJ booth, while struggling to remain calm as my eyes searched the crowd.

What if they were here? What if they were watching me?

I'd spent too long swallowing back my panic to allow it to consume me now.

I hadn't seen my attackers since the incident. The masked man remained a mystery to me while his accomplice had business elsewhere—his absence was barely noticed by the family. I promised myself that if he showed up, I'd spill all his dirty secrets. But he was a coward.

"Fuck." Lucky pointed towards the dance floor, watching on as his second-in-command shoved through the crowd towards Sienna.

I shook my head, concerned for anyone in Apollo's path. "He's pissed and she's drunk."

When would those two learn?

"Wish they'd either get together or leave each other alone." *Lucky drained his glass and tapped the rim at the bartender.*

"They'll figure it out one day. And it'll be the best love story—I'm sure of it." I could feel Peiro's eyes on me as soon as the words

left my mouth. "Or the worst kind of tragedy," I added on a laugh as Apollo stormed in our direction.

Since that day at the studio, things seemed different between Peiro and me, which had me wondering what our story would be… if we even had one. I had to admit I looked forward to our time together. There were still moments of indecision, when I was wrought with concern that he'd read too far into our interactions.

It was clear that my bodyguard was feeling a certain type of way towards me. However, the secret carved in blood across my stomach would never permit me a life of normality. Would never allow a relationship between me and anyone else, because there'd be too many questions that I'd refuse to answer.

I was fine being alone. It was all I knew anyway.

"You look beautiful," Peiro muttered as soon as my brother was out of earshot. "Thank you for the coffee."

I nodded in response.

Last week, I'd noticed that something wasn't sitting right with Peiro, so I'd asked to stop for a coffee, hoping I could pry it out of him. I ordered us drinks, then forced him to sit in a booth like a normal person and breathe for a moment. We'd shared lighthearted conversation that seemed to ease whatever burden was weighing heavily on his shoulders. And things seemed better since that day. Easier between us.

Apollo's abrupt entrance had me looking towards the door again. He ignored everyone in the room and made a beeline for the bar before wandering over to watch the crowd with a stiff drink in hand. I could feel his anger as he clenched the glass and focused in on my sister.

"A competent and self-confident person is incapable of jealousy in anything. Jealousy is invariably a symptom of neurotic insecurity," I muttered around my wineglass.

He stared at me for a beat and I thought I had him. "Robert

Heinlein? What're you reading?" Apollo asked, seemingly amused. "It's not jealousy when I see a potential threat."

"Hm," I hummed noncommittally. "Oh, is that not her security team taking control of things?" I attempted to hide my smile as I pointed towards the commotion breaking out below us.

Apollo portrayed a man of practical indifference—at least he tried. If it weren't for the clenching of his jaw, he might have succeeded. But I knew the man too well.

"I can read you like my favorite book." I giggled. "All of those thoughts racing across your mind don't have to come to fruition."

"What thoughts?" He sipped his drink while feigning ignorance.

"Imagining my sister with someone else. You spent so much time believing you're not capable of what she needs. But I need to ask... Have you met Sienna? She doesn't need a weeping man at her side. She's strong enough without your declaration of love. She just wants you."

He stared at me silently for a moment before setting his glass on the ledge. "Right."

"I know I've never experienced love, but I've read enough about it. After all these years, she understands you in and out. And even with all—" I waved a hand around him. "—this, she still wants you. But, hey, what do I know?" I hopped off the stool, offering my good-byes before heading towards the door.

"Thanks for coming." Lucky kissed the top of my head.

"I've got her." Peiro stepped up behind me, but Apollo shoved him back.

"I've got her." My brother's second-in-command motioned me out ahead of him.

I cautiously maneuvered my new heels down the stairs. The crowd parted for Apollo as he ushered me towards the door. The scent of sex, sweat, and booze made it hard to breathe as I chanced a glance at the dance floor. It was inviting. To stop for a moment, *take a twirl, and get lost in the music. My hips twitched, ready, if my mind would just give the command.*

For once, I didn't want to be the first one rushed out the door. I wanted to be like my sister, amongst the other partygoers, without a care in the world. But all thoughts of breaking my carefully constructed mold shattered the moment a firm grip on my arm thrusted me back. Apollo was vibrating with tension, clearly blocking me from someone's view. It didn't have the intended effect as the person in question stepped around my bodyguard to stare at me.

Holy. Shit. This monstrous figure was far more attractive and foreboding than any of the men I'd ever read about. Impossibly tall and wide. Covered in detailed tattoos while radiating the sort of violence that made my panties wet.

Fuck. Me.

The stranger's dark eyes lit with something I couldn't decipher. He took me in from head to toe while making no attempt to hide his intrigue. My body tingled, overly sensitive beneath the scrutiny of his gaze. I had to fight the urge to clench my legs together.

"What the fuck are you doing here?" Apollo's bark startled me out of my trance.

"Calm down, lap dog. Lucky invited me." The inverted cross on the stranger's face danced with his eerie smile. He was wearing black pants and a black button-down shirt that was rolled at the sleeves. Every inch of skin on display was covered in ink. His dark hair was gelled back in perfectly combed waves and his lips twitched as if he could read my mind.

"Then go to Lucky." Apollo motioned towards the balcony, pulling me tighter into his side.

"The youngest daughter," the man said and it wasn't a question. "I've seen you on TV and in the news, but not this beauty." He reached out a hand and I couldn't stop myself from shaking it. The moment our fingers connected, I gasped. The simple touch

caused an electrical current to crackle between us. "Hello, beautiful."

"Octavia, this is Carmine Ragetti," Apollo grunted while attempting to tug me out of reach. But Carmine held tight and the jerking motion had me stumbling on my feet. My bag hit the ground before I could stop it, and several books tumbled out between us.

"My heart be still…" Carmine snatched up the one closest to his shoes before I could stop him. "The Agostino secret has me intrigued." His eyes roved over my entire body as he spoke.

"Enough." Apollo shoved my bag into my arms and ushered me towards the door.

I chanced one last look over my shoulder, as he watched me leave, and I couldn't help but notice how his stare transformed from interested to… sinister. And for some odd reason, it made my heart beat faster.

Shaking my head, while trying to clear the memories, I stared into those same sinister black eyes. My sister watched our silent exchange with curiosity dancing behind her glare. "Sienna Agostino." She held a hand out for Carmine to take.

He turned to her for a moment. "We've met, Sienna," he ground out before finally releasing me from his dark gaze. "I suppose you wouldn't remember. You were inebriated on your birthday."

It was strange how many different sides there were to this man—a man much different from the one I'd met at the club.

Before me was a composed, Italian *uomo d'onore*. The same cockiness was there but it was presented in a more refined manner.

Why did I want to see every side of him?

"Hm." Sienna seemed to hum to herself. "And why're you interrupting my day with no appointment?" Then she motioned for Carmine to take a seat in front of her desk.

The chair groaned, clearly not accustomed to the man's larger frame. His expression was blank. Yet, somehow, I felt like he was cracking open my chest and reading my most personal thoughts.

I couldn't breathe. My head felt lighter and my vision was fuzzy.

His mouth opened and closed a few times. A moment of silence passed between us before he seemed to make up his mind. "I want to hire you," he said, and my sister asked him to elaborate.

Carmine was sent to New York by his father, tasked with surveilling a former business associate. When pushed for more information, he refused.

"Interesting," Sienna muttered under her breath while tapping her finger to her lip. "I need to discuss this with my father, then I will contact you."

When Carmine appeared as though he was going to argue, I rose from my seat. "I need to get back to work," I said before tossing my bag over my shoulder and offering my goodbyes.

"I'll see you later tonight." Sienna smiled, then turned back to Carmine as I exited as quickly as my legs would allow me. Peiro jumped to his feet, pushing the call button for the elevator the moment he sensed my approach.

Then I felt *him* at my back. Could feel his warmth in my bones, sense the sudden shift in his demeanor.

"Mario's fuckin' crazy to send a punk-ass bitch to protect his daughter." Carmine's words scorched the back of my neck, his speech pattern altered and off-putting to the ear.

"Step the fuck back." Peiro was barely half the man's size as he attempted to put distance between me and the native Californian.

Carmine ignored my bodyguard, all his focus on me, while Sienna and her secretary stood in the foreground, likely drawn forward by the commotion. Luckily the elevator dinged, breaking the tension, and I stepped inside. That should have been the end of it. But it was rare for things in my life to go on as they should.

In one quick swoop, Carmine threw Peiro towards my sister. They tumbled into each other as Carmine forced me farther into the elevator. The doors closed, and for a moment, I stood stock-still, pinned to the corner. My skin tingled as Carmine regarded me with something akin to desire. If he opted to attack, I'd never survive. Physically, mentally, and emotionally… I'd be destroyed.

"Like *that* was supposed to stop me," he muttered, forcing me further against the wall.

I licked my lips and his eyes followed the motion. "Wh-what are you doing?" My stomach lurched as the cable car continued to descend.

Tension hung in the air, almost sexual but leaning more towards violent. This hulking man could easily snap me in half with the flick of his fingers—the feeling was both terrifying and thrilling. When we finally reached the ground floor and the elevator doors opened into the lobby, I wasn't surprised to find security waiting for us, their guns drawn. One of the men stepped forward, his gun aimed directly at Carmine, who appeared nothing short of unconcerned as he reached out and pressed the *close door* button, cutting off their attempts to rescue me.

"Meet me tomorrow." The deep gravel of this man's voice did *delicious* things to my body.

I shook my head, but my throat was too dry to speak. His dark eyes emblazoned, clearly displeased by my answer. The doors opened to the basement this time, and Carmine stepped out, holding the elevator while he waited for me to follow him.

He leaned forward, nearly bent in half as he prompted, "Meet. Me. Tomorrow."

"No." My chest rose rapidly with the singular word.

"Ever get tired of being treated like a fragile little doll?" His minty breath ghosted over my face. "I'd bet everything I own that your family has no idea what you have locked away in that pretty little head." His grin was a mixture of malice and lust. "I'd give anything to meet the real *you.*"

I swallowed roughly as his finger lightly traced from my temple and down my cheek before ending at my throat. Stopping on my pulse, so he could feel the pounding of my heart. He dropped his hand and reached into his pocket, pulling out a cigarette and quickly lighting the end.

"I'll show you my teeth if you show me yours, little doll," he grunted as a finger stabbed at the button for the lobby. He continued to watch me until the doors closed, the inverted cross over his eye mocking me on a wink before the man disappeared entirely.

"What the fuck?" I muttered breathlessly while clutching a hand to my chest. I swore my heart was going to beat its way through my rib cage.

As a true crime enthusiast, I'd always had these strange thoughts—almost wants—within me. Sick and depraved thoughts that plagued my mind. I'd wondered what it would be like to be the *victim.* Stalked by a deranged man lost to his infatuation. Taunted by his need for her. I wanted to know what it felt like to be hunted...

I finally understood what that was like. At this moment. Standing in front of *him.* My body tingled, charged by the memory of his touch... his heated gaze.

The doors opened to the lobby to reveal Sienna surrounded by the building's security team. Peiro was on the phone—no doubt talking to my brother.

"I'm fine, Sienna. He didn't do anything."

"But…"

I spun on my heel to cut her off. "I'm. Fine." My fists clenched at my side.

All eyes were on me, glaring in disbelief, as I stalked towards the front doors. Another day, another situation, another person refusing to believe that I could handle this life. Another instance where it became harder for me to keep *her* at bay.

"We're going to the compound." Peiro ushered me to the closest vehicle.

"No. I need to return to work."

My sister was standing by the entrance to her building, offering me nothing. Her expression blank and her arms crossed. While I stood on the sidewalk, appalled at the realization that tears were burning my eyes. My emotions were all over the place. The thrill of the unknown, the fear of Carmine's dangerous presence, and the menial conversation all churned the acid in my stomach. At the same time, the scars that usually burned to life with phantom pain were numb to the touch.

A low rumbling caught my attention, drawing my focus to a sleek sports car. It was black-on-black and tinted. Peiro was too busy on his phone to notice the vehicle idling in the distance, the window opened just enough that I could see eyes marked by an inverted cross.

My feet itched to move towards him. But I questioned his motives and the type of cage I'd be rushing to close myself inside…

Peiro placed a hand on my shoulder, urging me to get inside the SUV. He ordered the driver to take us to the compound, and the sleek black car drove off before I slid into the back seat of our tinted vehicle.

Carmine Ragetti was getting under my skin. Though I wasn't sure if he wanted access to my heart or my veins. Both were equally appealing, depending on the party in question.

His eyes gave me no false promises; he'd destroy my presumed innocence and then break my heart without a second thought. I was well and truly fucked.

CHAPTER 4

CARMINE RAGETTI: PAST

"Pretty face, nice tits, and a brain. Who would've thought." I stared at the danger-seeking blonde standing in front of me with her chin raised in defiance. It didn't matter that she was dressed in only a G-string and a pair of clear heels—her nose remained in the air.

"Talk shit and I'll leave without helping you." Persephone baited me. She knew I wanted to hear what she had to say.

The heavy bass of the strip club beyond my office door seemed to dwindle to white noise as I tried to shove down the rage her snotty attitude stirred within my chest. I didn't take shit from anyone—let alone some fucking chick looking to order me around with her tits out on display.

"Lester was able to track down the shipping container. It landed on a dock in New York, intercepted by Mario Agostino."

My ears perked up at the name. "You fuckin' the computer geek for intel?" It was my turn to bait her.

Most women took one look at my height, wide muscular frame, and tattoos and ran in the opposite direction. But whores were whores and didn't think twice about trying to please me. However, every so often, I found myself wanting someone who wasn't afraid to fight me. Who wouldn't bend to my will without making me work for it.

"Just 'cause I'm a stripper doesn't mean I fuck everyone," Persephone grunted, crossing her arms over her chest in a move that only pushed her breasts higher.

"So, it was sent to the Agostino port… and what? They own it and people pay them to use it. Doesn't mean the container was delivered to them." I cracked my knuckles, ready to throw this girl over my lap with the bitchy glare she gave me.

"Duh. It was sent to a dummy corp with ties to the Morettis."

That had me sitting straighter in my chair.

Persephone sniffing around Moretti-Agostino business made me smile, made me crave their blood on my fucking hands. They could lie all they wanted, but my gut told me both parties were involved in my uncle's death.

Ya see, my uncle and I were close. A fuck of a lot closer than my father and me. Uncle Sal went east to meet his future bride, an arrangement made by my grandfather. Only he never came back.

Mario swore up and down that my uncle was the victim of a robbery gone wrong. That no one in *il famiglia* had anything to do with it. Once Persephone got me proof that the bastard was lying, I'd fucking kill him. Yeah, some nobody from the streets killed the man who was supposed to marry Serafina—sounded like fucking bullshit to me. Especially when, barely two weeks later, she was engaged to Anthony Moretti. The same fucker who was suddenly paying dues to Mario in some over-inflated deal about the docks.

Robbery… right. Nothing about that was fishy at all.

"So, you're moving to New York then?"

Persephone nodded, motioning to her packed bag. The girl was what I considered a stray, coming and going in my club for years. A top earner with her pretty face, tight body, and impressive moves on the pole.

"The fuck you thinking, Perse?"

She was too stubborn for her own good, set on killing herself for answers she might never get. "I have a lead and I'm following it." She flashed her trademark crazed smirk.

Something else about Perse was the fact she wasn't all right in the head. She was known for spiraling into dark places. I did my best to try to keep her kind of crazy locked down, but it took more time than I was willing to give. That being said, my brother had a thing for broken birds and felt responsible for her.

"You think they're just going to spill all their indiscretions to you while you're riding their dick?" My expression remained neutral as I held back my laughter.

"I'm done. Fuck your two weeks' notice." She turned to stomp out of my office, her heels lighting up with each step she took and forcing me to break my stone-cold exterior.

"Stop," I barked, making her turn abruptly with a snarl on her lips. "Let me get some shit organized and I'll send you support."

"I don't need your help, Carmine," she muttered, although her face showed signs of relief.

"Not now, you don't, but that could change quick. Plus, if you get *my* answers…" I waved a hand, leaving it at that.

Her voice grew somber. "If I hear anything on your uncle, I promise…" she said before exiting.

Our lack of a response when it came to my uncle made us look weak amongst the other made families. We may have owned the west coast but there were whispers constantly questioning our strength. I dared anyone to try to test that theory, though.

Growing up, I raised my brothers and my sister. They were the reason I'd fight like hell when I took over the west. Our father was fucking crazy, our mother distant, so my siblings' well-being fell to me as the oldest.

Just the thought of Anthony Moretti had me gripping my desk with pent-up rage stirring just below the surface. My knuckles turned white as I fought to keep from flipping the fucking furniture over. He did it. I fucking knew he did. And if the Agostinos were covering it up, I'd kill them too. I'd claim their oldest daughter for myself and murder the sons.

The sound of my phone ringing had my eyes flicking to the screen and my rage immediately simmered.

"Hey, *sorellina,*" I answered in greeting, using my sister's nickname. She wasn't the baby, but we still called her that.

Eva hated it, but my brothers and I didn't care. She was as dainty as they came, especially when compared to her three oversized brothers. Though that didn't mean she couldn't hold her own.

"Did you forget about dinner?" she whispered into the phone.

"Fuck. I did." Jumping to my feet, I started slamming shit into drawers.

"Dad's mad. Hurry," she added before quickly hanging up.

My father had a trigger temper befitting a toddler. And his rage didn't dwindle just because we shared his blood. If anything, it made him worse. He wanted total compliance, beaten-down submission. As the oldest, I took most of his wrath—learned every one of the *lessons* he taught with his fists. Our name was a curse, a burden thrusted on us from birth.

Matteo was second and picked up the unhinged parts of our father. He tamped down his outbursts, adopting a quieter tenacity to rip you to shreds, while Eva was the light of the family, far too kind and patient with us. Then the baby was Lorenzo, who—funny enough—was even larger than I was.

Our father, John Paul Ragetti, was known for killing first and asking questions later. He left chaos in his wake. The money and connections allowed him to walk away unscathed. Goddamn crazy son of a bitch.

Tree. Meet apple. Because those same traits followed me as well. Maybe I was born like this; maybe my father beat it into me.

"Have a goodnight, boss." The bouncer at the door motioned me outside a few minutes later.

My Bugatti Chiron was parked directly out front, in a reserved spot. Some called it ballsy, while others called it stupid. Not only was the car ridiculously flashy, since only five hundred were made, but I also parked it in a spot with my fucking name scrolled across the top.

I fucking dared someone to fuck with me.

My bones cracked as I flexed my hands over the steering wheel, my club just a blip in the rear-view now. The concern in Eva's voice was the only reason I was hauling ass.

As I drove out of the congested city, the lights and heavy traffic of Los Angeles disappeared in the background. I wove in and out of the lanes. The cops would take one look at the car and turn the other way. Money and fear, it did wonders.

I made it to my parents' mansion in Beverly Hills in record time. The estate was like something you'd see on a TV show about the rich and famous. My father never hesitated to flaunt his wealth. The old bastard was crazy, angry, and flashy as fuck.

The guard at the gate immediately opened the heavy steel doors. My family home sat on roughly thirty acres. It was basically a villa with over five thousand square feet of living space. That wasn't including the additional buildings on the property for the staff and guards, the garages, or equipment storage.

I hated it here.

I had a penthouse in downtown LA that was my main living space since it was close to everything. And a vacation home on the water in Huntington Beach that was predominantly used by Eva. All the shit his money afforded us didn't take away from his cruelty.

"Somebody's gonna get a spanking." Lorenzo flicked his cigarette at me.

I'd barely stepped out of my car when my brother began taunting me. Matteo, Lorenzo, and I were thick as thieves but fought twice as hard. We owned several businesses together and had each other's back.

I walked into the foyer where maids were scattered about with their cleaning supplies. They quickly disappeared as I passed. The moment I stepped into the dining room, everyone turned to my father, waiting for his reaction.

"How nice of you to join your family, Carmine."

Yep, murderous.

Just to piss him off, I smirked. "I was held up with some interesting news." I paused to see if he'd take the bait but his reddening face told me it wouldn't matter if he did.

"Bullshit. I know you forgot about dinner. Your sister can't lie for shit!" He glared at her. "Tired of dealing with her drama."

Gripping Eva's arm, I pulled her behind me and he snarled. He practically tipped over his chair as he rose to his feet to close the distance between us. His anger towards me was nothing new. At random times, when he thought no one was watching, he eyed me with a peculiar gleam in his eye. As if he was afraid of the man he'd created—me. The bastard ruled out of fear, not respect. My uncle taught me to evoke both. My men feared me but respected my work ethic. I'd go into battle right alongside them.

Everything my father hated about me was a direct reflection of himself. The same lack of control he exhibited was passed onto me.

Except when I blacked out in a rage, I didn't do it publicly. I was smarter than that.

"True. I did," I said, stepping around him, grabbing the closest glass, and taking a sip of the wine.

"You disrespectful asshole."

I waited for his own glass to shatter.

"Enough, John. The family is here and we are ready to eat." My mother smiled at me as my father grudgingly returned to his seat.

Family dinner went off as usual after that. The staff bustled around us. My mother and Eva filled the silence with endless chatter and the rest of us remained tight-lipped if not talking business. When JP started running his mouth midway through, my palms itched to pull a knife. Excusing myself, I headed towards the terrace instead. The bright city below calmed the festering inferno in the pit of my stomach.

To the outside world, I was John's prodigy, the future of the family. In reality, the old fucker couldn't stand me. He knew he had little control over my actions and was frightened by the monster I could become.

My thoughts wandered to Persephone and indecision settled into my gut. I'd always wondered why my father seemed to roll over and take it up the ass from our east coast rivals. His brother was murdered and the bastard took Mario at his word. It was customary to let Mario know Matteo or I would be coming to his city, which meant I needed to trick my father into thinking it was his idea to send me east.

"Having an issue with an associate I need found." My father's sudden appearance caught me off guard, almost like the fucker could somehow read my mind. "Might need you to head into Mario's territory. And you need to get your sister under control. I'm tired of her spoiled princess bullshit."

It took me a moment to calm myself. Eva was by no means a spoiled princess. Yes, she could have anything money could buy.

And, yes, there were moments where she acted like a little bitch. But she had a big fucking heart.

"About?"

"Her duties," he grunted, and I froze. "This life... you know women aren't worth shit without alliances."

"Like hell you'll marry her off to Lucky." The fucking self-proclaimed *Devil of New York* didn't deserve my sister.

"I didn't say that, now, did I? But if I did, you'd fucking fly her there and march her down that fucking aisle if I told you to do it." *Like fuck I would.* "Get your shit together, in case I need you to go," he added before walking off, leaving me annoyed and confused.

"Hey, I'm heading out." Eva stepped up to me a few minutes later and wrapped her arms around my waist in a tight hug.

"What the fuck aren't you telling me, Eva?" It was clear my tone caught her off guard. I was usually softer when it came to my sister. "What bullshit is JP pulling that you ain't telling me about?"

"He's been commenting on me bothering him more and more. Talking about an alliance, but you know he won't give me the details—just says enough to try to scare me." Eva's sweet, innocent smile took me down a notch. The old man was losing it; that was all it was. He wouldn't have the balls to arrange a contract without me knowing. "He's threatening to marry me off, but Mom says he's not serious."

Like I'd believe the woman who turned a blind eye to her husband abusing his children.

"It's too late to go back to the beach," I told Eva, knowing she'd want to put distance between herself and our father.

"Yeah, I know. Heading back to LA with Alessandro," she replied. In my crew, outside of my brothers, I had three men I trusted more than anyone else. Alessandro, Diego, and AJ had been in my inner circle since I was a kid. We'd go to hell and back for each other.

Alessandro was my sister's around-the-clock shadow, and I

knew he would take a bullet for her. He was also one of the few people who could tolerate her antics. The little girl wasn't raised with three wild brothers, only to remain demure.

Speaking of, I watched as Lorenzo crept up behind Eva and forced her into a headlock. "When ya going to New York?" He pinched her face when she lit up at the mention of her favorite city.

A few years back, I was meant to be taking Matteo and Lorenzo to New York for business. The plan was to leave our sister behind, but JP was on a warpath for something or another. So we let her tag along. It was better to keep her with us when our father was raging.

And then she met Mario's son.

Lucky Agostino. Easterners feared him. But I didn't need a fucking gimmick to instill fear; everyone knew who and what I was. The kid was a fucking chump, riding his daddy's coattails and hiding behind a stupid-as-fuck nickname. He was *il diavolo*, the Italian devil—sounded like a cheesy horror movie villain if you asked me.

"Go. And behave." I kissed Eva's forehead and walked her outside to where Alessandro was waiting. "I'm meeting Diego."

My brothers nodded as I hopped into my car and headed to my casino. It was a *members only* underground club. A few minutes later, my security team was buzzing me inside. Diego didn't give me much insight into what he needed to discuss. But as I made my way into a *certain* locked room, I knew it was going to be a good night.

I was greeted by the smell of disinfectant, heavy bleach, and the underlying hint of blood. The room was closed off to everyone but Diego and me—we trusted no one. It was easy enough to do, seeing as the only way out of here was in pieces.

"You fucked up, *cagna*." Diego handed me a manila envelope from where he was standing behind some fucker bound to the only chair in the room. I glanced at the contents with a low whistle parting my lips. "Two hundred thousand, on top of our cut and the additional fees, equals four hundred and ninety-four thousand, six hundred, and ninety dollars," Diego listed off his calculations. The dude was a modern-day *Rain Man* when it came to numbers.

"How will we get our money back?" I bent in front of the fucker's slumped-over form.

"Pl-please, I have a daughter! I… Just… Take her! She can make that money back in no time!"

Before I could stop myself, I launched a fist into the bastard's jaw, enjoying the explosion of flesh and bone matter against my knuckles. I was accustomed to pain these days, so much so that it took quite a bit for it to even register. The motherfucker's jaw broke with one more good swing. Not that it stopped me. Left, right, left.

The son of the bitch was already to the point of passing out, until I pulled out my knife and his eyes sprung open with a fresh wave of adrenaline coursing through his system. The glint of the blade in the dimly lit room had him expelling his bowels.

"You're supposed to protect your kids." My voice came out like a haunted whisper as I lost myself to the past. Instead of focusing on the prick in front of me. The sick son of a bitch reminded me a little too much of JP. They each had a *daughter* they were more than willing to hand over for their own benefit.

Disgusting.

I wasn't above hurting women. They were often collateral damage in our world. But as Eva's big brother, it was my job to protect her.

I jammed the blade into the fucker's gut before quickly tugging upwards. Whenever I killed a man, I stood directly in front of them. My face almost pressed to theirs as I watched the life extinguish from their eyes.

"What's up?" Diego leaned against the wall, lighting up a cigarette.

"Perse is headed to New York," I told him casually. Like we

were sitting in a coffee shop, discussing our day, and not surrounded by blood and death.

He nodded his understanding. "One call, and I'm there."

I didn't have to thank him. Diego knew how much I appreciated his support. It was an unspoken exchange between us, just like always.

Everything inside me told me that New York held the answers. I was going to rip that goddamn city apart with my bare hands. I'd been doing my research and knew that Mario's weakness was his family—specifically his daughters. I could only hope that the bastard knew how to protect them, because if he didn't, he'd regret it.

And as the days turned into months, all the little pieces started to fall into place, and it was high time I headed east. Those who got the fuck in my way be damned.

I slid into my blacked-out sports car, ignoring the way Matteo was staring me down. "Do I even want to know what that was about?" he asked, as we pulled away from Sienna Agostino's office and into New York traffic.

I refused to dignify his question with a response as we continued to drive in silence. Lucky had invited me to his club after I requested a meeting. I'd wanted to get behind enemy lines and my initial plan had been to connect with Sienna. What I didn't expect was her firecracker of a sister.

I almost didn't recognize Octavia, a little doll so different from the one they liked to portray in the media. One look at the sex kitten in disguise and my plans had shifted. I didn't need Sienna after all. The trap had been set, showing *that family* how easily I could take her.

The question was: what would they do with that knowledge?

The car idled in traffic just in front of the building just as my new target walked out with her security. Rolling down my window, I caught sight of how I'd unnerved her. She wanted to act like I was the Big Bad Wolf, but I saw the intrigue underlying the fear.

And I couldn't wait to use it to my advantage.

That's right, little doll. The wolf has his sights set on you.

"Persephone missed check-in." Matteo clenched the steering wheel, drawing my attention back to him.

"Pull over." We were a few blocks out from where we were staying—one of JP's properties—but the hair on the back of my neck was standing on end. "Something isn't right."

I jumped out of the car, checked my mag, and added another gun to my back. Matteo was right behind me, and soon we were both locked and loaded. We moved along the sidewalk, hanging in the shadows, until we saw the first sign of trouble. All the lights were out. Matteo pulled up our security app, confirming that the video footage was cut. Stepping inside the abandoned building across the way, we saw it.

"There." Matteo motioned to the upper east window, where a figure dressed in black was crouching down.

"Alarms have backups?" I whispered, and my brother nodded. "Set 'em off."

"Security breach, fire, bomb?" he asked, and our matching expressions gave him the answer. We were ready to send the Agostinos into a chaotic frenzy.

"All of 'em." My eyes narrowed in on the building. "Run, you fucking cockroaches," I muttered under my breath.

Men fled out every exit, searching for a threat that would never come. Nothing was going to happen, but they didn't know that. Matteo and I could've easily picked off half of them before they realized we were here. But we didn't.

Not. Just. Yet.

My cell rang in my pocket. I pulled it out and clicked answer. "Carmine." I knew who it was without even having to look. Mario's voice blared in my ear. "You don't touch my fucking family."

"What are you accusing me of, Agostino?"

My brother shook his head at my feigned innocence while lighting up a cigarette.

"Are you asking for war? 'Cause I'll fucking destroy your entire family." Little did the fucker know that his threats only made my heart pound in anticipation for more bloodshed.

"Well, that's a bit extreme." I licked my teeth, drawing out his rage. "A war over a little friendly fucking chat… don't seem real smart. Especially when the west has been patiently waiting to destroy *whoever* the fuck decided it was a good idea to fuck with our family."

"You know I didn't kill him." He was very careful when choosing his words.

"As you've said. But how does the *capo dei capi* of the east have no goddamn clue who did?" I grunted, but the son of a bitch didn't take my bait.

"You tried to blow up my men!" Mario shouted, his impatience more entertaining than anything else.

"Did I? It seems to me someone broke into JP's property." I could practically feel him seething. This was too easy.

I heard nothing but his heavy breathing for several long seconds.

"Come near my daughter again and I'll fucking kill you," he barked and then he hung up.

"That was rude." I smirked, while Matteo shook his head. "Seems Daddy played right into my fucking hand."

If I didn't already know I was right, Mario just confirmed it. Sienna wasn't going to be the ticket for their ruin. Once Perse fucked her way to my answers, I'd ruin the Agostinos using their perfect doll. And I couldn't wait to see how easily I could break her dainty little neck.

"Yeah." Phone pressed to my ear, I sat in the dark car. The only sign of my existence was the smoke billowing out from my cigarette.

"The fuck you think you're doing?" The old man didn't seem happy. "Mario-fucking-Agostino called up. Bitching about you." When I didn't give him anything more than a grunt in response, my father muttered a few choice insults in my direction and hung up.

Something had shifted between us. I couldn't put my finger on it. He seemed more crazed than normal—for him. The anger was nothing new, but his disconnection was. He'd cut me out, and I knew that met he was plotting something. One day, I was going to put him six feet under. It was only a matter of time. We both knew his clock was ticking.

Matteo wasn't himself after I paid Persephone a visit. She'd been missing our check-ins, so I sent a message, telling her to meet me out back of Dom Moretti's club. She was on to something but it didn't come without its consequences.

She was falling for the Moretti asshole. And there was a huge chance he was involved. Matteo had wanted to pull her out, but I wouldn't let him. We were too fuckin' close to the goal line.

Glancing at my brother and his obvious unease, I knew he was ready to snap. Whenever shit got him too frayed, there was only one way to calm him.

"I need to get my dick wet," he grunted, telling me I was right.

We both needed to release the pent-up tension building beneath the surface.

But not fucking together. This ain't that kinda story.

So we headed towards the perfect spot to cater to our depravity. As I expected, we dropped fifty large—a piece—at the door and were quickly ushered inside. The place wasn't overly ornate but had several options to choose from. Each of the rooms, whether you preferred a little voyeurism or wanted to keep things private, afforded you a waitress, unlimited toys, and a fine selection of tight cunts to choose from.

My brother liked watching and being watched when he played. I sure as fuck didn't. A woman on her knees was all I needed. We parted ways before I selected a booth in the corner and gave a passing waitress my order. Not for drinks.

She handed me a key and motioned me into a room. "Fuck. Me," I whispered more to myself than anyone else the moment I stepped inside.

The lighting was dim, while an assortment of restraints, benches, and toys littered every available surface, with a scent of disinfectant lingering in the air. The wall farthest from the door had long metal chains that hung from the ceiling and connected to the floor around a small wooden platform. Where a brunette presently stood in nothing but a blindfold.

I stepped forward and took notes, my nostrils flaring when I realized who she resembled. She was panting heavily, her naked breasts rising and falling with each breath. The fear of the unknown excited her. That much was clear. And I couldn't help but notice how her hair was wrapped in a high bun. She was also roughly the same height and body type…

My mind was playing tricks on me as I imagined this girl was Octavia, mine for the taking and ready to obey. The Agostino daughter was quiet, submissive, and completely sheltered—you could tell just by looking at her. And I was the man to take advantage of that fact.

I shook my head and tried to focus on the woman in front of me instead. My eyes dropping to the ball gag in her mouth that muffled each of her whimpers and pleas. Her arms were bound above her head and her feet were chained to the platform.

I quickly removed her gag and gave her simple instructions to follow. I'd enjoy seeing what limits I could push her towards. Then I turned her back to me and grabbed a round leather paddle before smacking it against my hand. Her body swayed with anticipation and I hadn't even struck her yet. I stepped closer as she steadied herself. Once she nodded her consent, I swung the paddle from one cheek to the other. Her ass started turning a gorgeous shade of red before I moved on to the tops of her thighs, just under her ass. Her moans increased with each strike, and my dick was practically breaking through my zipper.

She took everything I gave her and was more than ready to be rewarded. I freed her wrists and ankles, pulled her down from her makeshift display, and carried her over my shoulder to an obedience bench, where I strapped her down on her stomach. She lay bound on all fours, her reddened ass perched high in the air. Pulling myself free from my pants, I made quick work of sliding on a condom and ran my hands down her spine. I lined up my dick and slammed forward, burying myself to the hilt as she moaned. My dick was proportionally sized to the rest of me. Her walls hugging me tight and pulsating around my thickness. Slowly and precisely, I pulled out and pushed in, turning into a man possessed.

I pounded into her, releasing all the tension from the last couple of weeks. The bench was bolted to the ground, but it shook slightly each time I thrusted forward. The brunette cried and moaned. After her third release, she was rambling, none of it making much sense. She was practically in a coma of pleasure while I was still chasing my own high. My eyes dropped to the sight of the girl's flesh jiggling between the straps, as my mind wandered to thoughts of what Octavia's flesh might look like instead…

Two more strokes, and I came hard. My dick was still throbbing my release when *her* face flashed before my eyes. If I'd been one to vocalize my pleasure, it would have been Octavia's name on my tongue. But that wasn't me. I enjoyed the sounds I elicited much more than those driven from me.

I pulled out and wiped myself down in the sink, before loosening the girl's restraints. She refused my help to clean up, asking permission to remove her blindfold instead. Once I'd freed her from the bench, I conceded. She lowered the silk fabric from her eyes, her head tipping back to look me in the face, and gasped. I brushed my long hair off my forehead, smirked at her, and disappeared through the door. She was hot, but she didn't have the same doe eyes I wanted thanking me for making her come.

I couldn't wait to see what it took to break my little doll. Because Daddy didn't know it yet, but Octavia belonged to me.

The moment I met Matteo back at the car, something niggled at the edge of my brain. I'd always followed my gut—it had saved me more times than I could count. We'd just pulled into a hotel parking lot when my phone rang.

"What did you do?" Something told me the fucker was up to no good.

"Nothing that concerns you," JP snarled, barking commands at someone in the background—he was ordering a cleanup. "Where the fuck is your sister?"

"What? Why?" Silence. "Who did you kill?" I pressed. He hung up as Matteo's phone rang.

"Eva?" my brother asked.

"He's… he's dead!" she shouted. I could hear her through his phone.

Once she had calmed down enough to speak, her words had what little grip I had on my patience slipping from my fingers. JP showed up at my beach house unannounced, informing Eva she was being married off. When Alessandro stepped in, telling the old bastard to call me first, the fucker shot him.

"He told me I had to leave. Like right then. And I fought him. God, help me, I fought." She cried harder. "He shot him over and over and over!"

"Hey." Diego took over the call. "He's going to make it, but your sister won't if she doesn't sit the fuck down and shut the hell up." He paused and I could hear Eva whining in the background. "Alessandro is with us—alive. The doc is assisting with transport to a new secured location."

We all knew the old man was losing it, but now he was crossing a line. No one, not even JP himself touched my sister. Or my men. He was a dead man walking. Why the hell was he trying to wed Eva off? Only one thing came to mind. The bastard was trying to form an alliance.

"Diego," I barked into my phone. "I'm sending Matteo back to you." I snapped my fingers at my brother.

Diego would protect Eva with his life, but I didn't like the idea of leaving him alone with Alessandro injured. Shit was falling apart and I knew my clock was ticking in New York. It was time I prepared myself to take the next steps.

"No. It's too risky to be there alone. Lorenzo's on his way. We've got it."

As much as I didn't like it, Diego was right.

When I pulled the trigger and finally sent New York into complete chaos, I'd need Matteo and AJ. So I reluctantly agreed. Diego informed me of where they were headed and promised to check-in when they got there. Then we cut the line.

"Who the fuck is he brokering an alliance with?" Matteo grabbed a bottle from the hotel bar.

"Fuck." I rubbed a tired hand down my face. "My bet? It has to be the Lombardis."

"Ew, fuck. Hank Lombardi?"

We both shuddered at just the thought of that sick fuck. The family was a bunch of bottom-feeders. Hank was the oldest son, and a certified fucking creep. His love for outdated clothing, propensity for greasy hair, and affliction of pockmarks only added to his overall repugnance. Throw in his immoral compass when it came to innocent women and the whole family deserved to be terminated before they had a chance to procreate.

They'd sold all their properties in Italy and were apparently rolling in dough. Their most recent cash cow was a truckload of guns. But word on the street was that they'd stolen from the Russians. A death wish if I ever saw one—only a moron would mess with the head of the *Bratva*. But I was smarter than my old man. Everyone knew that, even if he didn't.

JP wouldn't give a fuck about anything other than the cash and having Lombardi's crew at his beck and call. While my sister would serve as his bargaining chip.

"What're you thinking?" Matteo rested his feet on the small table between us.

"We get rid of them." It was one thing to have a crew of bottom-feeders on your side. Another to have *the Russian Wolf* owe you a favor.

"You're going to call Nikolai." Matteo met my smirk with a devious grin of his own.

No one fucked with my siblings or my men and got away with it. Our father was no exception.

Carmine Ragetti's little elevator stunt had my family in an uproar. His sudden appearance, combined with his obvious interest, had me forced under lock and key at the compound. Even worse was how the man had been haunting my dreams ever since.

"I'll show you my teeth if you show me yours, little doll."

"Octavia." Apollo grabbed the bag I was pounding all my rage into. "Your father wants to see you in his office."

"Almost done." Left, right, left, right.

"Octavia!" He pushed me back a step, motioning towards my torn gloves.

"I'm fine." I tugged them off, revealing bloody knuckles.

It had been months since I'd let that dark part of me free. She was practically clawing at my guts, fighting her way out, whether I wanted her to or not. All the shit happening in my family was making all my dirty secrets harder to keep.

Apollo shook his head as I stormed past him and out of the home gym. My father had been basically locked in his office since… *the incident.* The one not to be mentioned unless you wanted to see a bunch of *made men* sulking in their expensive suits. His door was open, so I wandered in without knocking. My father was seated at his desk while my older brother stood by the far window. Apollo closed the door behind me as I claimed the chair next to Marco. None of them would look me in the eye.

"I know we've been over this more times than I care to count, but we need to ask you… about Carmine." My father's face twisted up, like saying the man's name tasted bitter on his tongue.

"What more do you want me to say? No matter how many times you ask me, my answer isn't going to change. I. Don't. Know." I aggressively rubbed my temples. "He didn't exactly share his master plan with me."

"And you're positive, other than the instances we've discussed, you've never seen him before?" Lucky positioned himself on the edge of my dad's desk, directly in front of me. "Nowhere else in New York? Just the office and the club?"

"Lucky, the truth isn't going to change just because you don't like it." I shifted uncomfortably, wringing my hands together as all sets of eyes were aimed at me.

Did they think I was too scared, too broken, to admit there was more to it than that?

My brother was perceptive, staring *through* me like he could somehow unravel the deception he thought he might find behind my calm demeanor. But it wasn't there. I was just as unnerved as the rest of them. I just wished they took me at my word.

Even now Carmine's words haunted me. *"Ever get tired of being treated like a fragile little doll?"*

I didn't have a response for him then. But I did now. The answer was yes. I was exhausted.

"I'm sorry we've been pestering you about this. We're just trying to protect you, baby girl." My father acted as if this repetition was helping anyone.

"I've told you *everything*. May I go now?" I huffed.

Lucky's white knuckles and hardened gaze told me I wasn't going to like what he had to say next. "The family is getting out of the city for a bit." His dramatic pause did little to help my growing unease. "Senator Daniels is having a little get-together over the bridge in Jersey and we're all expected to attend."

There was more to this than they were letting on. I could see it in my brother's eyes.

"Election season is over." Silence. "What's he celebrating?"

"His son's recent graduation. The kid will be working for his father, on the fast track to his own political success. We're expected to make nice."

The senator was already in our pocket so I called bullshit. Unless...

"You're arranging my marriage..." I was going to be sick. I could already feel the bile rising in my throat.

"I didn't say that, Octavia. It's just a party." Before he finished, I knew my father was lying to me. "However, it's something to keep in mind for the future. As you know, my marriage to your mother was arranged."

"As was mine." Lucky shrugged, appearing unfazed. But, of course, he was. My brother liked playing the good son.

"Not to an outsider!" I stood, knocking my chair to the floor in the process. "You're cutting me out of the family."

"We didn't say that..." My father walked around his desk, reaching out an arm in my direction. "*If* we were setting something up for your future, political ties are extremely beneficial to the businesses. Our way of life. And our enemies would be less inclined to target you and garner all that negative media attention."

White noise was filling my ears, muffling his words, while my mind raced, trying to keep up.

"But that's not why we're attending, Octavia. Like I said, it's just a little get-together with some good friends."

He was full of shit. The senator's son wanted to meet me. Our parents would flaunt us in front of the cameras before an "insider" would later give the scoop on our whirlwind romance. And then they'd pull the trigger. Boom. An arrangement to marry an outsider. Cut off from *il famiglia.*

I swiped an angry hand at a stray tear. "*If* you do this, you'll regret it."

"Octavia, calm down," my father ordered at the same time my brother asked, "Was that a *threat?*"

"I'm not a pawn! I'm. Not. Weak."

"Enough, Octavia. Your imagination is running wild." It was amazing how effortlessly Lucky could lie. I was aware he knew how to play the game but I guess I never fully grasped what it would be like to just be a piece on his board.

"Imagination? Like how I imagine how pathetic you are every time you let Tatianna back into your bed?" I was on a roll and couldn't stop the floodgates of anger.

"Excuse me?" Lucky stepped closer, nearly frothing at the mouth, until my father threw out an arm to stop him.

"Don't like hearing the truth? I see how you all look at me. Like I'm this pathetic little girl in the background of your lives. I can handle a lot more than you give me credit for and that doesn't make *me* the pathetic one." My heart was hammering against my rib cage. "Oh, and by the way, you're doing an impeccable job at protecting me—let me tell you." The scars felt like they were rising to the surface, burning through the long-healed flesh.

It didn't matter if I told them, because nothing would change.

"Jesus Christ, it's just a fucking party, kid." Marco chuckled to himself, ever the clown, no matter how grave the situation. I would have something to say back if his opinion was worth a damn. It wasn't.

"Carmine Ragetti isn't some little girl who's picking on you. He wants revenge against *us*. Do you know what his kind of revenge looks like, Octavia?" Lucky towered over me, leaning forward to meet my glare with one of his own, but I held my ground. "Rape. Bruises. Broken bones. Bloodshed—death wouldn't be the worst of it. He could smell your innocence from a mile away. But seeing as you refuse to recognize the beast standing right in front of you, I think we *should* arrange it. Send you away."

If only they knew… If only they understood… I'd seen it. Felt it all. And here I was. Beaten but not yet broken.

"Do it," I seethed, my chest heaving as I slowly rose from my seat. "I. Dare. You." My glare met each of them head-on. If *she* wasn't threatening to break loose, I'd laugh at their shock.

"Enough." My father sighed. "The Ragettis have a reason to hate me and I won't let them hurt you for it." His words sent a chill of foreboding and terror down my spine.

Why would they hate him so much…

"You know who killed his uncle…" I wasn't asking, and his silence told me I'd hit the nail on the head.

"All of us are spending some time in Jersey." He was evading my question, but I already had the answer whether he admitted it or not.

I nodded before turning on my heel and exiting the office. I couldn't stand to be around him for another second.

"Tomorrow!" he called after me.

Was it denial that plagued my father? Or had he pled his innocence for so long that he couldn't help but believe his own lies? If my suspicions were true, and my father had something to do with why this supposed beast was sniffing around the east…

Then no one was safe.

"You look gorgeous." My sister complimented me, but I remained tight-lipped.

I got up all by myself today. Did my hair. My makeup. And even picked out my own clothes. *Poof!* Magic had to be in the air because, despite being left to my own devices, I was still alive.

It was their blind ignorance that pissed me off most, I think. Didn't they realize that *they* couldn't keep me safe? How was some politician's son supposed to do what a bunch of made men couldn't?

The car ride to New Jersey was long and mind-numbing. After his fourth attempt at conversing with me, Lucky finally stopped trying. I was in the third row of seats with Apollo caging me in. Where the others were bothered by my silence, my brother's second-in-command was no doubt thankful for it. He stared off into the distance, content with his solitude.

But the moment we pulled up to the senator's estate and I stepped out of the car, I would have given anything to turn around and drive away—no matter how equally mind-numbing the ride back over the bridge promised to be. The hordes of people were the same at every event. Political. Powerful. All looking to get in good with the Agostinos. Make connections with the infamous family.

Aaron Anthony Daniels III was as pretentious and pervy as you'd expect a senator's son to be. He walked into this simple *get-together* extremely late, in a suit way too tight, with the swagger of a man who'd had his entire life handed to him on a silver platter. We weren't much different in that aspect, you could say. My siblings and I were given a lot growing up. But we also knew how to roll up our sleeves and work hard. More than that, we wanted to do it. We each wanted something that belonged to us and not our family name. While it was obvious this kid had never worked a day in his life. He was just another mediocre graduate, preparing to work for his father.

I wanted to vomit when he pulled me to the side a few minutes after making his appearance, acting like he didn't know all cameras were on us. He was using my attendance as a quick photo opt and assumed I wasn't smart enough to figure it out.

"Listen, Oct…" He scratched his thin beard. *The asshole didn't even know my name.* "We all know why you're here." He grinned before guiding me towards a private corner.

"And why is that?" I tugged my hand free from his.

"My name. You get a senator's son and I get a virgin bride with a decent enough rack. Win-win."

"Hm," I hummed to myself. I really didn't know what else to say. Well, I did but I couldn't say it at the moment without making a scene.

"They didn't tell you, did they?" he scoffed, and I stared him down. "This little setup is just the start, before the inevitable. But don't tell Daddy I gave up the goods." His smirk morphed into something more devious.

Perhaps that was why… why I suddenly didn't care anymore. Fuck tossing my anger into the wind. I'd set it on fire on his doorstep.

"Actually, Anthony," I started to say. He tried to correct me, but I talked over him. "I'm here because my family is looking for a *mediocre* name to be tied to. I won't be your *wife* in anything other than title. *If* we make it down the aisle. And before you bother with another interruption, I'll let you in on a little secret." My hesitance was for dramatic effect only. "The rumors about the Agostinos are true. Even their itty-bitty daughter is an apple not far fallen from the tree."

I lifted a hand, curling two fingers into my palm before cocking back my wrist and pressing the tips to his forehead. Then I winked as I pulled the metaphorical trigger. His entire body jerked, and I couldn't help but laugh as the growing crowd turned their attention to us. I closed a hand around Aaron's forearm and pretended to swoon. Aaron, noticing how all eyes were aimed on him, turned on his megawatt smile. He went to reach for my hand, to pull me closer, but I gracefully pivoted on my heel and walked away.

The ride home later that night was as uncomfortable and silent as it had been on the way there. Maybe more so. It was hard to tell.

"It was a nice party," my father said, attempting to cut the tension, but I didn't respond.

Lucky glowered at me from over the seat. "You can't ignore us forever," he grunted.

I traced the scars on my stomach through my shirt while thinking, *If only I could...*

"Would you even notice if I did?" Instead of continuing, I offered my brother a tight smile.

Apollo tried to hide his own smirk, but I saw it. It was clear no one knew what to make of my sudden noncompliance, and it was throwing the family dynamic off-balance. No one knew what to do with me.

Good. I wanted them to feel as uncomfortable as I felt in my own skin.

Stomping my feet wouldn't get my message across. But silence was golden. And to my family, debilitating.

Days turned to weeks as we all prepared for Lucky's pending nuptials. Though not one of them had mentioned the senator or his son again, I wasn't naïve enough to believe that their plan was put to rest.

Sometimes I didn't think my family considered their consequences. As if all the years spent on top had my father believing he was untouchable. They didn't understand the impact of their decisions. But they would. And sadly, so would my brother's bride. A contract with the devil would be the girl's ultimate demise.

Nothing we could do. I'm sorry. Bella has passed away.

I couldn't escape the words fluttering around in my head, a constant reminder of what this life did to us women. Chewed us up and spit us out.

I couldn't breathe past the devastation as my brother broke down in front of me. His wife of mere minutes, the only person he truly loved outside of his family, was gone. And hell hath no fury like a devil scorned.

My brother was out for fucking blood.

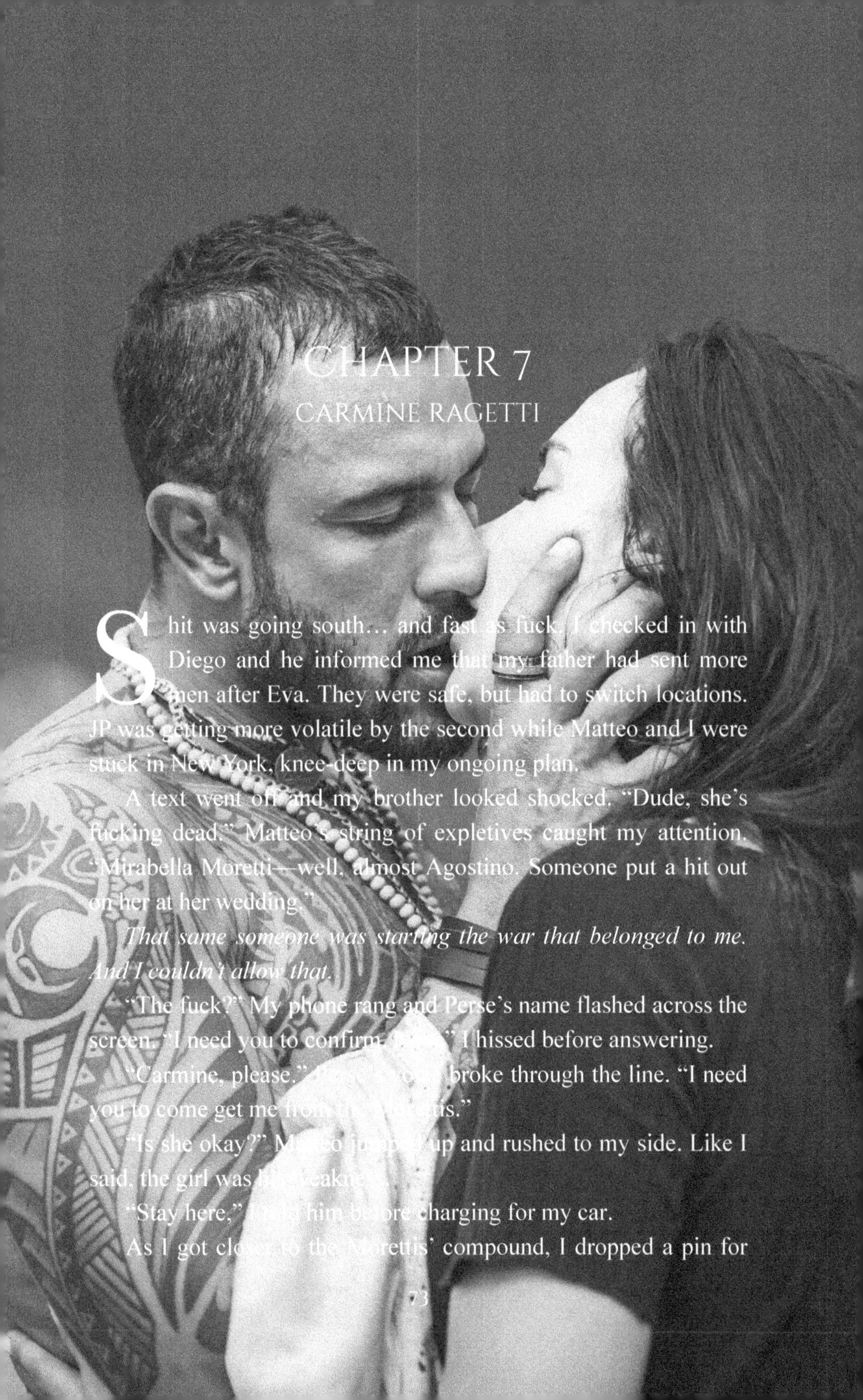

CHAPTER 7

CARMINE RAGETTI

Shit was going south… and fast as fuck. I checked in with Diego and he informed me that my father had sent more men after Eva. They were safe, but had to switch locations. JP was getting more volatile by the second while Matteo and I were stuck in New York, knee-deep in my ongoing plan.

A text went off and my brother looked shocked. "Dude, she's fucking dead." Matteo's string of expletives caught my attention. "Mirabella Moretti—well, almost Agostino. Someone put a hit out on her at her wedding."

That same someone was starting the war that belonged to me. And I couldn't allow that.

"The fuck?" My phone rang and Perse's name flashed across the screen. "I need you to confirm this," I hissed before answering.

"Carmine, please." Perse's voice broke through the line. "I need you to come get me from the Morettis'."

"Is she okay?" Matteo jumped up and rushed to my side. Like I said, the girl was his weakness.

"Stay here," I told him before charging for my car.

As I got closer to the Morettis' compound, I dropped a pin for my location and watched as a dirty little dream darted for me. There weren't many people I cared about outside my siblings. But Persephone was one of them. She was running towards my car like hell was on her heels. A panic attack weighing down her steps. I could see it on her face as she jumped into the passenger seat, and I pulled away. The little maid uniform that sick fuck made her wear was nearly torn off her shoulders.

"Breathe, girl. I need you to breathe and get your shit straight."

"It's all falling down around me…" She was muttering to herself and I could tell she was on the verge of passing out.

"Stay with me, Seph. Imma need answers, babe. Fucking hell…"

And then she was gone.

"Fuck!" I punched the steering wheel until I couldn't feel my hand anymore.

There was a time when I'd told the little blonde bitch that she could warm my dick, not my club. But then my idiot of a brother had to step in and offer her up like a sacrificial lamb to our cause. And now look at her… She couldn't function enough to do either.

"Goddamn it," I growled while carrying an unconscious Persephone into my warehouse.

"What happened?" Matteo asked, one arm shooting out to open the upper-level apartment door.

"The fucking Morettis, that's what happened." I placed Persephone on the bed before stepping out and closing the door behind me.

My brother followed me over to our makeshift bar, where I tossed back a glass of brown liquor, then pinned him with a glare—my fist was begging to meet the fucker's face. Deciding it was best to avoid spilling my sibling's blood at the moment, I turned my back on him and contemplated my next steps. I always knew this day would come. That these two families would have to be dealt with, and that I was just the man to do it.

"Don't put this shit on me. I told you no from day fuckin' one when she came clicking her clear heels on our doorstep. You didn't fucking listen *then,* so why should I listen *now*?"

"Really? I gave her a fucking job. You sent her on a suicide mission…" Matteo stopped short of approaching me, heaving out a sigh. "You're so focused on revenge you can't see anything else."

I reminded myself I couldn't kill my own brother as my eyes flicked over to the window and watched the sun slowly start to set. "It's them, Matteo. Both families are involved. I feel it. They need to fuckin' pay."

"And Eva?" He braced himself for my response.

"Leave her out of this," I grunted.

"What if they come for her?" His glass dropped from his hand and shattered against the floor as I turned on my heel and shoved him into the wall. "Tell me, big brother, what if someone wants to teach you a lesson? Through her," he hissed in my face.

"Shut the fuck up!" I barked back, but he didn't falter.

"JP's clock is ticking. That should be your priority." When I didn't immediately shoot him down, Matteo continued, "For Eva. Goddamn it, Carmine. He should be your focus, not New York. Uncle Sal is dead and the man is gonna stay that way. No matter what you do. But you know what you can fix? The rest of us who are still here. What will it take to make you see that?"

"JP is on borrowed time. I need to handle this first, to ensure that *when* I take over, nothing'll be in my fucking way," I grunted. "Then we will go back to Cali and handle *him.*"

My brothers didn't get it. They hadn't gotten to spend much time with Uncle Sal, the man more myth than actual flesh and blood. But to me, that man was everything.

"We need to take Persephone and go. Now. Go before it's too late. Diego is fighting too many battles, protecting Eva and Alessandro and we're in fuckin' New York."

I slammed Matteo into the wall a second time. But the fucker just wouldn't stop talking.

"And if you honestly think you will fuck with the Agostinos and come out unscathed, you're a fucking idiot."

I pointed at the thin wall separating us from Persephone. "Once she gives me answers, nothing will hold me back from declaring all-out war on those New York fuckers—a war I have no intention of losing."

I let him talk back but none of what he had to say mattered. A plan was already forming in my head. I had already done the groundwork. I knew exactly how I was going to ensure I came out on top. Killing the Agostinos was a risky venture. I had to destroy them from the inside out, take something from them.

"I don't like that look. You… you're not?" Matteo slapped a hand against his thigh. "Christ, you are. What if it was Eva?" His thoughts were running a mile a minute. My brother and I didn't have the same morals.

And that's exactly why I didn't tell him. I was taking over as the head of our family, so my word was law. There wasn't much more to be said. I was a ticking bomb just waiting to detonate: the fuse had already been lit, and the explosion was on the horizon.

The Agostinos believed they were only as strong as their weakest family member. Dumb-as-fuck statement if you asked me. They were basically admitting they had a kink in their armor.

Persephone finally stirred in bed, drawing my attention from my thoughts of revenge to her. "Welcome back. Did you have a nice trip?"

She jumped at the sound of my voice. "How long have I been out?"

"Shy of a day."

"Fuck," she groaned before rubbing a hand against her temple. "You were right. Dom is involved."

"Tell me everything."

And she did. She told me her entire story—and, fuck, was it a good one. But I was more interested in hearing how it all affected *me*.

"You were right."

"I always am, but what are you talking about?"

Here we go. Just fucking say it so I can kill 'em.

"Anthony… he talked about the Agostinos destroying him because… of a secret Mario knows. About your uncle."

Storming to my feet, I grabbed a chair and threw it against the wall. "Dead! They're all fucking dead!" I continued to unleash my wrath on the objects in the room, shattering anything within reach. When there was nothing left to grab, I started punching holes in the drywall.

And then, just like that, I stopped, cracked my neck, and slicked my hair back into place.

"Okay." I took a deep breath. "We've got answers, and now we act."

We worked out all the details over the next few days. My brain was focused and I was confident our plan was foolproof. The family was on high alert at Bella's funeral, but we were prepared. I watched them from my position and immediately knew something was off. Octavia stood with her sister and their little bitch of a guard—Peiro.

But she wasn't crying—something I found odd, considering the occasion. Her sultry body was hidden by a long black dress, her brown hair cascading down her back in soft waves and her face makeup free. As I shifted closer, I noticed she wasn't sad. She was pissed. She whirled around when someone approached her from behind, and I had to reposition myself to see who it was.

"I'll be damned." Matteo's voice came over my earpiece. "It's true. Mario is marrying the chick off to an outsider." Matteo chuckled into my ear as Octavia stepped as far away from the newcomer as she could get.

A younger man wrapped an arm around Octavia's shoulder before handing her a tissue. The little prick had a team of bodyguards at his back too. Whoever the fuck he was, it was clear she didn't want him touching her.

"Some senator's son," Matteo answered as if the fucker could read my mind. And a new rage settled in my gut like a roaring fire.

Who the fuck did this little shit think he was touching her?

It was obvious Peiro was thinking the same thing—I could read his body language even at a distance. There was something about the way Lucky's man stared at her that was as equally off-putting as the senator's kid.

"What the fuck?" The sound of gunfire had me moving quickly.

It took me a minute to realize what was happening. Gio-fuck-ing-Moretti had stolen step one of my vengeance. He'd killed his own father before I could. The man responsible for my uncle's death was gone and now I needed to come up with a quick Plan B.

People were screaming, colliding into each other as they scattered like cockroaches, while I ran full speed, weaving around parked cars before dumping my rifle inside my rental. Then I dodged around an idling SUV and rolled to the ground when the door opened and Apollo stepped out.

"Fucking hell, Bella. Car. Now!"

Tricky motherfuckers. Lucky's wife was alive.

A lone vehicle was sitting with the doors open about three hundred feet ahead. I charged forward, ignoring Matteo's protests as I closed the distance.

Victory was delicious and I was starving for a taste.

One swing and Peiro dropped to the ground, out cold. Octavia opened her mouth to scream until she saw it was me. A dark cloud hovered above us and she looked ready to kill. She could turn and run, but she was no match for my strength and speed. And her anger stalled her movements.

Before she could react, I was already taking her down. She didn't scream, merely yelped when she hit the ground. Even winded, the girl fought like hell. I jabbed the needle into her neck and that fight quickly dwindled. I scooped her into my arms and barreled back to my rental, where I tossed her into the back seat and calmly pulled out into traffic. My town car blended in perfectly with the fleeing masses. No one was the fucking wiser.

"Get to the jet, Matteo. I wanna be in the air within the hour." I yanked out my earpiece and stared up into the rearview.

She should be out cold until I got her stowed away back west. I pulled out a cigarette and turned up the radio, before sitting back in the seat and drawing up my lighter. The music calmed me as the nicotine burned my lungs.

The Morettis were getting theirs. Anthony was dead. Persephone was on Gio's tail. And Dom… well, Perse would deal with him in her own way. Everything was falling into place, and soon little Octavia Agostino would be kneeling at my boots.

"I hope you fight me, little doll. 'Cause it might be the only thing that saves you," I told her as my voice carried over the music.

She twitched on the seat, her dress lifting to reveal a perky ass. My cock hardened, looking to take a bite. The girl might have been my Plan B, but as it turned out, she was also my grand prize.

She'd beg me to fuck her and I just might oblige. Then I'd watch that Agostino blood of hers mix with her tears. And I had no doubt that when I was done, the entire family would be *wrecked*.

CHAPTER 8
CARMINE RAGETTI

The flight was long, but Octavia slept until I got her home. Now, she was presently sitting in front of me, wearing a hood and strapped to a chair. And I was fucking hard just looking at her. I wanted her bound and waiting for me in my bedroom, strung up to my crux decussata. She had an ass that was perfect for my large hands.

But I'd settle for this. For my revenge.

She'd slowly started to wake and the sound of her labored breaths incited something primal in my chest. I had a message to send to Mario and then I'd get this treat all to myself.

This was only the prologue; our story had barely begun.

She was just in time for her movie debut while Lucky and Mario were about to receive an advanced viewing. Me? I was eager to play with her for a bit, ready to make her bleed. I was dying to hear what she sounded like when she screamed, itching to mark her as my own.

"What did I do?" Her entire body racked in fright as she fought against her restraints. "P-please. Why am I here? What have I done?"

The panic I heard in her voice was such a fucking cock tease.

"Now's the time to confess your sins." The way the altering device distorted my voice grated on my ears, especially pressed up under this damn mask.

"How'd you—no, I… no, no, no…"

Now I was intrigued. There *was* something eating away at her conscience. And I'd rip it the fuck out of her.

"Maybe… it's not your sins that sent you to me. Maybe it's Daddy's that dropped you at my doorstep."

She was hyperventilating by this point. My favorite knife glinted in the low light and she trembled more noticeably with each step I took in her direction. In one swift movement, I ripped the hood off her head and gripped her face, forcing her to look into the camera.

"She. Smells. Amazing." Her scent was driving me wild. "Say hi to Daddy, Octavia," I growled against her cheek.

She attempted to twist away from me. Her eyes weren't covered anymore but the rest of her senses were still out of whack. I knew I had her family's attention and the thrill of their torment was the best high. The perfect prize.

"Even her blood smells innocent." The blade was sharp as it glided across her skin and flayed the first layer with ease. I had to be careful though, because with the way things were going, the girl was ready to pass out after a superficial scratch. And I needed her screaming.

"N-no. No. Not a knife… no!" she was gasping in air like a goddamn fish out of water and I'd barely touched her yet.

"Calm down. It's not deep," I hissed while wondering why the fuck I even cared.

"P-please, stop."

Fuck, that's it. Beg for me, baby.

"I-I. Can't take. N-not… again." The desperation in her voice did something to me, and it sure as fuck wasn't the usual *some-*

thing. For some reason, I wanted to end this almost as badly as she did.

"I'm sending demands, Mario. Pay up or she dies." I sliced her skin one more time, the sanguine eruption dripping from her neck as I cut the feed.

The knife dropped from my hand and echoed off the concrete floor. Her eyes immediately followed the sound, almost as if she were entranced by the blade, the blood it drew to the surface.

"Breathe. Octavia, breathe." If she passed out, it would really put a damper on my plans.

"I'm sorry i-if my panic is in-inconvenient for y-you," she stuttered out between clenched teeth.

Well, I'll be damned.

"My, my. So she does have a bit of fire in her after all. And here I thought Sienna was the only one with spirit." Apparently, that was the wrong thing to say if I wanted her present. I watched as she slumped forward, her breathing shallow as I cut off the ropes holding her in place. "Fuck."

She fell into my arms like a limp rag doll. Her small body rose with mine as I pushed to my feet, preparing to throw her over my shoulder as I bent down to grab my knife. Which was precisely when the fucking bitch jammed her skinny little elbow directly into my spine. Caught off guard, I didn't have a moment to recover before she kneed me in the face. Then the she-devil hopped over me and darted for the hallway.

She wanted a chase? Oh, this was going to be fun...

"Octavia!" I called after her, but she kept running.

A door opened and AJ stepped through. Clearly startled by her sudden appearance, he paused in his tracks and she once again used it to her advantage and kicked him in the balls. And part of me had to wonder if this was bigger than her fight-or-flight instincts kicking in. Maybe there was more to the girl than she was letting on.

She made it to the end of the hallway by the time I called out to her once more. "Not gonna lie, Octavia." I kept my distance, my mask gone and voice taunting. "I picked you because the whole submissive thing turned me on. But, damn, little doll. Your fire is even hotter."

She turned and the truth of her predicament appeared to slap her in the face.

"'Ey, baby." I grinned as several emotions crept across her features.

"You motherfucker." The delicate little doll left, and as her pupils dilated, she held herself differently.

"Ouch. No name calling." I tsked my tongue at her. "Now, be a good girl and drop that knife before you hurt yourself."

Fight me. Please. Do it.

Tossing the blade from one hand to the other, she thought for a moment. "No, I think I'll hold on to it." She pinned me with a glare, and I smirked.

Game on.

"Do not. Push me. Give me. The knife." I stalked forward, one calculated step at a time.

"Fuck you!" she snarled, and I sang her name as I closed the distance.

Any other woman would've shriveled up on themselves. Not her, though. It was like she was ready for this, waiting for it her entire life. She was half my size but the blood still dripping from my nose told me this was just the start.

And, fuck, if I wasn't right. She threw the knife, and I had barely enough time to sidestep it before the blade scraped across my arm.

"Bitch."

If she wanted to fight like a man, then I'd treat her like one. I slammed her into the wall, with just enough force that I knew she would feel it without cracking her teeny-tiny ribs. A hand around her throat kept her in place, while I tipped her chin up so she had to look at me.

"Yeah. You're gonna regret those stunts you just pulled." I pressed my body closer to hers.

Her body sagged, submissive. "Just kill me." She already sounded so defeated, and we'd barely begun.

"Where's the fun in that?" I shrugged, watching as her gaze dropped to my lips and back up again.

"Fuck. You."

"Don't tease me, little doll. I'd hate to break that dainty neck of yours." One side of my mouth curled up, and the bitch spit in my face.

"Fuck you, Carmine!"

I lifted a thumb and pushed her saliva past my lips, staring through her as I did. She mewled against my hold, unwillingly pinning her thighs together as she watched me.

That's right.

My dick was painfully hard and her fight rejuvenated. She thrashed against me, the fire between us burning bright. I liked this version of her. I liked to see how far I could take her anger.

Because I would take everything from her. And she'd give it willingly. Dirty little dolls like her always did. But it was mine regardless. Every piece of her was mine.

I tugged her forward by her throat. She stumbled, and I threw her over my shoulder with a sharp slap to the ass. She fought me harder with each step I took up the stairs while all eyes shifted in our direction. My brothers ignored her cries for help. Thankfully Eva wasn't here. Diego had her holed away, out of my father's long-reaching grasps.

Octavia kept fighting all the way up to her room and past the threshold. Eventually, I'd give the girl more comforts. But for now, the only thing laid out across the bed was a singular t-shirt. Mine. A physical representation of my ownership. She'd fight me, but it was either that or nothing.

"Doesn't it get tiresome, little doll? Fighting all the time?" My hair fell into my eyes as I stalked across the room. "You submitted to Daddy and now you'll submit to your *new daddy*." I dropped her onto the bed with a little more force than necessary.

She rolled off and landed on the other side with the grace of a dancer. She shuffled into a fighting stance, but then appeared to take in the room as she lowered her fists. The very bare room. A bed, a dresser, no décor. This wasn't her palace. She'd have to earn her luxuries.

"Typical," she scoffed while crossing her arms with mock arrogance. "Bland. Boring. No class. Just what I'd expect from a Rag—"

I lunged forward, leaving her insult to die in her throat. Before she could scream, she was pinned to the wall. One hand in her hair, forcing her to look at me, the other against her chest, keeping her subdued.

"Watch what you say, Octavia. This isn't New York and these men are loyal to me. Not you. You better be smart if you want to survive. My suggestion? Get on your knees." I shoved off her. "Now you need a shower. You smell like piss." When she didn't immediately move, my teeth clicked in my jaw. "Shower. Now."

"Clothes?" she questioned, her eyes flaring when I motioned to my shirt. "Pants?" Her face burned bright when she saw where her words took my attention.

"That. Or nothing." I shrugged a single shoulder. It was her choice.

"Right. Give me *clothes*, Carmine," she growled, and the sound of my name on her lips sent a new thrill up my spine.

"I guess Sienna *is* the smart one." I sighed and tossed the shirt at her face. "Clothes, Octavia."

She rolled it into a ball and threw it on the floor. Then, to add an extra *fuck you*, she kicked it across the room.

Guess it was time to show her just how shameless I could be.

I stared at her. My expression blank, my body relaxed, my mouth set tight. And her resolve crumbled. Her hands flexed and her shoulders twitched as she kept licking her lips.

"So beautiful. And so dumb." I shook my head. Then I was on her.

Her shirt stretched as I latched a hand around the material and tugged her to the bed. She bounced once before I landed on top of her. She thrashed wildly but couldn't find purchase on the bare mattress. I'd removed everything from the room she could have used to cover herself. She was at my mercy. My little doll, delicate and sweet. I couldn't wait to see how she'd crack.

Would she be just as beautiful? More?

"Just remember." I pinned her arms above her head and sat on her hips. "This would've been easier if you just *obeyed*." That last word introduced me to a wildcat. "That's it. Fight me," I urged her before freeing her hands so she could claw at my skin. "Tsk, tsk, tsk." I caught her wrist right as she tried to slap me. "That wasn't very nice."

Her little gasps only beckoned me to continue. Her shirt shredded in my grip, while the cups of her bra gave way to olive skin and perky nipples. My hands shook, wanting to caress and explore every part of her. She held onto the remnants of her clothing, pinning it to her stomach in an attempt to cover herself. When I went to yank it away, her eyes flashed with *something* that had me pulling back.

This girl was *fuoco e ghiaccio.* The way her skin turned a slight red to match her face, but her touch was frigid. The way her chest jiggled as she panted. Her eyes were saying no, begging to hate me. Yet her body couldn't hide how much she wanted to be tainted— ruined by a Ragetti.

Lifting my hips off her, I slid lower, my fingers digging into the waistband of her pants. My knife came loose, and with one vicious tug, both her pants and panties tore from her body. She glanced at the floor, suddenly staring at the shirt she claimed to not want like it was a beacon of hope. Her hands did little to cover her glistening mound, with breasts far too large for one arm to maintain their modesty.

"Nothing it is," I hissed, then gestured an arm towards the bathroom. "Shower. Now."

She didn't move. I knew she wouldn't. I yanked her down the bed by the ankle and she shrieked, her body making a loud thud when she hit the floor. She clawed at anything nearby, refusing to comply despite knowing she would lose the battle against me. Her insults, in both Italian and English, were creative. I'd give her that. But they were also pissing me off.

I didn't let go as I dragged her across the room by one leg before dropping her in the shower stall. Her cries echoed off the tiled walls the moment the ice-cold water pelted against her bare skin.

She tried to crawl to the door. I watched the view for a few seconds. My cock wanted nothing more than to shred that delicate hymen she was protecting. She just didn't deserve it yet. So I shucked off my shirt and tossed it to the floor before shoving her under the showerhead.

Once she was scrubbed to my liking, I turned on the additional faucets. The water blasted her from three different directions, igniting more of her screams. Which eventually died out as she curled into the fetal position. I waited until all the suds were washed away before I opened the door and stepped out again. Left a soaking mess of limbs and matted-down hair, Octavia glared up at me from the tiled floor.

Her body shook as her red skin glowed in the overhead light. Her lips turning blue. Then I noticed how she continued to clutch the remnants of her shirt to her stomach. I bent down to tug it away again, and the moment my fingers grazed the skin of her abdomen, she shrieked and scurried back.

The fuck? It didn't make sense. This wasn't about modesty anymore. *What was her deal?*

I exhaled my frustrations. "Submission. Obedience. *Conformità.* And then you'll beg me to stay." My original plan was to lock her in the basement, but the idea no longer interested me. "Listen and give me what I want, then I'll return you to *Daddy.*"

"W-what do you want?" The chattering of her teeth matched the trembling of her body.

"Everything." Giving her my back instead of more explanation, I didn't spare the girl a second glance as I left the room and locked it behind me.

She could yell, scream, break shit. It wouldn't matter. No one was going to help her. No one was going to come to her rescue. The windows were barred and the door locked behind me, while every inch of the room and bathroom was monitored by cameras.

Securing both locks, I turned to the thermostat, dropped it ten degrees, and laughed. My little doll would learn very quickly that I wasn't going to tolerate her tantrums. Matteo watched me as I secured the plastic seal over the white box. He followed me into my room as I turned on my monitors. She dripped water across the bathroom, no doubt in search of a towel. It wouldn't take long for her to realize that the closet, cabinets, and drawers were all empty.

Mario's precious daughter was about to learn what it was like to live as my hostage. I'd spent more than a decade uncovering details in my uncle's death. And I knew once I figured out who was behind it, I'd revel in ruining them. Beautiful Octavia Agostino was the perfect prize for my revenge.

"The fuck you doing, brother?" Matteo glanced at the monitors, his eyes shifting away in obvious disgust.

"That family took everything from us." I clenched my jaw into a snarl. "Now I'll take everything from them. From her."

"At what cost? What if they had Eva?"

I told him to fuck off and the bastard stormed out. I didn't bother to look up as the door slammed behind him. My eyes were glued to Octavia, who was huddled in a corner of the room, her arms wrapped tightly around her knees. The air was pumping full blast and she had nothing but a torn piece of thin t-shirt protecting her stomach. It might have been a step up from downstairs, but that didn't mean I was gonna make her time here pleasant.

My uncle's death sure as fuck wasn't. An eye for an eye and all that. He was the man I'd wished was my father and protected me from his brother.

"John, he's your legacy. Beating the shit out of him is only teaching him to hate you." My Uncle Sal's voice still played in my head.

That day was just one of many ass-kickings my old man had dished out on me. JP's fists had been torn open to match the assault he'd unleashed on my body. Couldn't tell you what I did wrong that time. The fucker had never given me a reason. He hated me for breathing. It didn't matter what I'd done. He was the jury that found me guilty. And if it had been my siblings at fault, I'd do something worse to protect them—suffer the consequences so they wouldn't have to.

"Mind your fucking business, fratello. *This doesn't concern you."* My father's voice haunted me just as much.

"I'm taking him with me for the weekend."

JP had looked like he wanted to argue, but eventually the sick fuck stood down. As future capo, my uncle had final say. His word was law.

If only he were still alive, maybe I'd be different. Maybe everything would be different. And that was why the Agostinos would fucking pay. Mario didn't just deserve to die. No, he deserved to suffer like I'd suffered for years.

His lies had officially caught up to him, and his daughter was going to pay the price.

What the hell was I doing? When he stripped off his shirt, I wanted him to take me on the bathroom floor. His harsh words and crude treatment were everything I didn't know I needed. *Wanted.* His powerful muscles flexed and his tattoos danced and taunted me as he leaned into the shower.

Then he left.

There was something about wearing his shirt that rattled me. I understood what he was doing, staking a claim. It was the one small act of defiance I had at my disposal.

Now it was goddamn freezing in here, and I'd give anything to have that shirt back. I clung to what was left of the torn pieces of fabric. Begging it to conceal all my secrets. To serve as a barrier between my body and the man that some sick part of me wanted to surrender it to. I promised myself that I wouldn't allow someone to take from me anymore. What was left of me was under my control.

As the sun set, then rose again, I was lost with my own thoughts—my own self-loathing. All the while I remained huddled on the floor. Unmoving. If Carmine planned to use the solitude to drive me crazy, he'd lose. The silence of my own company was comforting. But I was left freezing, hungry, naked, and growing fucking desperate.

"How're we doing, little doll?" My captor, tormentor, loomed above me with a cruel snarl. "Cold? Hungry?" He was chewing on a cookie with something balled up in one hand.

Approaching with the swagger of a man set to destroy you mentally and physically, Carmine smiled as he held out what I now saw was a shirt—the material taunted me like a white flag urging my quick surrender. Instead, I turned up my nose and refused to meet his glare.

"Fine. No skin off my back." He chewed, the crumbs landing on his toned chest. "We've only just begun and you'll give me the satisfaction I want before I dump you back at Daddy's door."

Carmine laughed and left, the air kicking on as the locks slid in place. My skin burned from the bitter chill. I could practically feel each degree dropping with the temperature. The camera in the corner of the room remained pointed at me the entire time. I waved a middle finger at the little blinking light, moved to the side of the bed, and curled up, hugging my legs to my chest.

The sun set again and I found myself drifting off into a restless sleep, my tormented mind and weakened body too plagued by nightmares to gain anything from it but more exhaustion. By the next morning, my throat was raw and scratchy, my skin moist and warm to the touch. This was it. This was where I died.

At some point during the day, Carmine appeared with the same shirt and a tray of food. I didn't bother to get up.

How many days had it been?

I couldn't remember. Honestly, I didn't care. I wasn't wearing his fucking shirt or eating his probably drugged or poisoned food.

A man obsessed with revenge wanted you to crack, to snap. He took the wrong girl. I'd come close to ending my own life shortly after I'd gotten the scars. Let the secrets be buried with me. Once they found my corpse, my family would move on and they'd be none the wiser of all the shit they'd caused.

I crawled to the bathroom, drinking straight from the faucet. The shower wasn't an option—the only setting was blisteringly cold. My resolve was slowly cracking, and I feared I'd break the next time he came in.

When I limped out, I saw Carmine sitting on the bed, watching as I ignored both him and his offering. I barely blinked as we continued our silent standoff. His jaw ticked, the only sign I might be winning. A few more moments of suspended silence before he stood tall.

"Ready to give up, little doll?" His arm shot out, the shirt hanging between us before the scent of something warm and flavorful floated in behind him. His eyes were alight with excitement as I stepped forward. His need for my submission was intense.

My plan had been to snatch the damn shirt and shred it. Instead, my legs gave out and large arms reached out to grab me before I hit the ground. His skin was warm and I couldn't help but try to get closer. I could sense his suspicion. His body stiffened, but I just longed for the warmth he offered.

The cold had shattered my resolve and I knew I wasn't strong. The feel of his body stalled some of the ache. My brain struggled to concentrate past the terrible headache and congestion sitting on my face. Death seemed welcoming at this point.

"I-I g-get it." My teeth were chattering. No matter how much I willed them to stop. "It's b-because of your uncle. And I-I'm paying for it."

That reignited his rage, flaring it to life, as he stalked towards the bed and deposited me on the bare mattress. My frail body bounced with the movement, and a resounding cackle of pained laughter ripped from my dry throat. I laughed until the sound was hoarse, mocking. Chest heaving, Carmine watched me lose my mind before storming to my side.

Hit me. My stare taunted him.

He squatted in front of me, pinching my chin to look at him. "So beautiful. So dumb." His dark orbs held me captive. "Game. On. Couple more days and you'll be on your knees begging me to save you." His back muscles tensed and flexed as he walked out, the door slamming shut behind him.

"Only as strong as your weakest link," I whispered to myself, tracing a finger along the stars and moons that dangled above me. I repeated the words over and over again, as an involuntary tremor took hold of my body.

A bee danced above my head. I reached out to touch it, jolting when the insect landed on my finger. The buzzing noise seemed to calm me, like we were trapped here together while beady little eyes stared back, as if they understood me.

Until, like everyone else in my life, it stung me too.

The ache had settled so deep within my bones it hurt to breathe, let alone move. Death lingered like a welcomed reprieve. Something warm settled over me, my head rolled back, and I felt like I was moving. Flying. A throaty laugh broke free as someone whispered kind words into my ear.

Kind. I didn't deserve kindness. If they gave me a weapon, a choice, I'd end it all here and now.

Then I felt the burn of water pelting my skin, ice picks stabbing every part of my damaged body. I fought, cried and begged for the pain to stop. Anything to get away from the agony.

"Octavia, don't fight me." Calloused hands pinned my arms to my sides. "We need to bring down her fever. Lorenzo, call the doctor."

"He's going to be pissed," a voice sighed, and I recognized the sound. I was an inconvenience.

"I don't give a fuck. If she dies, we're all fucked."

Then I felt myself being pinned to a chest, and my fight drained as my agonized limbs begged for relief.

"The Agostinos are going to start a fucking war."

"No. Nope. They won't," I said, my finger following the bee. "It's better this way."

"What way?" I didn't answer, too entranced by the insect just out of reach. "What's better, *piccolo ragazza?*"

"If. I. Die." I slid from his grasp, turning my face to the water. "Then it all dies with me…"

My entire body tensed when I felt a fingertip trace across my abdomen. "Octavia, who did this to you?"

"She still burning up?" The second voice was back.

"Yeah. She's hot as fuck," he spluttered, quickly clarifying. "Temp wise."

"Nice tits too."

"Get the fuck out, Lorenzo." Heavy feet stomped from the room as something soft and warm was wrapped around me. "The doctor's almost here."

As I seemingly reached the eye of the storm, the only thing I could hear was the thundering of my own heart and the torrential downpour of my tears. Tears I was weeping for myself. For everything I'd lost before I even stood a chance to gain it. The Octavia they left behind, broken and bleeding, was someone I prayed would die.

She needed to be dead and buried.

If Carmine didn't do it, someone else would. Death was still waiting for me at the end of a narrow hallway filled with flames that licked at my skin. It wasn't a fever that was consuming my physical body. It was my soul heading home to the fiery pits of hell. Running full steam ahead toward a flickering red light.

There was no salvation for sullied girls like me.

"When was the last time she had something to eat?" Cold hands were poking and prodding me.

"I don't know." The bed dipped and a much warmer hand stroked my cheek. "She's been talking to herself, reaching out an arm like she was trying to paint the air or something."

"That's normal. She's hallucinating. Her body was shutting down to contain the infection and battle the fever." Something was swiped across my forehead. "Temp's lowered to one hundred for the last two hours. Change the bags one more time after they've cycled through and she should come to in a day or so. Maybe sooner."

"Matteo!" a booming voice called out, and I whimpered.

In fear? In need?

"Call me if her temperature changes." The first man's voice vanished as a door slammed.

"The fuck ya think ya doin', Matteo." There was the distant shuffling of feet. Boots. Followed by grunts and more arguing.

"You almost fucking killed her. Look." The covers were ripped from my body, as a breeze of cool air prickled my almost-bare skin.

"Why is she in your fucking shirt, *fratello?*"

"Because you left her naked, dehydrated, and battling an infection in a goddamn icebox." Careful hands positioned me onto my side before gently shifting the thin material covering the top half of my body. "Her back was fucked up from your kidnapping."

"That's not my problem." Two heavy footfalls approached my bedside.

"No."

"The fuck did you just say to me?"

"You fucking heard me. I never fight you, Carmine. I always have your back. But not with this. You're going to kill her and start a fucking war we don't need."

"War has casualties."

"And karma is a bitch, Carmine. You've got her suffering for what her father did. What if this was Eva? What if someone wanted Eva to pay for JP's bullshit?"

Silence was the only response before heavy steps retreated from the room, followed by the sound of the slamming door.

When the fever finally broke, I was slowly coming back from the dead. Matteo and Lorenzo, Carmine's brothers, had saved me. Well, Matteo saved me and Lorenzo was kinda just there. He'd play on his phone and watch over me when Matteo was busy. Carmine was nowhere to be found.

Was he with *her*? That Eva girl… And why did I care?

Too many questions plagued my mind until I finally got the courage to ask one of them. "Is he going to kill me?"

Matteo paused, before releasing a long sigh. "A few years ago, I never would've thought he'd be capable of it. Now… now, I don't know." He closed the book he was reading. "But I will do my best to stop him. Even though you begged for it."

My head dropped back to my pillow. "What else did you hear?"

"I'll tell you." Matteo paused. "After you tell me about those scars."

"I was in an accident," I answered too quickly.

"I'm well-acquainted with knife wounds."

I turned away from his scrutinizing glare.

"My brother hasn't seen them, has he?"

I shook my head.

"Get. Out." Carmine's lips curled into a snarl as Matteo seemed to hesitate. "Fuckin' leave, Matteo!" The brothers stared each other down.

"I'll be outside," Matteo said to me, and Carmine scoffed as the door closed us in.

"You get he ain't gonna protect you forever, right?" The beast of a man stepped closer to the bed. The same man who'd shredded my skin and sniffed around my insides. There was no hiding from him. "I'm not letting you die—not unless it's on camera so that Daddy can watch the life drain from your eyes." He reached out a hand, twirling a piece of my hair. "The last thing he will see is you choking to death with my thick cock jammed down your teeny-tiny throat."

"Do it." My voice was unrecognizable. "Go ahead, Carmine. Do it." I kicked back the covers, climbing from the bed.

"Don't tease me, little doll." He turned away.

There was a moment when I could tell… he wanted me too. A man barely restrained, ready to attack.

"Is this what you want?" I ripped Matteo's shirt from my body and dropped to my knees. "My submission?" Slowly, I crawled towards Carmine.

His hands shook and his need hardened, pressing against his zipper. When I'd closed the distance, I slapped my hands on his thighs, sat back with my ass on my heels, and looked up at him. He wasn't in charge anymore. Carmine Ragetti would have to work a hell of a lot harder than that to break me.

The days of people taking from me were done. I welcomed death.

"Don't fuck with me, Octavia. These hands have broken little dolls like you before."

"That's fine. You won't be the first to hurt me," I said as I pulled down the zipper on his pants, popped the button free, and reached inside.

I gulped as my eyes took in the size of him, which I could only assume was larger than most. Spitting into my hand, I wet my palms as my mouth enclosed the head and I sucked. Then I hollowed out my cheeks so I could take him down, deep into my throat.

My head was woozy and my body ached, but right now I felt invincible. Even when his hands slipped into my hair and he directed the rhythm. Back and forth, he took control while the pain and resentment I felt slipped away.

For once, I. Felt. Free.

I stared up at him, and his dark pupils seemed to eviscerate the white around them. Low growls came from deep within his large chest as he ripped his shirt over his head. My eyes followed the various paths of black ink before landing just north of the delicious V that made up his lower abdomen. The words stared back at me in thick script.

La famiglia prima di tutto. Family above all.

And here I was. On my knees, paying for my family's misdeeds. The vengeance having brought us together. The irony wasn't lost on me.

His panting became erratic, his grip on my locks tightening. A man craving power was being controlled by his little doll. On the cusp of his release, until his growl echoed as I bared my teeth and raised my hand. His desire hit the back of my throat and the scalpel in my hand sliced into his thigh.

Carmine's body jolted and I ripped the scalpel out and drove it back in. Repeatedly. When I finally let go, he shoved me onto my back, going for the piece of metal protruding from his leg. I paused for too long, his blood magnetizing. Drawing my eyes to its dark hue.

Throwing on Matteo's shirt, I started chuckling—the sound low and crazy—before tiptoeing towards the door.

"You act like a god." Using my thumb, I smeared the little droplets of his blood across my cheek before licking my finger clean. "Yet you bleed."

"You fucking bitch." He tucked his hard dick back into his pants. "I ain't your pussy of a brother. I don't pretend to be god *or* devil. I bleed just like everyone else. Just. Like. You."

Before I could move, he was on me. Pinning me to the wall. A large hand around my neck as he squeezed. My body hummed from the lust. From the terror too.

What was wrong with me?

He pushed his mouth to my ear, bucking his hips against me. "Keep it up and I'll never let you leave." He laughed as I shoved against his hold.

A moment of insanity turned into several and I punched his thigh. His attention on his wound as I darted into the hallway and slammed the door in his face. I limped my way towards the stairs. The door opened just as my legs gave out and I collapsed onto the floor. Matteo shouted but I couldn't understand anything past my exhaustion.

Carmine came up behind me, looking murderous. And I laughed, the sound loud and cathartic while my legs shook as I stood. I'd gotten one up on him. Just one. And I knew he'd made me pay for it. But…

"Fuck. You." I gestured for Carmine to come get me. He lunged, my foot slipped, and my scream echoed across the walls.

CHAPTER 10

HOODED MAN

Her screams were figments of my dreams and I couldn't wait until the next time I had her writhing under me. Octavia didn't understand that she belonged to me. She'd assumed it was a onetime visit, but I would be back.

Especially now. Especially because of her silence.

When I'd marked her, it was because I wanted Mario to see I'd forever own his little girl. To show him that he wasn't untouchable. That he couldn't protect his most prized possession, his children. Octavia had been handpicked for her innocence and soft spirit.

The more I watched, the more I waited. And the more she'd become my obsession. She'd consumed every part of my day. Where was she? Who was she meeting? What book was she reading?

I knew how she took her coffee, what her favorite meal was, which of the hundreds of classics in her library she preferred. I knew how hard she worked to perfect the dances she wouldn't perform for anyone. And most of all, the sounds she made when my blade touched her skin. How her body caved to my ownership. The screams of terror mixed with desire. It was intoxicating…

Each stroke of the sharpened blade was mesmerizing, each thrust of my hips heaven.

Mario thought he owned everyone and everything in *his* city. Well, I was fucking owed what was mine. Everything. A self-proclaimed king because of a fucking *birthright*. In reality, the man was a liar, a cheater, and a son of a bitch. He took everything from me. Mario Agostino was the bastard who ruined my life. And I was going to take it all back now.

Just like I took her.

Staring out the window, I watched the entire family moving about their days as if an integral piece of their unit wasn't missing. They were trying to show power, but I knew they were falling apart. I watched. I waited. I listened. There wasn't a single one of them who wasn't feeling the effects of her disappearance.

The only problem was that she had been taken by someone else. Though it was only a matter of time before I found out who. Then I'd kill him.

"What the hell are you doing?"

I turned towards the sound of my father's voice, fighting the urge to flip him off. The man was a coward, using me to do his dirty work. He'd suddenly learned of my existence and showed up like I owed him the world for getting me out of one hell and dropping me into another. He wouldn't tell me who my mother was, dangling it over my head to keep me in line.

He wanted his revenge even more than I wanted mine. It was a fight to force the man to see past his anger. He'd finally claimed me as his own, but it wasn't because he loved me. It was because I was his key to take New York. To destroy that family. He just didn't get that my going along with his plan wasn't for him. It was for her.

"I have my men out looking for leads," I said, refusing to glance in his direction.

"You're a fucking disgrace. You had one job. Own her. Instead, the little bitch kept her mouth shut, and now we're back to square one."

"No, we're not. I will find her. Then we'll make the last move to end this."

"Then get it done." He stormed from the room, once again leaving me to my thoughts.

Octavia was my scarred beauty. Every part of her belonged to me. It wouldn't matter if someone else touched her now. I was her first and her blood had coated my soul.

She was my forever and soon enough she would realize I was hers.

CHAPTER 11
CARMINE RAGETTI

My mind was consumed by my little doll. Was she miserable? Was she begging? Calling out for me? Did she have any idea what I'd planned to do to her? Hell, did I?

I'd been gone longer than I intended and was practically salivating at the thought of having my hands on her. Her supple skin was soft, innocent. My inked palms ran callouses over every inch of her in my mind. And now I was finally back to do the real thing.

I pulled up, eyeing my father, who was seconds away from walking into my home. "Where is she?"

"Who?" I shrugged, feigning ignorance while knowing it would only piss him off more.

"Don't fuck with me, *boy*. You know who. Living in my fucking house with the enemy." His words were spitting at my feet.

My fists clenched. It was my fucking house. Not his. I wanted nothing from this man or the empire he was running into the fucking ground.

"Who?" I repeated.

"Eva… the *disgusting bitch*… Take your pick. They all seem to flock to you and then… *poof*. They're missing." He lit the cigarette in his hand, and my eyes dropped to the blood on his shirt. "Fuckin' pussies. The lot of you. Some sons I raised."

"You've got an amends to make," I grunted, and he glared at me. "Shooting one of *my* men."

The pause was pregnant. Then he laughed. "Amends? Fuck you. That motherfucker should've known his place. She's my daughter. On my order. Never should've interfered." His eyes were wild, manic, and I fought to keep calm.

The image of my fist flying into his face was interrupted when his phone rang. What he did to Alessandro wouldn't go unanswered. I just had some other shit to deal with first. And then… JP would get his.

I paced in the front yard, watching his car pull off. He didn't deserve to fucking breathe. But I had to bide my time. Make sure all the Ts got crossed first. Rage, so much rage, was bursting through me, and I had someone that I could take it out on.

The moment I closed the door to my brother's room, my little doll thwarted my plans. My teeth threatened to shatter as I watched the way her breasts swayed as she crawled on all fours towards me. A ripe, perky ass at the cusp of two wide hips begged for my hand. Those delicate lips opened for her tongue to trace along my dick.

Tangling my hand in her hair, I took control. She was inexperienced and a strange sense of pride consumed me at the mere thought of all the depraved things I wanted to introduce her to. I was buried deep in her throat while the muscles there worked me over as she tried to breathe. Once. Twice. On the third thrust forward, I came, my body shaking with pleasure.

Pleasure and a ripple of… pain?

Her teeth scraping along my cock only made me come harder, but then an inferno tore through my thigh. She ripped the blade free and stabbed at me again. I lowered a hand and gripped at the nape of her neck, forcing her backwards.

Matteo had told me she begged for death. Seemed almost at peace with it. Now I *really* wanted to kill her. I was going to tie her up and fuck her till she bled. She wanted knife play? Fine by me. I'd mark every inch of that supple fucking skin.

I watched her dart through the door, thinking she'd won. And I let her. I craved the chase. She made it down the hall, all the way to the stairs, by the time I caught up with her.

And then she screamed.

Her legs were weak, shaking from all the exertion. A foot slipped and she fell backwards. The sluggish part of her brain appeared to sense the danger too late. If she didn't break her fucking neck, I was going to wring it. She hit the steps and tumbled, rolling down a few before Matteo caught her. She was out cold when I ripped her out of his arms. Her unblemished skin in my scarred, tattooed hands. My biceps shook, wanting—no, needing to teach her a fucking lesson. To remind her of her place. With me.

And where was that?

On. Her. Fucking. Knees. Just devoid of a weapon this time.

My large California king bed with black silk sheets seemed to swallow her whole. She had curves for days, but she was so tiny. Not very tall with tight muscles stretched over a slight frame.

"The fuck… Carmine?" Matteo glanced at my leg, my jeans soaked with my own blood for once.

"I need stitches." I kicked off my pants and plopped down on the edge of the frame to take a look at Octavia's handiwork.

Make that several.

That fire in her was admirable. It was also the same thing that would end up getting her hurt.

"She did that?" Matteo barked out a laugh before walking into my bathroom and coming back with a needle and thread.

"She's got… *spirit.*" I stared down at the small bundle sprawled out under my sheets.

"She still alive?" Lorenzo sauntered into the room, eating an apple like I hadn't laid him out on the floor less than an hour ago. "The fuck happened to you…?" He glanced at my leg, then over to Octavia and started chuckling between bites. "Brother, you're fucked."

"That girl is somethin'." Matteo ignored my hiss of pain as he started piecing my thigh back together.

"Shut the fuck up." I followed his line of sight. "She'll pay for it. Later."

And I couldn't wait to start. But first thing was first. My father's impromptu visit meant I needed to be ready and focused on my family right now. I quickly filled my brothers in, and they agreed.

"He's fucking lost it. Straight batshit crazy, dude." Lorenzo chucked the apple in the bin before leaning over Octavia as if she might just jump up and bite him. "Should hand her over. She can be his fucking problem."

"Fuck no," Matteo and I both grunted in unison as my eyes flicked over to my brother. His concern was getting under my skin. The mere idea of my brother attempting to touch what belonged to me made me murderous. I'd never kill the rat bastard, but I'd hurt him if he tried.

Matteo tied off the last stitch before peering up at me. "If Eva gets word of this—"

"She won't. She barely comes here and now she won't be welcome."

"If you tell her to stay away…" Matteo started, only to be interrupted by a tiny groan.

"Who's Eva?" Octavia sat up, Matteo's shirt falling off her shoulder as she eyed us from my bed.

"Out," I hissed, and my brothers didn't spare her a glance as they left.

"Guess you're mad, huh?" Her breasts pressed against the blood-splattered white material. "Like I told your brother, why don't you just kill me and get it over with?" Then Octavia dropped back against my pillow, the circles under her eyes turning a dark blue.

"Mad. *Mad?* Mad doesn't even begin to describe it." I rolled my shoulders and cracked my neck, wincing when I pushed to my feet and put pressure on my thigh.

"You should rest that leg. You'll just tear a stitch." She was staring at my cock through my boxers.

I towered over the bed, watching the way my little doll trembled beneath the covers. She'd made me bleed but I wasn't innocent either. And it was time she learned a lot more about me.

She looked up and something she saw there had her freezing to the spot, her breath stalling in her lungs. "Calm down, and fucking breathe. You did this to yourself, you know."

Before she could respond, my housekeeper breezed into the room. Kate gave me that *thirsty* look she always had on her face whenever she saw me, until she noticed Octavia.

"What is *it* doing in your bed?"

I snapped my fingers, drawing her attention back to me. "Who the fuck do you think you're talking to?" She jumped at the sound of my voice but didn't move. "Get the fuck out." Then I pinned her with a glare that finally sent her running.

My brothers had warned me about her. She'd been growing a pair of balls in *my* house. She was cruel to the other staff and acted as if she ran the place. Besides that, she'd made it known that she'd help me with *anything*. I fucked her here and there, on the occasion when I was bored, which apparently was the wrong move, seeing as she seemed to think herself my equal now.

I'd always wondered what she told herself after we'd fucked. How she justified my treatment of her. The first time, I'd come home drunk and needing to take a piss. Kate had just finished cleaning the toilet and I fucked her from behind, pushing her face into the bowl to drown out the awful sounds of her screams. Then there was the time I fucked her after I'd just lost one of my men in a random shooting. I was enraged and she was on her knees scrubbing the dining room floor. I'd fucked her on her stomach, using her body like a fucking mop as she sloshed around the puddle of cleaning product she'd just dumped on the floor.

Apparently, she thought that made her special. When, in reality, it just meant she was convenient. She was also out of a job, and if she didn't lose her little attitude towards Octavia, she'd end up dead too.

"I didn't disobey," Octavia mumbled under her breath, before her eyes flicked to my thigh.

"No. That I enjoyed." A slow smirk curled my lips, and she shivered as exhaustion had her settling back against my sheets.

This girl made it hard to breathe. Focus. My anger and need for her constantly consumed me, debilitated me. Much like mixing kerosene with an open flame, it was a goddamn explosion set to destruct. All while her contented sigh made my dick hard. I couldn't deny how much I liked the way she looked in my bed. Except I wanted to be between those creamy thighs. Give her fire a little gasoline.

"That your housekeeper?" she asked, and I quirked a brow, wondering where this conversation was going. "I've never seen her before." Octavia closed her eyes and drifted into a fitful sleep as I was sent into a rage.

That little fucking cunt…

I'd left Kate very explicit instructions, a timed schedule of when I wanted Octavia fed and watered.

Okay, that sounded like she was more horse than human—though if that were the case, the girl would be a prized thoroughbred.

Once I was sure Octavia was sleeping, the sound of her soft breathing telling me as much, I locked the door behind me and went in search of my brothers. Matteo was already in my office when I stormed inside and headed straight for my computer. Pulling up the footage from Octavia's room, I reviewed the feed during the time I was gone.

"She's fucking dead." My anger took hold as I thought of how to punish her.

"Told you that bitch was getting ballsy." Matteo's words filtered into my brain, barely stifling my anger and making it hard to think.

Drawing my phone from my pocket, I sent Kate a text, sat back, and waited. My brothers took up their usual spots, spread out around my office. I glanced at my watch and tapped my foot impatiently. I wasn't sure how long Octavia would be asleep and she was loose in my room.

A slight knock and each of us rivaled the other's smirk. "Enter," I called out.

Here was the thing about the business my family was involved in. You had to have many talents—many faces—to remain at the top. Behind closed doors, I was the big brother to two little assholes. And Eva. I was whoever I needed to be to protect them. I was myself. Laid back and carefree in a sense. I was the version of me my father hated the most. Wearing jeans and slinging slang words. I was a chameleon because on the other side of it all was the future boss.

Suits. Slicked-back hair. Proper English and a tense silence that made our enemies squirm in their seats. And Kate… she was my enemy right now. The little whore had no idea what the fuck she was in for.

The moment she entered the room, I saw what everyone else was seeing. Eyes for only me and a seductive sway to her hips as she approached my desk. I'd never willingly invited her into this room. It was only when she had crossed nearly half the distance that she noticed my brothers' presence.

"Yes? Um?" Kate glanced at each of us, her shoulders hunched.

I let her fidget for a moment, then two. Without a word, I hit play and turned the monitors in her direction. Did she really think I'd leave Octavia without surveillance?

Kate started to back up towards the door, fear replacing the lust in her eyes. Her cry of shock as she bumped into Lorenzo's chest made me smile. She was absolutely petrified and she fucking should be. Because standing tall behind the desk, palms flat against the gleaming wood, was the future boss of the Ragetti family. The man who could break her neck with a snap of his fingers, which would be the least painful option.

"Speak," I barked and she jumped.

She remained tight-lipped, and for a second, I didn't think she would comply. But when the floodgates were finally released, she poured her truth all over the room. "She's filth! Filth! She doesn't belong in this house, let alone upstairs. I know what her *family* did and she didn't deserve to eat. She doesn't belong in my—*your* house," Kate repeated, catching herself but not before it was too late.

"Whose house?" I tilted my head with the question, my teeth gleaming under the harsh light.

"Y-yours, sir."

I walked around the front of the desk, leaning against it. "Kate, you've been with me long enough to know I don't tolerate disobedience." She nodded. "However, I thank you for your service. Devotion." Her shoulders sagged in relief, until I added, "Though illplaced, as it seemed to give you a false sense of security. The belief that you could disobey me. In my own fucking house!" I roared.

"Knees," Matteo commanded. When she stalled, he tapped the back of her legs and she crumbled.

"Will you show the three of us how sorry you are?" I hummed, dropping my voice to that even pitch.

"I... Sir... I..."

We let the suspense linger a little longer, the three of us glancing at each other until we all burst into a fit of humorless laughter.

"None of us have a taste for rape. But whores like you wouldn't say no, would you?" I asked the question, not expecting a response. She remained silent. "No. I don't rape. But…"

I lunged for her. My grip was tight on her throat, a silent message that one wrong move and I'd end her life. My breath wafted heavily over her face, the same face that was slowly turning red with the lack of oxygen. She tried to swat at my arm, but I gripped her wrist. Applying enough pressure to cause pain. I held her throat until she was just about to pass out.

At the last second, I released her. And Kate fell, crashing to the floor. A mess of tears, desperation, and snot.

Had she always been this pathetic? Fuck if I could tell you.

Bending down to cup her cheek, I whispered into her ear, "You're no longer welcome in my home. Yard duties and the guard quarters only." And then I spit in her face. "Get out of my fucking sight."

If she were a man, I'd fucking kill her for this. That cunt between her legs was the only thing that gave me pause. At least for now.

As she took off from the room, I sat back in my seat, rolling my neck until it cracked in several places. It had been a fuck of a few days and the tension seemed to settle in my shoulders.

"Wanna acknowledge why you *behaved* like that?" Matteo crossed his arms and shot a glare in my direction.

"Octavia's pain and torment is *mine,*" I grunted, and he raised a brow. "As the oldest, I fucking called dibs on this little plan of ours. I put in the work. I set it into motion. Mine."

"Sure that's all?" Matteo laughed as Lorenzo turned on a heel and left.

"Shut up." My tone and the glare that came with it would be his only warning.

"We've got another problem thanks to her." Matteo turned his phone to me. "He's been seen sniffing around Cali, hitting a few of your properties."

"Peiro. That little-fucking-shit. Call it in. I want him picked up."

Pride caused a man to do dangerous things. And if he was in Cali, it meant the son of a bitch had a fucking death wish. I'd watched. I'd waited. It was clear how he looked at her, craved her. Octavia might've missed it, but I hadn't. I wouldn't let the little motherfucker anywhere near her.

A minute later, Lorenzo returned. "Might want to get upstairs, brother. *Tempesta mortale* is tearing through your bedroom from the sounds of it."

"Fuck." I darted past him. The farther up the stairs I went, the louder her screams became. Followed by various crashing sounds.

Matteo laughed at my back. "Sounds expensive." His amusement was quickly cut short when my fist clipped his jaw and he tumbled to the ground.

I unlocked the bedroom door and had just opened it a crack when glass shattered by my head. My little doll was breaking everything that wasn't bolted down. The sheets were strewn about the room, the dresser drawers upended, my glass tumblers and liquor smashed while an expensive bottle of bourbon was dripping down the wall beside me.

"Little doll, you've made a mess." Her chest was heaving, her thin shoulder peeking out of the neckline of Matteo's shirt. "Get the fuck over here and lick it up."

She laughed as if I'd said something funny.

This creature was bizarre. I watched her. Researched her. Mommy and Daddy's prized little doll. She dressed, acted, and smiled just like the image they depicted. But the bitch was a wolf in sheep's clothing. I'd heard the rumors all suggesting that if Sienna had a dick swinging between her legs, she'd give Lucky a run for his seat…

But something told me it was Octavia they should really be keeping an eye on.

L ick. It. Up.

As if the man hadn't gotten to know my teeth first-hand, he taunted me further. The bastard had the nerve to come back in here, wearing no shirt with the top button on his jeans popped open, and demand things of me? His naked chest was making my brain short circuit.

You did make a mess, I told myself while eyeing my handiwork. Good. Fuck. Him.

When I'd woken up in an unfamiliar place, it only took a second for reality to set in with the speed and velocity of a freight train. So I decided to share the damage. Anything I could pick up, I broke. Shattered. Threw it against the wall. I screamed at the world. Released all the anger, pain, and resentment until I was nothing but a vessel for the emotions that were trying to consume me.

My entire body hurt and my resolve was disintegrating. The strength I exhibited was all a farce and I was one hell of an actress. I couldn't make things easy on him. He'd bled… but how long before he returned the courtesy?

"Lick. It. Up." Carmine stalked forward, each word gritted between clenched teeth. "No? Where'd those heavy balls go, little doll?"

I narrowed my glare at him, the pet name grating on my nerves. Picking up another bottle of expensive liquor, I took a large gulp. My hands shook while the liquid warmed my soul and fizzled in my brain.

Carmine stepped over the mess I'd made. His eye on his *prize*. My airway constricting the closer he drew. Stopping in front of me, he moved far too gracefully for a man of his size. He took the bottle, his lips sensuously wrapping around the rim and giving me pause.

He snatched my hair and forced my head back. He ran the tip of his nose down my jawline. And when he leaned in to whisper in my ear, his dark eyes seemed to glow. "Your family plastered their little doll all over the media. So sweet, innocent. Your delicate porcelain face was painted so purely, to cover what they didn't want the world to see. Daddy dressed you to please the image of incorruptibility to cover his tainted name. Well, you're my little doll now. And, baby, I'm your new daddy." A chill went down my spine and a fire lit between my thighs.

"Be gentle." My voice was soft, but I was ready for the fight that hadn't dwindled.

"Why? Too afraid of the face behind the paint? The body under that shirt? Baby, I want to see it all… Daddy won't be gentle. I want to see how many pieces are left behind when I crack the mold and reveal the goddess underneath."

I'd read about this in far too many books. The female lead, frozen to the spot, transfixed by his proximity. She wanted to run, flee to safety. But the throbbing between her thighs held her in place.

And I promise you… I couldn't move. I couldn't think. I couldn't do anything other than swallow past my need for him.

My mouth opened but nothing came out. I'd been raised to be demure and silent, allowing men to take the lead. But this man was leading me straight down a path to my own destruction. And here I was, just waiting for him to command me. Wishing this wasn't our story. That we were anyone else.

My fight disappeared as reality settled heavily on my shoulders. "Do it already." No one would want me for anything other than revenge. "Rape me. Kill me. I don't care. Just stop talking about it and finally fucking do *something*."

If he wanted to hurt me, then he needed to get on with it. I'd survived this once. Let's see if I could survive him too.

"Is it rape, little doll? 'Cause that would imply you don't want it. Want *this*." He grabbed his erection through his jeans.

"I don't." I bit my lip to keep back more lies.

A vicious circle of steps matched each subliminal message as Carmine prowled around the room. His hate was heavy like a humid storm, drowning me until I was unable to breathe.

"No, I—"

This time my lies were cut off by a shattering of glass and an echo of screams as a haze of bullets tore through the window. Carmine was on top of me, pinning me to the floor before I could focus on the chaos. His brothers were shouting down the hall as a war embroiled outside.

"Help! I'm in here!" I shoved at his chest.

Carmine glanced out the window. "They're not here for you." He pulled me behind him, heading to the hall. "You ever fire one of these?" He held out a nine in my direction.

"You really wanna give this to me?" I countered, grabbing the gun before he could think better of it. Carmine might think otherwise, but Mario Agostino raised his children to survive this lifestyle. Even me.

The barrage of bullets seemed unending, glass shattering and wood splintering in every direction. All while Carmine shielded my body with his. It was the oddest sensation, the most irrational thought. *Was he protecting me?* There was no reason he wanted to save me outside of killing me himself.

"Front has been breached," one of the brothers shouted as heavy boots charged from the far end of the hall towards us.

The gunfire ceased and Carmine climbed to his feet, reaching out a hand for me to grab. "Get up." When I didn't move, he barked at me, "Now, Octavia."

What happened to *little doll*?

I hated the fucking endearment, hated it even more when he didn't use it. Whoever this girl was that wanted to ride his cock with a knife to his throat, she wasn't Octavia. My fingers pressed against my temples as an internal war raged in my head.

"Do not let go of my back, and if you see anyone that isn't my brothers, you pull that trigger."

"And then?"

"And you don't stop until the magazine is empty." His long, quick strides had me stumbling behind as I fought to keep up with him.

A patient man would've asked if I understood. A kinder man would've made sure I was okay. A protective man would've told me to stay put until he slayed the dragons. But Carmine was none of those things. He was a bloodthirsty brute who made my heart race, while his reassuring glances told me he knew I could do it. And suddenly I realized my enemy had more faith in me than my own family ever would.

How was this terrifying stranger able to see into my soul and call to my needs?

The door opened, his two brothers firing down the hall as Carmine stepped out with a gun in each hand. No one coming up the stairs stood a chance. Men were lying in pools of blood at the end of the long corridors, bent over the stairs, and sprawled out over every surface.

"Carmine!" a deep voice bellowed from below. "Call off your hounds. Let's talk."

"You shot up my motherfuckin' house, Hank? I dare your dumb ass to show your ugly fucking face." Carmine bristled in front of me.

"Don't be fuckin' stupid. I got a lot more firepower down here. Trying to be civil. I just want Eva."

There was that name again, and all three brothers seemed to be on edge at the mention of it.

"Russian firepower, right? The fucking Bratva is onto you, *cazzo di asino.*" Carmine shoved a fresh magazine into place.

"Chiudi il becco!"

The three brothers had a silent conversation that consisted of nothing more than a few broody expressions and quick hand signals. Then, all at once, they moved. Carmine—not feeling me at his back—turned, grabbed my hand, and put it on his shirt, silently ordering me to follow his lead.

"She's bought and paid for! Take it up with your father after you hand her over." We shuffled closer. "She belongs to me! I want her! Now!"

I felt bad for Eva, whoever she was. This man-child was literally stomping his feet and whining like a toddler who needed a nap.

My head was pounding and my body was weak. Gunfire and shouting surrounded the house, but I felt myself fighting to stay in the present. Exhausted, while my anger seeped through my central nervous system. Teetering on the brink of madness, until I heard her.

Let me out. The monster was beating on the door again.

A warmth consumed me, my mind clearing. Peace settled over me as I let go of Carmine. Floating from behind him, I ignored his brothers' shouting. *She* was craving blood and it was time to collect. Carmine tried to grab me, but I stepped out of his reach. Peering over the rail, I looked down on the man below.

"And who are you?" he asked, his hair greasy and slicked-back and his eyes beady like a snake's.

"You have a really annoying voice," my empty hand raised to rub the heel of my palm into one eye. His greedy gaze followed the slight lift of my shirt. "I don't want to listen to you anymore."

He was so focused on my bare thighs he didn't notice the barrel aiming in his direction. Chaos broke loose as I started firing. My shot missed the target between his eyes. It connected with his shoulder as I stepped to descend the stairs.

Heart racing. Adrenaline coursing. The need for blood made me smile. I could practically smell their death. And then… Carmine pulled me back.

"The hell was that?" His expression morphed and blurred, then went black.

I was jostled awake. Inside a car.

I eyed the leather interior, noticing the brothers were in a heated debate. Carmine and I were in the back seat. I was sprawled out across his lap. I moaned and he glanced down at me.

"Go back to sleep." The authoritative tone would've been enjoyable if I weren't so exhausted.

"JP is a problem we need to handle," Matteo said from the driver's seat while Lorenzo sounded bored—detached.

"He won't stop until he gets them both."

"He's not gonna get either," Carmine snapped.

"Give him the Agostino bitch. It'll keep him busy for a bit."

"Shut the fuck up, Lorenzo. Before I break your goddamn jaw." Carmine shifted in his seat, forcing me to move.

I rolled over, my face buried in his lap, and curled my arms around him. Soft touches stroked my hair and I fell blissfully back to sleep.

I opened my eyes and saw I was alone in an unfamiliar room. Rising slowly, I looked out the window and noticed that we were at the beach—the water crashing just beyond the glass. It looked beautiful.

I felt physically rested but my mind was wandering. I'd blacked out again. Carmine had attempted to protect me, but I'd refused to cower. The weakest link was forced into the shadows and I felt confident in whomever stepped forth. Or rather *what*…

But why had he protected me? He couldn't be—

Idiot. I'd read too many love stories. You could call me beauty and him a beast, but outside of being well-read and a moody asshole, that's where our similarities ended. Carmine wanted to kill me himself. That was all there was to it.

"You're awake."

I didn't turn away from the window, even as I felt him approach. "It's so blue. Nothing like the beaches at home."

"Because the east coast dumps its waste into all the rivers that feed into the ocean. The Pacific is nothing like the Atlantic." A meaty hand gripped my hair and turned me around. "You look well." That dangerous glare was back and a shiver of fear gave me goose bumps.

"Where are we?"

He ignored the question. "You thought your family had come for you?" he hummed, and I remained silent. "Poor, naïve Octavia." He stepped closer, enjoying the way I flinched more at his words than his touch. "I look forward to breaking Mario's precious doll."

"You can't break me, Carmine. Someone already beat you to it."

We became locked in a silent stare down.

"Get a fucking shower. I'll leave clothes on the bed."

I didn't fight him, just turned to walk towards the open door. His grip on my wrist stopped me. Before I could turn around, he grabbed the hem of the shirt and ripped it over my head.

We're back to this again? At least it wasn't cold in here.

His hand caught my wrist when I tried covering myself. A soft finger traced my collarbone before pressing down—hard. I flinched at the pain while dark swells threatened to drown me in his hatred. His free hand dropped to my hip and in one swift wave, his fingertips traced along my scars. I looked away and he grabbed my chin, forcing me to meet his glare head-on. Another soft touch and I gasped. The phantom pain and embarrassment were too much. He was invoking too many harsh memories and I was hanging on by a thread.

Instead of holding me tighter, he let me go, his glare burning the skin at my back.

Running into the shower, I allowed the water to hide my shame. Oxygen barely met my lungs and I struggled to breathe. My chest was heavy and tight. I was floating through life and I felt ready to crash back to earth.

"Let's go, Octavia." When I didn't respond, Carmine ripped open the stall door and shut off the water. "This isn't a fucking game. Let's. Go."

"Leave." My voice sounded stronger than I felt.

"No wonder they aren't paying the ransom. You listen for shit."

Sadness ripped from deep within me, and tears ran down my cheeks. Gripping my shoulders, he licked the trail before biting my jaw. My arms dropped to his thick waist to hold myself upright as my legs shook.

I wanted his hate. I deserved it.

There was something wrong with me. Because the worse he treated me, the more I wanted him. My hands went to his belt and I pulled him closer. His grip on the back of my neck was painful as he continued to mark my face with his teeth before lowering his lips to my mouth and capturing it in a harsh kiss.

His rough touch lit me on fire. Carmine picked me up and I wrapped my legs around his waist. My hands threaded through his hair, tugging as I bit his lip. His groan was animalistic, and he moved faster, tossing me onto his bed as a thumb swiped at the blood dripping from his mouth.

"You're going to pay for that, little doll," he hissed. I crawled backwards on the bed, my legs spread and naked. "Blood for blood, baby. I'll be your first and make you Daddy's little whore."

And like a bucket of ice water being dumped all over me, he ruined the moment. One knee on the bed, the other bracing him on the floor, Carmine was reaching for my ankle when he stopped. Only a moment of hesitation before he yanked me towards him.

"Don't be scared, little doll. Once the beast gets his blood, he'll make it better." His warm mouth devoured my mound, my folds, exploring—all while assuming he was the first.

The moan of pleasure that parted my lips sounded like a different woman. Someone who needed the pleasure. This escape.

His tongue hit just the right spot, one I didn't know existed. And all I could do was hold his hair, pull him tighter, closer to the part of me that needed the attention. I'd let this man suffocate before I'd let him move. My breath stalled, my heart beating out of control, and I couldn't force myself to suck in air. I stared at the ceiling, my entire body seizing up as my thighs gripped the sides of his face. That climax was better than anything I'd ever done alone, and it wasn't over yet as another wave rippled through my body.

"Fuck." Carmine crawled up the bed, his pants thrown to one side as he hovered over me.

I'd seen my brother's second without a shirt before, but Apollo's ink didn't hold a candle to Carmine's. Nothing compared to this man—this animal. Every inch of his skin was covered, leading up to his erect dick, while the inverted cross had me praying to the devil. My hands shook as I registered just how equivalent each part of him was to his overbearing height and width.

"Come here." Carmine braced himself on one arm, as he reached between his legs. "Get it wet for me, baby." His tone was husky, his eyes smoldering, his entire body coiled. Prepared to attack. And I was going to be his victim.

I opened my mouth, licking him from tip to end before swallowing back the head. His tree trunk arms gripped the headboard as he pushed his hips forward.

"I need to be inside you." He lifted my legs, pushing them into my chest as he settled his length at my entrance. His mouth opened before a long strand of spit seemed to move in slow motion. Palms remained on the backs of my thighs, holding me in place, as we watched the trail of saliva land on flesh. The head of his cock smeared it around before settling back between my thighs. "This is gonna hurt, little doll. And I want to hear you scream." One thrust of his hips and he buried himself deep.

The sensation was a lot. He was so long and thick that even with the orgasm I still wasn't prepared for him. Once, then twice, he pumped into me until he stopped, sitting back on his heels as he stared down at where our bodies met with his head cocked to the side.

"I won't bleed for you." My jaw trembled with the admission.

"My little doll has a secret."

He had no clue.

There hadn't been a moment of rebellion against my parents. No pact to break my hymen, just to break mafia law. If only that were the story, but it was a much more graphic picture. I couldn't stand the embarrassment. The questions I knew were coming. So I did the only thing I could think of…

I lifted onto my elbows, my face an inch from his. "My father knew who killed your uncle," I hissed, and his hand immediately went to my throat. "And he lied to you. It's only right that he feels a semblance of your pain, that he knows what it means to lose something he loves."

I was a stupid girl, but I needed his rage.

His grip was brutal, the strokes of his cock painful as he punished me. Restricting my breath as he thrusted his hips. His harsh movements forced my head to slam against the headboard and added to the pain radiating through my body.

"You fucking bitch." His breath came out in fast pants, while random gasps of air made their way into my lungs, stalling my death. We stared at each other, him with hatred in his eyes and me with nothing. Because I had nothing left to give. To anyone. Not even myself.

All I could focus on was what he would do next. Would he strangle me to death? Tie me to the bed and take me again? Send a message to my father?

Despite the agony, my body tightened around his cock and I came, screaming just like he wanted.

"Look at my little whore. If Daddy could see you now," he grunted as my eyes rolled into the back of my head when no air filtered in. Then Carmine abruptly stopped pumping into me, his body tight and his chest heaving.

Stars burst behind my eyes as darkness settled over me. Everyone died. It was how life worked. Though I never anticipated being strangled and fucked to death.

Guess no one could predict how they'd die.

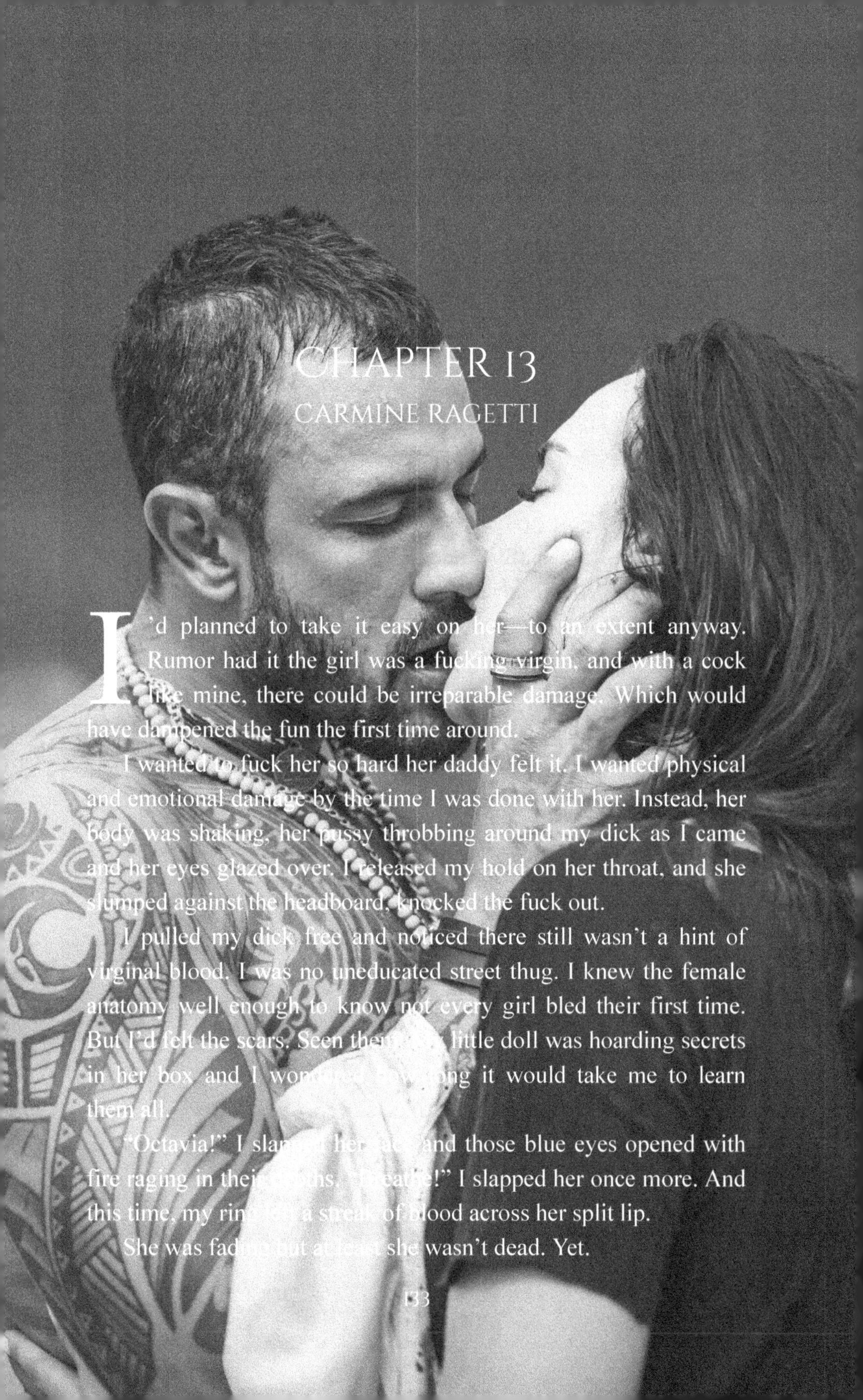

CHAPTER 13

CARMINE RAGETTI

I'd planned to take it easy on her—to an extent anyway. Rumor had it the girl was a fucking virgin, and with a cock like mine, there could be irreparable damage. Which would have dampened the fun the first time around.

I wanted to fuck her so hard her daddy felt it. I wanted physical and emotional damage by the time I was done with her. Instead, her body was shaking, her pussy throbbing around my dick as I came and her eyes glazed over. I released my hold on her throat, and she slumped against the headboard, knocked the fuck out.

I pulled my dick free and noticed there still wasn't a hint of virginal blood. I was no uneducated street thug. I knew the female anatomy well enough to know not every girl bled their first time. But I'd felt the scars. Seen them. My little doll was hoarding secrets in her box and I wondered how long it would take me to learn them all.

"Octavia!" I slapped her face, and those blue eyes opened with fire raging in their depths. "Breathe!" I slapped her once more. And this time, my ring left a streak of blood across her split lip.

She was fading but at least she wasn't dead. Yet.

She panted as I loomed over her. A vantage point that gave me a better look at the scars on her stomach. It was clear Octavia liked pain. It was why she'd taunted me. Her tight little cunt gripped my cock like a goddamn vise as soon as I started choking the life out of her.

My fingers traced along the thin, raised lines that marked her skin. A man like me knew a healed-over knife wound when we saw one. But this wasn't self-mutilation. The angles were all wrong for that. No, this was done with precision, meant to cause harm. To leave a message.

So what the fuck happened to her?

I shook the curiosity away. It didn't matter. The girl's welfare wasn't my concern. Not when she knew the shit she spewed would send me over the edge. She wanted my rage and the bitch got it.

"Daddy's going to love seeing his little whore." I chuckled as I threw my jeans over my still-hard dick. "How many men have you fucked?"

She didn't answer, wrapping her arms around her legs.

"Lost count, huh? Good. Glad you aren't new to this. Because things are about to get a lot more painful."

She didn't say a word as I stalked towards the door. My mind was in a goddamn tailspin over this new information.

And then it clicked.

Octavia was smart. Much smarter than she let on. Everything she'd said, done, was intentional. Meant to redirect me. Stop the questions I'd wanted to ask. I'd played right into her fucking hand. And suddenly I despised the stabbing feeling in my chest that in no way could be guilt over what I'd done.

Slamming the door behind me, I headed downstairs to the bar. My brothers were already a few fingers deep.

"How was she?" Lorenzo asked, rubbing his hands together. "Heard those fucking screams all the way down here. Love virgin screams."

"She wasn't a fucking virgin." I tossed back a glass, immediately refilling it.

"So?" Matteo's inquisitive stare was tenacious.

"'Ey, baby," Lorenzo answered his phone before quickly stalking out of the room while Matteo's eyes continued to drill into me.

How the fuck was I even supposed to explain it? The look. The feeling. Whatever it was that transpired between us… How I was fucking dumb and played into her games.

When I couldn't take his silence any longer, I snapped. "I think she was raped. And… she's covered in scars."

"Did she tell you anything?" he asked, not seeming the least bit surprised, which told me the motherfucker had seen her fully naked before I did.

"No. It was her reaction." I stormed behind the bar, pouring a third glass. "She was into it. Then, when I noticed she wasn't bleeding, she baited me. Wanted me to lose control, and I fucking played into her goddamn hand."

"Did you hurt her?"

"She wanted me angry, like she wanted me to forget that she wasn't—" *The fuck, dude?* "She threw Uncle Sal's death in my face…"

"During sex?" He was just as disgusted with the situation as I was. "Carmine, that's even more reason… she's gotta go."

All of this changed things. Which left me in an uncomfortable place. When this all started, I knew what I wanted to do. What I was going to do. And no one would fucking stop me.

Now? Now I had no fucking clue.

Then there was that question still screaming at the back of my mind. Why? Why was she trying to get a rise out of me? I could've ended her on the spot. Ruined everything I had been working towards for years.

She was more dangerous than I'd thought. A momentary lapse in judgment that I wouldn't allow to affect me again.

"Put her in the basement," I grunted before pushing to my feet. "Now, Matteo." I needed to get my head back in the game and I couldn't do that when she was sitting around tempting me.

"You can't be serious." He followed me out of the room. "Carmine, you just said the girl might've been—"

I turned on my heel. "Did it sound like a request? Like there was room for a fucking debate? It was an order."

He cursed at my back, but too fucking bad. Octavia needed to learn her place. She was an Agostino. Nothing more. My little doll, broken wide open.

Who did she think she was fucking with?

Raped. Beaten. Abused. None of what happened to her was my fucking problem. Clearly, I'd been too soft on her. And then an image filtered into my mind and my dick got hard.

Octavia chained to the stone wall. An open-mouthed gag locked around her face, her chest covered in spit. Whimpering and waiting for me.

My office door rattled as it slammed closed a few minutes later, and I charged towards my room. Seeing that Matteo had followed orders and Octavia was gone, I went to the shower. Before I knew what I was doing, I stripped down and stepped inside the stall with a tight grip on my aching cock. One hand on the wall, the other rapidly stroking. I hated that I had one girl on my mind as I grunted and came. Her scent lingered everywhere.

I eyed myself in the mirror and shook my head in disgust. "Fuck that bitch."

Then I quickly threw on a tee and a pair of jeans and headed for the basement. Thankfully, none of my brothers were around. The steps creaked under my weight and the soft glow from the hall lights made out her tiny shape. Cells lingered down the hall, but she was huddled on the bed directly in front of me. Her sparse amenities were a far cry from the luxury she was used to.

I stood outside the door, watching her cocoon herself with her arms, her tiny frame curled up on one side. Her hair was spread out and I could see the dark bruises on her neck. The lock echoed and the door creaked as I stepped inside. She didn't move, didn't speak. Just stared as I towered over her. One long, tanned, toned leg peeking out.

"Stand," I barked the single-word command and watched as she didn't move a goddamn muscle. "Octavia. Fucking. Stand. Now." Where I was looking to instill fear, she glared at me like more of a hinderance than anything else. "Take off that shirt."

She didn't hesitate this time, tossing it at my feet. My fingers skated across her clavicles before trailing down between her breasts. I wasn't lying when I'd told her she was beautiful. Octavia was innocence mixed with something else. Something darker and wanton. Her eyes weren't cold like the rest of them. They were deep with secrets. Secrets I was just beginning to unravel.

The room was brighter now, but the added light cast shadows across her face. The infamous Agostino blue-steel eyes seemed dull and vacant.

I'd barely begun and she was already falling apart.

Goose bumps broke out across her smooth flesh, trailing behind my touch. Even from a foot above her, I could smell her desire. My hand traveled farther and farther south before finding the wet heat between her thighs. Her whimper was just audible, her body bucking as my finger ran through her folds. When I shoved a finger into her channel, she molded against me, her tiny hands gripping my forearms.

She'd wanted to be strong. But she would *never* survive me.

My fingers played with her until she came all over them, tremors rippling from her toes to the base of her neck. She was damn sexy when she came. My lips wrapped around hers and she opened for me, our tongues and teeth clashing as the intensity reached its peak. I lifted her into my arms and her legs wrapped around me. Using one hand, I popped the button on my jeans and she used her heels to shimmy the material down my ass. I placed myself at her entrance and stopped.

Looking into her eyes, I noticed how much lighter they suddenly appeared. A crystal blue. Her brows pinched as she tried grabbing my dick. I made her pause. I wanted to hear her say the words. To tell me to fuck her. Because for some goddamn reason, I'd drawn a line between being her captor and her rapist.

The darkness between us was a welded door she slammed in my face. Harsh. Angry. She pulled me close and I knew what she was about to do. This time, I didn't give a fuck. If she wanted to play this game, I'd make it hurt.

"Too much of a pussy to fuck me? Thought the Ragettis were so tough. So fucking strong?" she hissed, and I squeezed her hips. "Do it. Fuck me, Carmine."

Now was that so hard, little doll?

She didn't have to tell me twice. Maybe it was twisted. Maybe I didn't care. Because each time I tried to give her *something*, she forced my hand.

The moment my dick was buried deep inside her, I bit her shoulder hard enough to bleed. She moaned, nails scratching my back as I pushed her into the unforgiving stone wall. Her face pinched with pain as I forced her down a road of infamous pleasure.

"Shit. I-I... Carmine." Her body tightened around me and I found the same release.

I didn't pause to take a breath, tossing her onto the mattress and watching her bounce. The teeth marks on her shoulder were dripping blood across her neck and her back was torn from the exposed brick. My pants were stuck around my thighs and my dick had barely calmed. I should feel bad. Instead, I felt hatred. I felt the need to make her suffer.

To make her father suffer.

Smiling deviously, I pushed Octavia flat to her stomach, using the sheet to swipe up some of the blood smeared across her body. Once I was satisfied, I tucked the thin fabric under my arm and planned to stomp right back up those stairs.

Until. That. Ass. Had me pausing in my steps. Before I knew what I was doing, my hand was on the center of her back, pushing her into the mattress. Her hips tilted up and her ass on display.

Did she just grind on me?

"Please." That one word severed the thread of hesitation that was lurking in the back of my mind and enlivened the fantasy that had sent me down here in the first place.

Lifting Octavia from the mattress, I went to secure her to the wall with the mounted cuffs. But something about her face when she saw them—the panic—had me choosing rope instead. She didn't fight me. I put the metal in her mouth and her jaw opened wide. Then I secured the leather behind her head, picked up the bloodied sheet, and locked the door behind me. A single glance through the bars had my dick hardening all over again.

"Beautiful. On your knees for me. Mouth waiting. I'll be back, little doll." Bounding up the steps, Mario's present tucked under my arm, I smiled as I headed towards my office.

"What is that? And why is it covered in blood?" I spun around at the sound of my sister's voice. "The hell is going on, Carmine?" She crossed her arms over her chest and glared at me.

My little sister had wormed her way into something that was clearly none of her business. And Diego knew he was fucked. I'd told him to keep her away. Yet here she was, with my two most trusted men avoiding eye contact. Eva was a terror, and when she spotted something that intrigued her, she didn't back down.

"I'll take Alessandro to the first-floor guest room. The doc should be here soon." Diego gripped him under the arm and the two scurried away.

Pussies.

She tapped her worn sneakers at me and I smiled at the comparison. Sienna and Octavia were raised in designer clothes and heels, while Eva was raised in a skate park, rockin' Vans. JP had been unhinged our entire lives and I didn't like to leave her home. Where I went, so did my siblings. Until now.

Now I wished her annoying ass would learn her place.

"What the fuck, Eva?" I found a box in my office and dumped the sheet inside. "Told you it wasn't safe and you show up anyway. *With* my men bleeding all over my floor."

"It's not his blood on *that*." She pointed at the box. I ignored her. "Fine!" she huffed before adding in a softer tone, "You know I don't like us being apart too long." She was sitting on the edge of my desk with a pout playing on her lips.

"I cannot deal with the Lombardis and the Agostinos at the same time, Eva!"

"Lombardis I get, but why are the Agostinos a problem *now?*" She was being a fucking smartass and she knew it.

"Again. Not your business." I leaned back. "I will let you stay here if you remain out of sight and out of my business. JP could roll up at any minute and I don't want you hurt."

"He doesn't know about this place." *But for how long?* When I didn't reply, she knew she'd lost. "Fine! I agree to your terms." She hopped off the desk, her sneakers squeaking as she went.

"Little shit," I muttered, trying to hide my smile.

"I will find out what you're hiding though." She skipped past Matteo and down the hall.

We'd attempted to shelter her from this life, but she wasn't dumb. She heard the whispers, felt the animosity in school. We were outsiders and the blood that surrounded us wasn't a secret.

"Thought she was supposed to stay away." Matteo laughed, glancing at the box in my hands. "Jesus fucking Christ. The hell is this?"

"A gift for Mario." I chuckled.

"This isn't good, Carmine. JP keeps calling. And you know Eva is nosey as fuck."

"No one goes to the basement but me. She doesn't know about the hidden door. Keep it that way."

Just thinking about Octavia naked and bound with my cum dripping down her legs… It was pure torture ignoring my need to fuck her again. But right now, I had to get this package to New York and then it was time my little doll and I took a trip.

Octavia couldn't hide her reaction when I told her the ransom went unpaid. She didn't need to know that was because I hadn't made one. My silence was killing her father far better than making demands. Her family was trying to maintain face in the public eye, moving as if nothing happened. But I think it was time she saw just how little her family cared for her.

I'd crack away at her porcelain skin until there was nothing left but a pretty dress and a broken smile.

What the hell was wrong with me?

Every time Carmine was near, I became this insatiable deviant. I wanted his anger and his hate. It made me feel *something* after years of cold detachment.

The rage I saw staring back at me warmed my insides. My heart ceased to pulse and the blood in my veins hardened. Turned to stone. His hatred was the only thing I wanted because it was far better than his pity. Every time he caressed my skin, looked at my scars, I could see the hundreds of questions filtering through his brain. It didn't matter. Because the answers were my secrets to keep and I would hold them close to my chest.

Several of my father's business associates were at dinner along with my brother and his friends. Sienna was too busy pissing off Al and Apollo to pay attention to me.

I ate and then milled about with my extended family. Uncle Rick, Al, Apollo, Peiro, and a few others were standing in the center of the large dining room with me. We laughed and danced, the conversation flowing easily with such a small crowd. Someone shouted and the staff bustled into the room with tray after tray of champagne. The group was growing drunker by the second.

"Ma'am." One of the waiters handed me a drink before turning away.

"Three. Two. One. Happy New Year," everyone shouted together and then the music grew louder, the lights dropping low.

I quickly tossed back my glass and set it on a nearby table. I was feeling a bit tipsy, and I suppose that was why I couldn't stay off the dance floor. Usually, I'd let Sienna do her thing while I stood off to the side and watched. Tonight, I didn't care. As the style of songs changed, my dancing adapted. Until I found myself twirling on my toes and smiling at the applause.

I loved dancing. It was the closest thing to freedom I would ever get.

The next song began to play and someone stepped up to my back, pulling me into their body. I leaned against the figure's strong chest and swayed to the rhythm of the music. Whoever was behind me, he was a good dancer. I went to turn but then stumbled.

"Woah, there!" Peiro caught me. "You okay?" His eyes filled with concern.

I laughed and leaned into his embrace. He'd become such a good friend over the years. He'd always been kind to me, even when my sister pushed his patience.

"Thank you for the dance." He smiled, holding me against him. "Would you like another?"

When I nodded, he twirled me onto the floor. We danced for two more songs before my head started spinning. I'd drank wine plenty over the years, but apparently bubbles and I didn't mix. My head was spinning and I suddenly felt exhausted.

What time was it?

"Come on. Let's get your sister." Peiro helped me over to Sienna, who started laughing at me.

I mumbled my incoherent response and she laughed harder. Then things went blank before I woke to a nightmare.

The tearing sensation of the blade slicing across my stomach was unbearable and I'd do anything to fight the pain. Each time I felt my body slipping under, they'd pull me back. I was permanently marked.

"He likes it when you fight." The voice laughed, as the thrusting became faster. It was like sandpaper was being shoved inside me. Raw and painful. And then he stopped, pulling out of me.

Terror was something that settled deep, but if you could survive it, you'd be okay. It was the deceit. The treachery. The fact that I knew this man and he didn't give a damn what was happening. He'd selected me for a reason. Because he saw me as weak. They all did.

He would pay for this. One day. Once I knew the identity of his counterpart, the man who raped me.

"I will unlock these cuffs. But you will count to fifty before you remove the pillow from your face." When I didn't answer, he slapped my ass, forcing me to agree. "Be a good girl. Or Sienna is next."

"Don't!" I startled, shouting through the leather bite in my mouth.

"What's that, little doll?" Carmine stood just outside the metal door. "Don't what?"

My chest was coated with my own saliva, my jaw aching. The skin around my wrists was raw from the unkempt rope but suddenly all I could see were cuffs. I could feel the phantom blood dripping down my arms as I felt the sting of cold metal. I flailed, screeching past the gag as I pulled to get free. No cuffs. Not again.

Carmine watched me as I lost control, before transforming into a wild animal. The beast stormed into my cage, yelling but I couldn't hear him over the sound of my own screams. I needed my arms free.

The cuffs... I couldn't take the feel of them. Too many memories were flooding to the surface. Carmine freed my hands and I stumbled onto the mattress. Crawling into the corner and scratching at my face. The metal in my mouth was too much. I needed to be free.

"Stop, Octavia. Let me get it off." Carmine gripped my hair, holding me in place as he tugged at the leather. I twisted away from him as soon as it was gone. "What happened to you?"

My chest heaved. My memories were sending me over the edge. Ripping off his shirt, he handed it to me. And for once, I didn't fight him. Instead, I wrapped myself in his scent, curled into a ball, and shut out the entire world.

I would never be safe.

I hadn't seen Carmine in days. Lorenzo had been the only one to bring food and water. If the solitude and boredom didn't kill me, it would be the diet of peanut butter sandwiches.

Pulling my knees to my chest, I sobbed into my skin. And rocked. I wasn't cold but freezing. The air was chilled down here but it was the memories that made my insides frigid, the pain too much to bear.

I'd removed the dirty and stained shirt at Lorenzo's command. Then he allowed me a quick shower in the basement. Thankfully. He was kind enough to not look. But I was escorted back to my cell the moment the water stopped. Without anything to change into.

Whenever Lorenzo did come around, he didn't stay long enough to speak to me. I was losing myself to the solitude. A broken mind was something you didn't want to be alone with. And that was all I had.

My thoughts. My memories. The constant reminder that I'd let my family down.

"I knew it! That son of a bitch!" A female's voice startled me from my negative thoughts as a figure stepped up to the cell door. "Are you okay?" she asked.

It didn't take a genius to realize who the small woman with the dark hair and terrifying eyes was. She stared slack-jawed, and if I didn't know any better, I'd believe she was appalled. I pulled my legs closer to my chest, shielding my naked body from her view.

"Do you know where the key is?" She started looking around the room, finding and flicking on the light switch. "Shit."

My curly hair was wild, my skin still mottled with bruises and teeth marks from her brother while my eyes were red and raw from the constant tears.

She was wearing a red and black flannel over a tank top. She took it off and thrusted it through the bars. "Here."

When I didn't take it, she chucked it onto the mattress. She was one of *them*. I couldn't trust her. Matteo had been kind, but you know what they say… Apple. Tree. And all that. The girl wandered down the hall of cells, muttering to herself as she went.

"I can't find the keys but don't worry. I'll make one of them get you out of here. I promise." Her confidence was loud and then she was gone.

The shirt remained on the mattress and I kept staring at it like it might bite me. I tucked myself into the corner when I heard movement on the stairs. My hands were shaking and my neck twitched.

Have you ever tried so hard to focus on something and yet your mind wandered?

I couldn't stick to a single thought, my emotions taking me down. Confusion being all I knew.

"They fucking locked her down here naked. Naked, Diego." The girl was back with a tattooed man I didn't recognize.

"Not your business, Eva," he growled and then it clicked.

Eva. This girl was Eva. Their sister. They were angry and trying to protect her. She was the one who had the Lombardis shooting up the house. It made my skin crawl, just thinking about what would've happened if they'd found her.

"Like hell it isn't. We don't hurt women, Diego."

"Take it up with your brothers."

"Where is the key? I know you know where it is." She was tiny but fierce.

"This key?" He was back. Carmine's voice sent another chill down my spine. "You mean this?"

"Carmine, let her out!" she hissed before turning to the second man. "Get her out of here, Diego." She started shouting question after question about me.

And a few simple words had her concern turning into aggression. "Uncle. Sal. Her family covered it up." Carmine tilted his head towards me.

The girl gasped in shock and took a quick step towards the cell. "Look at me," she ordered, and I glanced up, her head snapping back when I opened my eyes. "You're… an Agostino."

"She is." Carmine shoved her into Diego. "Now get the fuck out of here, Eva. Octavia and I have a flight to catch." He opened the cell door and tossed another one of his shirts in my direction.

"Carmine," Eva ground out, but he interrupted her.

"Out, Eva! Get up, Octavia."

My limbs creaked as I moved. I threw the shirt on before anyone could see my entire body and limped towards him. I missed dancing. It was an odd thought, but how long had it been since I'd freely danced? I used to dance five days a week. It was the physical activity I enjoyed and I could feel my muscles itching to move— needing the exertion.

I walked into the hallway, past Carmine, as Eva and Diego watched me silently. I'd expected anger or resentment from Eva, not sadness. Her disdain was fine. I would have understood it. But I loathed pity. Before I could take another step, Carmine grabbed my shoulder to stop me. Handcuffs slipped around one wrist and then the other.

"No," I whispered, my body already trembling.

"What's that, little doll? Don't like them? Too bad. Now walk."

He shoved me forward, but my legs were frozen to the spot, and I fell.

The hard cement floor shot a fresh wave of pain through my shoulder, my jaw scraping across the cold surface. I started convulsing like I was seizing, my mind consumed by my past.

Make her bleed, son. Take her. You own her now.

"Octavia, look at me!" someone hissed, but I couldn't see him. "Fuck!"

My eyes rolled into my head and I started whimpering. Begging, pleading for them to stop.

Don't touch me. I don't want it. Please, stop.

"You fucking raped her?" Eva screamed as Carmine kept shouting my name.

"It's the cuffs. Take them off!" The tattooed man's voice broke through as I screamed. "Please!"

The shackles were removed from my wrists but not my mind. Feeling the sudden relief, I shoved from the ground and darted to the stairs. I paid little attention to anything as I froze in the light. All around me, the sun was filtering into the room. The smell of the ocean and the cry of the waves called to me. Open doors took me outside and I felt compelled to run towards the water.

I could still feel them. Their cruel hands all over me.

The sand was hot under my feet, yet it didn't slow me down. Rocks and shells cut into my soles, but the sounds of waves crashing called to me. I was so, so dirty. I needed to wash them away. From my skin. From my mind.

No matter how many times I told myself that I was strong. That I was a survivor. It didn't take away the agony.

The water was cold as I sloshed through it, slowing the deeper I went. Carmine was still behind me, shouting for me to stop. But it didn't matter. A thousand showers or drowning in an ocean, *they* were still here. Forever marking my flesh. Worse than that, my soul.

Water splashed behind me and I dove into a wave. A million icy knives pricked my skin as I went under. I exhaled, the bubbles pouring out of my mouth as I willed my body to sink.

They took so much from you? Why're you giving them the power to keep hurting you? Open your mouth. Tell your story. It was time for the traitor to face his judgment. My own voice filtered through the water.

My body shook as my lungs ached for air. I opened my eyes and only saw darkness. This was it. This was my time to choose what I wanted to do. If I wanted, this could be how I died. I closed my eyes again and drifted, the waves pummeling above me, sending my body farther out into the ocean. The darkness was my peace.

But the peace didn't last. It never would. Not for someone like me.

Strong arms wrapped around my shoulders, pulling me to the surface. "Goddamn it, you crazy bitch!"

I gasped for air, water expelling from my lungs as I struggled against him. "Let me go."

The last word was drowned out as a large wave beat down on us. The momentum knocked the air from my body and I inhaled more water.

Swim, Octavia. Fight! Don't let them win!

Carmine found me once more and pulled me back to the surface. This time, I clung to him. I couldn't let them win. It was time to free myself of the burden they inflicted on me.

Clean. I felt clean. And I felt ready.

For the first time, in a long time, I stared at someone and felt like they *saw* me. Carmine didn't say anything as he carried me out of the water. Staring into the dark depths, I recognized his understanding. The anger, the hate, none of it mattered. I was far more damaged than he thought, and we were akin to the other.

Dumping me on the sand, his large hand slapped at my back as water purged from my depths. Everyone circled around us to witness my humiliation.

"She's just as fucking crazy as you are!" Eva shouted, staring at me in shock. And...

Was that amusement?

"What the fuck?" I looked up at Carmine, trying to catch my breath.

He shielded me from the bright sun hanging in the sky above us. A dark god looming over me, both my protector and my executioner. I had no doubts that this man had plans for me, and suddenly I didn't care anymore. I felt imprisoned and empowered all in the same breath.

He should've killed me for so many reasons. Yet here I was. Still being a pain in his ass. A garbled, crazy fit of laughter settled between us as the past few weeks replayed in my head.

"Definitely fucking crazy." The tattooed man, Diego, shook his head while motioning for Eva to follow him back inside the house.

"Good luck with that one, dear brother." She laughed. "Think you've met your match!"

"The fuck was that, Octavia?" Carmine grunted as I lay on my back, making a sand angel and laughing at his discomfort. "Speak. Now."

"Or what?" I sat up, cupping a hand over my eyes as I watched him.

He ripped off his shirt, those intricate tattoos once again mine for the viewing. Water dripped from his trimmed beard onto his hard chest before glistening along his toned abs. The waist of his wet jeans ate it up and I itched to unbutton his pants.

"Keep looking at me like that and you'll get fucked," he snarled. My brows danced, challenging him. "How does that sand feel?"

I looked down and realized I was in a wet shirt without panties.

"Yeah, a sandy snatch ain't fun for either of us, babe."

He extended a hand, and I took it as he pulled me so roughly I slammed into his bare chest. Carmine looked conflicted right before he muttered *fuck it* and claimed my mouth. It was both precise and panicked, his hands holding my face to him as I gripped his wrists.

"Don't you ever run from me again, little doll." The sincerity in his black orbs had me nodding without meaning to. "I don't like it. And I sure as fuck don't like whatever *that* was."

I shook my head, unwanted tears burning my eyes worse than salt water. I wasn't ready to talk about it. I couldn't. Sure, his pity was bad, but his disgust would be even worse.

"One day. One day, you'll confess all your sins. Tell me all your deepest, darkest secrets."

I laughed at his lopsided smirk. That damn inverted cross dancing.

"But right now, you need to wash all that sand out ya crack. And then we got a flight to catch." Carmine slapped my ass and grabbed my hand, dragging me back towards the house.

Those weeks alone with myself and my memories hardened me. I wouldn't be the weak little girl anymore. Carmine had brought out a new side to me. I'd no longer be a victim.

One moment he was the terrifying mobster. The next, he was suddenly human—charismatic, charming, concerned. The constant back and forth was daunting at times, but it also made me giddy, excited to see exactly who I'd be getting.

Beauty fell for the beast, not the man. And, shit, if she and I weren't bred the same.

This time, Carmine guided me to his bedroom, not the basement. I showered all the sand from my body and let the nightmares drip from my skin, collecting in the drain. It was time to wash them away, once and for all.

Until I faced them head-on. Until I faced *him*. The traitor to my family needed to give up his son, then I'd end them both.

I soaped myself up again, the shower door opened, and Carmine stared at me. His glare devoured every inch of my skin, following the path my hands took over my body. A moment of confliction passed behind his eyes before I grabbed his wrist and tugged him inside the stall with me. It was the only invitation he needed to lift me into his arms and claim me.

We didn't make love. Neither of us were capable of something so soft, gentle. We were monsters, akin to each other. One born, the other made.

And as I allowed my body to revel in the pleasure he invoked, I released all the demons. I was ready to take back control of my life.

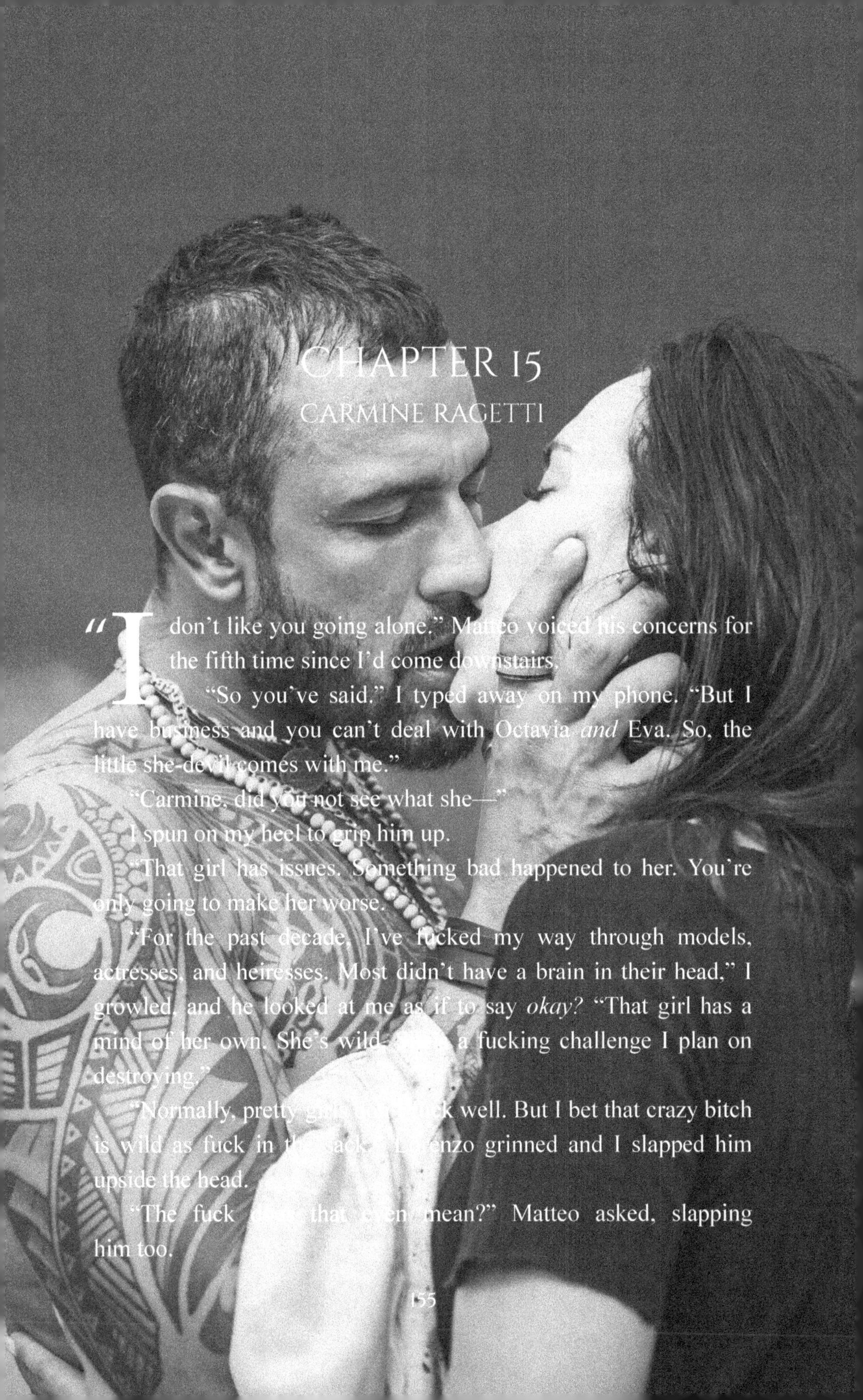

CHAPTER 15

CARMINE RAGETTI

"I don't like you going alone." Matteo voiced his concerns for the fifth time since I'd come downstairs.

"So you've said." I typed away on my phone. "But I have business and you can't deal with Octavia *and* Eva. So, the little she-devil comes with me."

"Carmine, did you not see what she—"

I spun on my heel to grip him up.

"That girl has issues. Something bad happened to her. You're only going to make her worse."

"For the past decade, I've fucked my way through models, actresses, and heiresses. Most didn't have a brain in their head," I growled, and he looked at me as if to say *okay?* "That girl has a mind of her own. She's wild [illegible] a fucking challenge I plan on destroying."

"Normally, pretty girls [illegible] fuck well. But I bet that crazy bitch is wild as fuck in the sack." Lorenzo grinned and I slapped him upside the head.

"The fuck does that even mean?" Matteo asked, slapping him too.

Octavia walked into the room, interrupting our brotherly banter. "Pretty girls have it easy. An inviting package that you want to claim. Once you open it, they've already ensnared you in their grasp," she said, opening the fridge—as if she fucking lived here—and guzzling down a bottle of water. "Then, they lie down and take it because their beauty did the work for them."

"The crazy bitch gets it." Lorenzo laughed, clapping a hand on my back before walking out of the room.

"Maybe you're right. Maybe New York is a good idea," Matteo said, motioning between the door and Octavia. "I don't need her and Lorenzo becoming friends." He shook his head and followed our brother's shadow.

"I see the clothes fit." It was the first time I'd seen her in anything other than a man's shirt in weeks. Her hips had a delicious flare and her ass was plump and inviting.

"What're we doing?" she asked, and I didn't answer her. "Are you taking me home?"

Apparently, her little dip in the ocean had fixed her head. She was different. Her eyes were clear, her spine straight, and she seemed… at peace. For now.

"You don't have a home." My words did their job, landing like a punch to the girl's gut. "Mommy and Daddy don't want you back. They've had more than enough opportunity to make a move, and they've ignored it. They've seen you bleed on video, accepted the delivery of bloody sheets, and still… radio silence."

"You're lying. This is all part of your sick game."

I could tell that, as much as she thought I was lying, the damaged part of her brain believed me. "I am a liar, a thief, a murderer. I'm also the only one who seems to give a fuck about you." I grabbed her wrist, walking her out to my Bugatti. "I can't trust you to behave without me."

"Just let me go," she whispered, sliding into the car.

I leaned so that my face was a breath away from hers. "Life in New York has gone on without you. No. One. Cares."

"You're lying." Those pouty lips pressed into a thin line.

"Am I?" I gunned the engine and took off towards the airport.

Octavia rolled down her window, her long dark locks flying in the air. It was the first time I saw a true smile play on her lips. She was a gorgeous girl with a dangerous glint in her eye.

"Fuck!" she screamed as a car slammed into the rear bumper.

Little pings echoed off the metal sides right before a window was shot out. Octavia unhooked her seat belt and slid to the floor. Looking out the back of the car, she offered me a devious grin.

"Life moved on, huh?" she taunted.

Fuck.

"Or does your father just not like to lose?" I countered, watching her tense. "Hold on." I punched the gas and the engine purred as we took off.

The gates to the private airstrip were opened and we flew through. I veered to one side, away from my jet, taking the chase farther into the field. The car attempted to follow but cut the wheel too hard and careened into the rough terrain, the sudden momentum sending the fucker rolling. I slowed down before pulling around and stepping out. My back against her door, I crossed my arms over my chest and waited.

A slow fire was already burning across the hood when I heard someone moving. I could tell the driver was dead, but the passenger was crawling out. Octavia watched from her open window, and it was clear the moment she recognized him. Because I did too. I'd done my research after all. These guys were Agostino men, from her bodyguard's crew. Peiro had some balls on him. I'd give him that.

My hand rose to my hip, pulling my gun free as I approached, hearing Octavia's door open behind me. The passenger was covered in blood and stumbled onto the ground, rolling onto his back. I pressed the heel of my shoe against his hand, prying his cell phone free. I used his face to unlock the screen and read through the call log and the messages. Peiro didn't know anything specific. Yet.

Following now. Can't tell if it's her or not.

He didn't give up the goods. Which meant New York was none the wiser. Octavia charged at my back, trying to shove me out of the way. I tugged her behind me, and one slug between the eyes ensured my secret was kept.

"You bastard!" She swung but missed.

"That isn't nice." I shoved her into the car, closing the door and heading back over to my plane.

"You didn't have to kill them." She glared at me, as I escorted her up the steps.

"You're right. But I wanted to." I shrugged, and her face mottled red before she huffed and stormed inside.

My little doll curled up on one of the sofas, making herself tiny as I sat beside her. She glowered, and my lip twitched at her agitation. She'd yet to realize she couldn't get rid of me that easily.

The plane was filled with three of my most trusted armed guards as well as Diego. I didn't care for the way he watched me with Octavia. If he were smart, he'd keep his fucking comments to himself.

My little doll startled as the plane started descending several hours later. She jolted awake, her small hand grasping my own. My knuckles were covered in ink and her tanned flesh was a stark contrast.

The doors were opened and my men filed out. Octavia went to walk past me, but I grabbed her arm. Staring down into those blue-steel eyes, I hardened myself for the fight I knew was brewing.

"You will behave. Got it?" I ground out as she tried shrugging from my hold. "I fucking mean it, little doll. Don't mistake the fact that my dick likes your tight pussy for anything other than emptying my balls."

"You're disgusting." She pulled free, her chest heaving as I caged her in against the wall of the plane.

"And you love how fucking filthy I make you." With both hands, I grasped her face. "I mean it. Behave. We're meeting people that won't care who the fuck your daddy is. Don't make me hurt you. 'Cause if you disrespect me, I'll make it fuckin' hurt."

She finally nodded and I allowed her to take the stairs in front of me.

"She's going to be a problem," Diego grumbled after closing Octavia inside the waiting car. "AJ's protected Eva and dealt with her antics…"

I nodded, understanding what he meant.

Eva was just as much of a pain in the ass as Octavia was. My sister didn't like having our men hanging around her and would play games, losing her tail as often as she could. AJ and Alessandro were the only men who could handle her bullshit.

The ride to my warehouse was quick and Octavia practically vibrated in her seat. As if being back at home was going to save her. I studied her profile as she watched the city pass us by, and something caught my attention. Maybe it wasn't excitement after all. Her small hands were in her lap, a slight tremor running through her fingers as she squeezed them together. Her jaw was clenched shut and her lip quivered.

What was she so afraid of?

Though the answer to that question wasn't all that hard to figure out. New York was home to those who hurt her. I licked my lips, trying to swallow back my agitation. She needed to fucking tell me her secrets.

As soon as we pulled up to the warehouse, I took her up to the makeshift apartment that would be her newest prison. Ushering Octavia into the kitchen, I opened it to find several premade meals. Without asking her what she wanted, I dumped the contents of a stir fry into a pan and popped open a bottle of wine. She stared at me curiously from the other side of the island.

"Domesticated." She hid her laughter behind a fake cough.

"My father had a very interesting concept when it came to raising children," I admitted, a fact which seemed to grab her attention as she moved closer to sit on a stool. "My mother was very loving but was never home long."

"Didn't that bother her? To be away from her kids?"

"I'd assume to a small extent, yes." I dumped the stir fry onto two plates, depositing one in front of Octavia. "JP *raised* me to take over. Considered my brothers assets to building a strong *famiglia,* while my mother would come home and try to humanize his actions."

"Clearly, that worked." Octavia flicked a mocking wrist in my direction.

"For Lorenzo and especially Matteo, it did. But they weren't my father's target."

"Of course not. You're the oldest, the heir." She nodded, and I had to admit it was nice having someone *get it.*

Typically, I'd be arranged to marry a woman from our world. But JP didn't care much for tradition. So I stuck my dick in the Hollywood elite. I'd put on a façade of the type of dangerous businessman those sorts lapped up. Then I'd enjoy tossing them aside for the next one.

Until now.

I wasn't lying when I'd told my brothers how I craved Octavia's insanity. This woman had the ability to get under my skin and enjoyed what she saw. The real me. Just the thought of her swallowing my dick and stabbing the fuck out of my skin turned me on. I was two seconds away from shoving the plates aside and throwing her onto the island. Let her be both my dinner and my dessert.

"Sir, Bianchi is here." Diego walked in, causing Octavia to almost fall out of her chair.

"Sorry, little doll. Business." I tossed back my wine and scooped the last mouthful from my plate. "And, no, don't even think about it. Romano won't save you." I buttoned my suit jacket, hating the way the thick material restricted my movements. Then I left Octavia standing there, her mouth gaping, as I followed Diego from the room.

I motioned to AJ and he nodded and placed himself outside the apartment door before I crossed the hall with Diego at my back.

"Romano. Romeo." I greeted the two men as I entered the office. "How's business?" I asked before placing myself behind my desk. When I looked up, my eyes fell on the woman sitting in one of the leather chairs in the corner. Romano was seated at my desk with Romeo at the girl's back, clearly protecting her.

Who was she?

She was absolutely gorgeous, with dark blonde locks and a well-shaped body. Her hair shielded part of her face as she looked at the ground, but I could tell that her features were delicate. Her tight, short black dress was alluring but also sophisticated. Or perhaps it was the way she held herself. She sat straight and poised, ankles crossed with her purse on her lap and her hands clasped on top of it. But there was something else about her…

Romano coughed, making me smirk at his annoyance. "Business is good. I've already been to the building you suggested and had my attorneys write up a proposal."

And then we were off discussing things as usual. Time passed quickly as we ran over every detail of our plans. Romano hated Mario just as much as I did. Whatever transpired between them wasn't my business, though it certainly was my gain.

"Now that, that's settled…" I stared pointedly at the woman who hadn't moved or spoken since my eyes first landed on her.

Romano smirked before turning to peer over one shoulder. "Kennedy, come say hello to Carmine." He motioned for her to sit on his lap in front of my desk. "Carmine, Kennedy."

"Nice to meet you." She leaned forward to shake my hand, and I noticed the scars up her arms.

"Kennedy has agreed to be my wife." Romano smiled, as the girl glanced down at him adoringly before turning back to me.

I got lost in her bright eyes, an evil smile dancing across my lips. Romano tightened his hold on her, a clear sign of ownership.

How the fuck had he managed to get her?

"Mario has no idea, does he?" I asked, and Romano shook his head. "How?"

"I could ask you the same." He laughed. "Kennedy, love. Why don't you head back to the car with Romeo? We're leaving shortly." She obeyed without question, following his second out of the room.

"And that ploy to get Sienna?" My mind reeled with the tricks the bastard pulled.

He lit a cigar. "I didn't think I'd ever get Kennedy in line. I saw you looking at her arms… I needed a backup plan. It was supposed to be Sienna, but that asshole Apollo was in the way."

Before I could speak, however, the door opened and Octavia stormed inside.

"Carmine, I—" She froze, seeing all eyes turned to her. My little doll hated the attention and I used it to my advantage.

"Come here." I patted my leg, offering Octavia a seat.

Romano's jaw dropped as he watched her approach. If she thought he'd help her, she didn't seem to show it.

"You—" Octavia began to say and then stopped as she perched

herself on my leg. Her blue-steel eyes flashed with so many unspoken words. No doubt shocked by Philly's obvious treachery.

"Octavia Agostino." Romano slapped a hand over his mouth to cover his amusement. "It's true."

I nodded. I was indeed a merciless man.

"I… I… I'm sorry. I shouldn't have interrupted." My little doll was fumbling over what to say. She went to get up, but I held her against me.

"Don't you dare. You're exactly where you belong." I squeezed her hip, enjoying the growing shock on Romano's face.

"I'll be damned." He laughed. "Mario doesn't know, does he?"

I ignored him, turning to the prize currently perched on my lap. "I'm glad you came in, little doll. This will make this easier to explain. Do you understand now?"

She glanced between Romano and me before looking at Diego, then back over to me. I could tell Octavia was slowly putting it together in her head.

"Your father loves to turn his back on the people he should care about most. Now do you see that you're just another casualty?" I asked, but Octavia still appeared confused. "*Daddy* was arranging Sienna to marry Romano. A man… meeting with the enemy."

"But how? Why?" She directed the question to Romano.

"Not your business, little doll." I pushed to my feet, making her slide down my body. Then I pinned Romano with a glare. "If you don't mind, I think we've accomplished enough today."

He stared at Octavia and the way she was leaning against my side. I might be an animal, a monster, a beast but she knew I'd protect her if they stepped out of line. This was my game and she was *my* prize. She continued to watch them carefully, her mind twisting and turning. The truth of her situation was smacking her in the face. Daddy didn't care about his family as much as he liked to claim he did. And she was finally starting to believe me.

"Diego, take her across the hall to AJ while I see Romano out,"

I instructed, and he motioned for Octavia to walk out first, as the rest of us went downstairs.

Romano looked at me like he wanted to say something. A look I supposed matched my own.

"And here I thought I had all the tricks up my sleeve." I pulled a box of smokes from under my jacket and lit one. "How the fuck did you find her?" I asked him.

"Right back atcha," he grunted. We stood in silence for a moment, the smell of my cigarette filtering between us. "Fuck Mario." He laughed and slipped into the car before it pulled away.

"I wouldn't have believed it if I didn't see it with my own two eyes." Diego laughed, walking back inside with me.

We'd just reached the top of the stairs when we heard Octavia screaming and AJ shouting. I ran to the door, my key struggling to get into the lock before I pushed my way inside and froze. AJ was standing in front of a knife-wielding Octavia, presently handcuffed to one of the exposed pipes in the brick wall. Her eyes were wild and unfocused, her thick hair haphazardly strewn around her face.

"The fuck is going on here?" My voice seemed to take her legs out from under her and she slid onto her ass.

Octavia lifted a cuffed arm, her toned belly on display as her chest heaved. Her grip was tight on the blade that was pointed towards AJ as she watched him from under a veil of hair.

"I was in the kitchen when she attacked. I had no choice." He was holding his bleeding arm. "She came at me with a knife and I didn't want to hurt her so I cuffed her to the pipe."

"Fuck. Diego, get him stitched up," I barked, and the two men headed out as I circled Octavia.

Her back was pinned to the brick and her body trembled. However, the hand holding the knife was strong, calm. Someone had hurt my little doll and I was going to return the favor. Before I fucking gutted him. Her eyes had darkened with challenge and my dick came to life. Ever since I pulled her out of the ocean, I was seeing a different side of her. I'd seen the fight, the internal battles, and felt her attack. But this woman was even sexier. Wilder.

"Little doll, it's time to drop the knife," I urged. She didn't move. "I will get you out of those cuffs once you do."

She appeared to consider it for a moment, but still made no motion to relinquish her weapon. Acting as if I was giving up, I turned away. Then, the moment the knife dipped slightly, I turned back and kicked the blade out of her hand. Octavia jumped up from the ground, ready to attack one-handed and unarmed. She fought like a wildcat, even as I subdued her.

As soon as her hand was free, she ran to the other side of the room, walking in circles, breathing heavily, and staring at the ceiling. Her face pinched in pain as she cried nonexistent tears.

I walked around the island and sat on a stool, allowing her to release all that pent-up energy. "I'm not a patient fucking man, Octavia. For you, I've been far more than I'm used to," I said honestly. "This shit ain't easy. I get that. You went through hell and I'm putting you through more of it. But I'm done waiting. I want answers."

"Why the fuck do you care?" She paused, then scoffed at me. "I know why. So you can laugh, throw it in my father's face." She walked around the island and closed the distance between us. "I'm not dumb. My family wrote me off a long time ago, and soon you'll get your revenge and do the same."

"Enough." My fingers broke through the gel in my hair, the dark mass falling freely onto my forehead. "You're angry. You're hurt. I fucking get it. Hate me all you want, little doll, because it makes my dick hard." Her eyes followed my hand as I grabbed myself through my slacks.

"I do hate you," she whispered while staring at my cock.

I stood up, removing my suit jacket, then my tie, before unbuttoning the top of my shirt. She followed my every movement, barely breathing as she watched me. "Come show me how much you hate me." I pulled the shirt over my head and walked into the bedroom.

Without hesitation, Octavia stepped through the doorway and was on me. Her hands were shaking as she tugged at my belt. My slacks dropped to my ankles and her pants got stuck at her knees.

It didn't matter. I didn't need her naked. Thrusting her face-first into the plastered wall, I slammed her hands above her head in a way that told her to keep them there. Then, twisting her dark locks in my hand, I moved them to one shoulder. I bit the tip of her ear, licked and nipped my way down her back, and took a bite of her ass.

Octavia writhed against me, softly begging me to take her. This little doll was so broken, but her shattered remains were more than enough to get me off. Each piece cut me open and made me bleed. Which meant neither of us would walk away unscathed.

I thrusted deep inside her, getting lost in how warm and tight she was. Her hands remained on the wall as I continued to fuck her senseless, spurred on by the sound of her screams. I couldn't wait for Mario Agostino to see what a little whore his daughter had become. I wanted him to hear how she called out my name and came on my dick.

Glancing up at the camera, I smirked. I wouldn't send him the video, just clips of the audio. Enough to shatter him when he's forced to hear his baby girl beg the terrifying beast to fuck her senseless.

And that, ladies and gentleman, was how you won the fucking game.

Was it possible to die from pure, muscle-exhausting ecstasy? If the answer was yes, then I wanted to be reborn just to do it all over again.

This man. I felt like I'd drowned in that ocean, and once Carmine had pulled me out of it, something within me—with us— changed. Though I had yet to figure out what it was.

"Tell me." His demand broke the spell as we lay together in bed. I was under no illusion that he was asking out of actual concern. He wanted to know who had stolen his chance to really hurt my father. This was just a game and Carmine Ragetti was playing to win.

"What?" I tried to feign innocence, to pretend I didn't know what it was that he was asking me.

The bed was a California king—as was the beast residing in it— but the mattress seemed so small in comparison. It was the strangest sensation to lie naked, next to a man, especially one I was supposed to hate. It was like he held this power over me, and no matter what I did, there was no point in fighting it.

For the first time since *that night,* I didn't feel like I needed to hide. When Carmine said my name in that deep, gravelly voice of his, I didn't stop talking until I expelled my deepest secrets. It was like touching a hot stove. It burned like hell, and for a moment, you didn't know how to let it go. But overtime the pain would lessen and only the scar would remain.

I had barely gotten through all the sordid details before that question was leaving his mouth. The one I knew was coming. "Who. Was. It?"

"I never saw their faces." I wiped away a single tear.

"Octavia." Carmine rolled over, one arm by each side of my head. Looking down at me was a snarling monster.

"Just, stop. I'm exhausted." I sighed. After all, he deserved nothing from me. I'd just told my enemy my saddest truth. The very man who abducted me now knew something that no one else had ever been privy to.

"We're going out. Get dressed," he hissed before climbing off me and disappearing into the connected bathroom. By the time he came out again, I was already dressed in jeans, sneakers, and a hoodie. This ensemble he'd given me somehow fit the new me. "You look fucking sexy. But that won't work for tonight." He went into the closet and pulled down two boxes. "We're going *out*."

And then he was gone.

There was a pair of black stilettos in one box and a tight, glittery material in the other. The red Givenchy dress had spaghetti straps with the center cut out, a simple piece of diamond fabric keeping the whole thing together. I slid into the dress and stepped into the shoes before staring at myself in the mirror. This wasn't something I'd pick for myself. But I felt… different. And I liked that.

"Leave your hair down," Carmine commanded from the other room.

I noticed the small bag of makeup within reach and made quick work of applying some eyeliner, lip gloss, and a little color on my cheeks. My hair was wild and wavy. With a little water on my hands, I ran my fingers through the dark mass and watched the curls bounce.

"There she is." Carmine looked me up and down as I walked out.

He was dressed in a tight black shirt, dark jeans, and black boots. I think I preferred this version of him to the soon-to-be mafia Don he would often portray. Right now, he appeared much more… relaxed and down to earth.

A few minutes later, Carmine was holding open the door to the SUV for me while Diego and AJ sat up front. As we moved through the familiar city traffic, my chest ached at just the thought of seeing my family again.

"Little doll." Carmine's pointer finger stroked my chin, urging me to look up at him. "Don't make me regret doing this. Got it? You watch. That's it."

"But I thought…"

He laughed and dropped his hand. "Thought what? I was sending you back? How easily you forget who owns you. Behave yourself or your sister will suffer."

He wouldn't…

But that glint in his eye and the pleased expression on his face told me he would. He definitely would. And the bastard would enjoy hurting us both.

"We aren't—" I didn't have to finish the thought, as the car made a left and the familiar building appeared in front of me. The words glowed back at me like an ominous sign in the night sky. My brother's nightclub.

How was a seven-foot monster and a glittering red damsel supposed to remain in the shadows? There'd be a neon arrow pointing at us the moment we walked through the door. But then we drove past and turned another corner, pulling into the alley.

"Carmine?" I didn't know what I was asking. But this… this was too much.

"Come on, little doll. Let's play." He grinned, grabbing my hand and pulling me out of the car.

"They never noticed me anyway," I whispered, but his tightening grip told me he heard.

The place was packed, but Carmine's crew moved people out of a booth located just off the dance floor. He grabbed my hips and tucked my back to his chest.

"I don't understand how they've never *noticed* you before," he spoke softly into my ear. "When we met, you were all I could see."

I sighed and leaned against him, watching the crowd move around us. Diego and AJ lurked close by, but I felt *alone*. I glanced around the room, waiting and maybe even dreading that I'd see them. Then, suddenly, there she was. My sister. Gorgeous as ever in an insanely short dress. I laughed at Al's expression as he followed her onto the dance floor. I itched to get closer to them. To see her. To have my sister tell me Carmine was lying.

"Let's dance." My eyes went round as Carmine pushed me out of the booth. "Behave, little doll."

I couldn't act out if I wanted to. If Sienna saw me, what was I supposed to say? She'd realize I'd stopped fighting to come home. That I'd somehow become a willing participant in my own captivity. She'd see what the Italian beast did to me, how he made me feel. And the betrayal I would see on her face would be far worse than watching him kill her.

Carmine pinned me to his front and we swayed, lost to a slow song only the two of us could hear. My hands gripped his forearms, needing him to hold me up. To anyone looking, the gesture was intimate. Just another couple.

"Open your eyes," he grunted, and when I did, I noticed my sister was within arm's reach.

She was leaning back against another one of my brother's men, Rocco, and he appeared less than happy about it. They were so close I could hear their exchange. Still, they had yet to notice me.

"Sienna. Gross." Rocco gripped my sister's shoulders to keep her from grinding on him. Her smile was devilish and I could tell she was drunk.

"I can practically see your… your…" Al couldn't bring himself to say the word.

"Pussy?" *Yup, she was hammered.*

"Sienna!" Al gagged as Rocco shouted, "Ew!"

Carmine turned us, his back to them as we kept swaying. Then he spun me once more and I realized my sister was gone. I sagged into his embrace, releasing a breath that was somehow choking me.

"Look up."

Once again, I complied, my eyes finding all three of them glancing down at the crowd from my brother's VIP booth.

"Now watch." Carmine gestured to my family, and I froze. Because it was obvious no one saw me. I was just as invisible as I'd always been. Carmine licked my ear, and a shiver coursed through me. "That night we met was the start of this game. Until you. Until those innocent eyes looked up to thank me for saving your books…"

I spun in his arms to face him. "You were here for Sienna." A new wave of jealousy roared to life in my chest.

"Until. I. Saw. You." His hands warmed the open back of my dress, keeping me tight to him. "Look at how fuckin' selfish they are. If someone had taken you from me, I'd burn this fucking city to the ground."

Why did he sound so sincere? And why did I so desperately want to believe him?

When he lifted me off my feet and stole my breath with a dirty kiss, no one noticed. No one gasped, tried to pull me away. No one was appalled.

That was the thing about my family. I loved them more than anything. But they'd clipped my wings and stuffed me into a cage. As long as they could glance at me, appraise their sheltered prize, they were happy. And I was miserable. Night after night, I'd woken to the same nightmares, and they never came in to check on me.

That's just Octavia.

I was the nuisance they ignored, while the monster under my bed now resided in it. Carmine had seen through my façade. He'd seen past the performance I gave the world and knew there was something *else* there. They never did. And suddenly, I was angry.

Really. Fucking. Angry.

I slowly pulled away, feeling every hardened muscle of Carmine's front as he finally let me go. My legs were burning, itching to pull him back onto the dance floor with me and move like the rest of the world wasn't watching. Until our moment was ruined when someone bumped into us.

"Hi." She licked her lips, giving Carmine an obvious once-over before a boney finger reached out and stroked his chest. The girl acted as if I wasn't there. A fact that seemed to dig the dagger in my chest that much deeper. Without a thought, without a care, I reacted.

Her pained shriek had my lips curling into a smile as she held her broken finger to her chest. I could see her moment of indecision, wondering *if* she should fight back.

"Run along!" I mouthed and waved my hand at her, watching as she practically sprinted from the club while our laughter nipped at her heels. I was done being ignored.

Carmine pulled me tight against him. A look of pride mixed with a dangerous need lingered behind perfectly straight teeth. Teeth that should've been sharp like an animal, and I wanted him to rip my flesh from my bones. A singular taste of violence and I'd wanted more.

"I need to be inside you. Let's go." Carmine grabbed my hand, and I followed behind him.

Why did that feel so good?

Because I stood up for myself. Something I only now just real-ized I had been doing this entire time. I'd gone toe-to-toe with a dangerous man. I'd made him bleed and survived weeks of his torment. If only my family cared enough to see me now…

But it was my time to step from the shadows and bare my teeth.

The crowd seemed louder, drunker, busier. Carmine attempted to weave through the horde, shoving people out of our way as he held my hand. Suddenly, his hold was gone and I was surrounded by a group of men, pushing me backwards through the crowd. Terror drowned me. I knew what they wanted.

"Happy to see me, baby?" The asshole smirked.

A singular moment of fear was instantly eviscerated when my beast loomed over his shoulder. My amused smile gave the man pause, and I was ready to see what Carmine would do. The rage in his eyes gave the black orbs an eerie glow.

"You picked the wrong girl," Carmine growled, a promise of murder lingering in the air. Diego and AJ were at his back within seconds, but their assistance wasn't needed. Carmine had taken down the newcomer's friends and was quickly honing in on his target.

"Did you mean happy to see *him*?" I asked, while jutting my chin towards Carmine.

"S-sorry, man! I didn't know."

Carmine's grip tightened as the man visibly flinched and hunched his shoulders, while the look on my beast's face had my stomach filling with butterflies.

"Didn't know?" I leaned closer to him, nearly nose to nose. "Didn't know I was owned by someone else?"

"Didn't know touching her meant death?" Carmine added.

I patted the man's cheek, and the poor bastard begged me with his eyes, as if I would be the one to save him. Instead, I pulled back with Carmine's blade in my grip. Ready to strike.

"Tsk. Tsk, little doll." Carmine's large hands wrapped around the guy's neck before I had time to inflict my damage, and he twisted until that sickening popping sound filled both our ears. Then Carmine slowly lowered the guy's body to the ground.

"Got it." Two of Carmine's men approached as Carmine rushed me away from the scene.

My heart was racing and the adrenaline was doing funny things to me. We stepped into the alley when suddenly Carmine shoved me back into the door. Diego and his men swarmed in front of us.

"Two men. End of alley." That's all I heard as we waited.

"Clear. Let's move."

We stepped into the rain. The spike heel of my shoe got stuck on the cobblestone and I felt myself slip. Carmine caught me before I hit the ground, pulling me to his chest. I swiped his hair back to see that same dangerous smirk on his lips. He righted me on my feet and urged me towards the waiting car.

This time, when I stalled in my steps, it wasn't because of the uneven sidewalk. It was fear that gave me pause as my eyes landed on the man standing a few feet in front of us. Then I felt the cold snare of a cuff on my wrist. Glancing down, I rubbed my empty arms as my demons resurfaced in my mind. Challenging me to save myself. My breathing spiked, my eyes unable to look away. We were too far, and I was shielded by the door to the idling SUV. But it was *him*. He'd been scarce since he allowed his partner to ruin me, but his face still haunted my nightmares.

"Octavia," Carmine barked, but I couldn't answer him. "Speak."

"One a traitor the other a mystery," I muttered to myself while peeking out from behind the door.

"Who is it?" Carmine gripped my face, the rain making us slick. "Speak."

"No one," I grumbled. But his expression told me it wasn't enough. "My uncle."

"Uncle?" Carmine glanced down the alley, recognizing the man immediately. "You call Ricardo your uncle? Your dad's right hand?"

I nodded and turned to get into the car. But Carmine's tight grip stalled me in my tracks. "Let's go." My smile was so fake I wanted to vomit. "It's raining," I added as if the weather somehow mattered now.

"One a traitor the other a mystery?" Carmine repeated my words, and uncomfortable laughter settled in my gut. Then he pulled his gun from under his jacket while I grabbed for his wrist, only to have my hand slip. So I reached for his jaw instead, trying to force his attention back on me. This wasn't his fight—his moment.

"Carmine…" His attention mirrored far too many things and a silent understanding settled between us. I needed him to stay with me. Carmine glanced over my shoulder as my uncle got into a town car at the end of the alley and disappeared.

"Get in the fucking car." The snarl of his lips told me this wasn't over. He didn't understand. I didn't even understand entirely. *That man* had promised to ruin my family, and I needed to protect them. His men filed into the cars and we slowly started to pull away.

More importantly, I needed a name. I'd spent so much time avoiding him, proving I wasn't broken. That I wouldn't cave. Just a little longer and I'd end it.

"Get down!" Diego shouted before the SUV stopped a mere inch from the vehicle presently blocking our path.

"Shoot that motherfucker!" Carmine ordered. The windows lowered and then gunfire lit up the night sky.

"Don't!" I cried out as soon as my eyes saw him. Peiro didn't stand a chance against two car loads of trained killers.

I had to protect him.

Honestly, I was getting cocky bringing Octavia here. I was self-aware enough to realize that. But her siblings played right into my hand. Which had my little doll seeking solace in my embrace.

She could've yelled. She could've screamed. She could've caused a war on that dance floor. Instead, she stood quietly by my side. Octavia didn't want to go home. She was mine. We were coming down to the final inning, and as I gripped up on the bat, I knew that a home-run was right around the corner. My men saw it too.

It wasn't just enough to steal Mario's daughter. I wanted her heart. I wanted her begging Daddy to give her back to me. Her siblings were so fucking selfish and self-absorbed, they didn't even notice her. I wasn't lying when I told her I couldn't take my eyes off her.

Especially when she threatened that bitch who touched me. And especially when she was ready to cut through the asshole who touched *her*. The night was perfect.

And I was basking in my victory until reality seeped through again. She didn't have to say it. Her body. Her fear. It told me everything. She knew one of her attackers, and the asshole in the alley told me all I needed to know.

Her father's right hand had fucking raped her.

That motherfucker was dead and I was going to goddamn enjoy being the one to do it. That look on her face couldn't hide the lies she spewed. How had her family missed it? The fact that Mario's best fucking friend took his youngest daughter's virginity? How couldn't they see she was rotting away in her own head?

My forehead slamming into Diego's seat as the car jolted to a stop snapped me out of my haze.

Peiro. The son of a bitch had some fuckin' nerve showing up here. Especially now, after his crew had fucked up in Cali.

"Shoot that motherfucker."

Octavia could beg all she wanted. It wouldn't save him. Gunfire echoed in the alley, the bullets hitting the car. My men moved quickly on foot. He was no match by himself, shooting at my crew like he had a fucking chance. A bullet grazed his arm and he ducked behind the car. Shoving Octavia back from view, I grabbed her hands and quickly subdued her with a pair of zip ties.

"Shut her up and hold her down," I snapped, and AJ quickly placed a strip of tape across Octavia's mouth.

I stepped out of the car, seeing that my men had the scene controlled. Diego motioned towards the end of the alley and we approached with caution. I walked around his car and Peiro raised his barrel and took aim.

"You little prick." I kicked the empty gun from his hand. "Pack him up," I called out, knowing we'd caused a scene and needed to move.

He yelled and cursed all the shit I'd heard a million times before. From a million stronger men. All who'd died very painfully at my command. Peiro tried peering into the SUV as he was dragged towards the rear car. He was met by tinted windows and silence.

Opening my door, I came face-to-face with a wild, furious woman. It was funny for a minute. Until a tiny fist hit me across the chin, her knuckles cracking against the bone. Diego and AJ eyed me from their seats as she continued to rage. My hands shook as I reached out and grabbed her by the throat. I enjoyed the way her tits bounced as I slammed her down beside me. When I snarled in her face, she finally quieted down.

"Trying to protect that piece of shit? You should be begging me for your own life—not his. You're mine. My. Toy," I hissed, and her eyes widened as she tried to shake off my hold. "You fucked up, sweetheart. You've just lost your freedom." Then I shoved her away from me, ignoring the way she whimpered and twisted against her binds.

"Boss?" AJ asked as we pulled into the warehouse a few minutes later.

"Get her out of my fucking face," I replied, and he nodded. "The ties and tape stay on."

AJ gripped her shoulders and escorted Octavia up the stairs. That fire in her eyes quickly dissipated as she followed his commands. My little doll forgot her place and I was just the man to remind her.

"Bring him," I barked out. The doors opened, and Peiro was dragged inside and quickly tied to a chair.

He spit and cursed at every man in the room. My lip twitched, entertained by the dramatics of it all. Two more seconds and I was on him. One punch, then two. His agonized moans helped to heal the image I had of him in my head. The image of him trying to take Octavia from me. I slapped his face to bring him back each time he drifted off—a true testament to his weakness. A man who was used to abuse, used to a good fight, wouldn't break this easily. I'd survived JP's lessons and it hardened me to pain while this fucker was nothing more than mediocre muscle.

"You're really pissing me off." I spat in his face. "I took her from you. Twice. She's. Mine."

"I'd die for her."

Aw, ain't that sweet.

"You will. Slowly. Just like those assholes you sent to Cali." I stepped back to look down at him. "Mario doesn't know, does he?" It wasn't a question. The wannabe bodyguard was on a suicide mission.

"He'd find out when I brought her home," he grunted, and my men laughed. "With your corpse."

"And now you'll die for being a dumb fuck." I shrugged as AJ walked back into the room.

"Tied to your bed. She'll be waiting," he said, and Peiro started cursing louder.

"Gonna be a long, painful night for you." I cracked my knuckles and took a deep breath.

Each punch to his face eviscerated some of my anger. I got lost in the fight as my mind cleared and I planned my next attack. Riccardo. As Peiro's blood dripped across the floor, I knew I'd make it worse on her *uncle*. He'd beg me for death, but it wouldn't be fast. Then my little doll could bury the memories six feet deep— alongside his body.

"He passed out again." Diego peeled back Peiro's eyes but it was clear no one was home.

"Leave him. We'll grab a drink, then come back." I didn't want this to end too quickly.

Locking the door behind us, we headed up to the apartment. The bedroom was silent and I assumed Octavia was passed out. Diego and AJ updated me on news from Cali as we sat around covered in blood and drinking expensive bourbon. Alessandro was better and

Eva was safe. However, JP was becoming an even bigger problem in my absence.

"Wasn't that her bodyguard downstairs?" Diego asked, and I nodded as I brought a glass to my lips and took a long swig. "That's fucking hilarious."

"Fuck him." I twisted my wrist as the amber liquid swirled in front of me. And then I heard it. The unmistakable growl of my Bugatti. Sitting up, I realized the key hook was empty. "Fucking bitch!"

We all moved into action. I hurled over the back of the leather sofa, charging for the bedroom door. The room was empty except for a broken zip tie and a discarded piece of tape on the bed. We darted downstairs only to find that both my car and the bloodied man I left tied to a chair were gone.

"Kill him, but don't you dare touch her," I shouted commands as my men filed into their cars. "She's fucking mine."

Diego followed the Bugatti GPS tracker as I seethed beside him in the passenger seat. "You gotta admit." He glanced at me. "Shit was boring until she came along."

"They stopped at… the fucking hospital." I dropped the phone into my lap.

"Smart." He shook his head while I refused to respond.

It wasn't long before our tires were peeling into the lot just outside the emergency department. We found my Bugatti idling by the double doors as Octavia appeared to be dragging Peiro inside. The moment her eyes flicked in our direction, she pushed him inside and went running towards the car again, aggressively holding down the horn before taking off on foot.

Clever girl. The commotion would force us back. But it wouldn't stop us from following her completely.

We came upon a divider and I jumped out. Her short legs were no match for my size as I quickly gained on her. Then she unwittingly darted down a dead-end corridor between buildings. A door opened behind the dumpster and she disappeared inside. A second later, I charged through it, slamming into the wall as pain erupted across my face. We made eye contact as Octavia lifted the board and struck me again. The blow was just enough to send me stumbling as I tried to blink past the blurriness.

She darted back the way she came, only to curse under her breath when she heard the sound of screeching tires. Diego blocked her escape route. So she took the chance and turned to run towards me. I remained on the ground, daring her to risk it. And my little doll took the bait. As she went to jump past me, I grabbed her and she screamed. She fell onto my chest, fighting like a wildcat when I pinned her down. She twisted my arm and pulled, but her strength didn't compare to mine.

Daddy may have taught her how to grapple but not with a man my size.

I was toying with her now. Grabbing her ankle, I pulled her towards me. She rose on an elbow and glanced back. Her eyes were the brightest blue and the sight of her fire made me burn for her. I just noticed the smirk on her face a little late. Her sneaker-clad foot kicked at my nose, and she was lucky I didn't want to fucking hurt her too bad or else I'd have responded by breaking her fucking neck. Then, clearly thinking she'd won, Octavia took off running. I slowly pushed to my feet, straightened my shirt, and stepped outside.

Diego pulled up behind me, and I jumped into the car. "Like I said, she does keep shit interesting." He laughed again.

We hauled ass down the alley, barely decelerating at the cross streets. And just when I thought we'd lost her, movement caught my attention. Diego went around the block and we slowed our approach as we noticed men circling her. I jumped out of the car and approached the scene. The fuckers were so entranced by their would-be prey they didn't notice me. And then I struck.

One started wheezing when two fingers assaulted his throat

before the man at her back collapsed on top of her when I sent my knife through his head. By the time I was done with the third guy, the one I'd seen groping her, Octavia had managed to crawl out from under the pile of corpses.

Her face flashed with indecision, and I knew she was itching to fight me. To run.

"Don't even fucking think about it." I held out my hand and she took it. A quick tug and Octavia slammed into my body before I tossed her over my shoulder.

The moment I deposited her into the SUV, she slid across the seat, putting distance between us. This time, she kept her pretty mouth shut. One word and my dick would've silenced her the rest of the trip. I could feel myself harden at the thought.

The car ride was cloaked in tension. When we finally pulled into the warehouse, I gripped both her wrists in one hand and I forced them behind her back. She bent forward awkwardly as I yanked her arms into the air and watched her try to shuffle up the steps.

Diego stopped me before I could follow behind her. "I ordered the cleanup but I got news." He glanced at Octavia, who remained rooted to the spot.

"Give me a minute." I escorted her into the apartment and charged for her the moment the door closed us in. "I want you naked and sprawled on that fucking sofa." When she didn't move, I barked, "Now!" And watched as she jumped and slowly started stripping.

Once she was naked, she glanced between me and the sofa. I pointed towards it, once again daring her to disobey. One wrong move and I'd snap. She sat down, leaning into the plush leather. Her heels on the table and her legs spread wide. I stepped between them. She was already soaking wet and waiting for her punishment. My little doll had no clue what she was about to get. I'd gone easy on her until now.

"Don't fucking move, Octavia," I gritted out, and she flinched at the sound of her real name. "This little fucking stunt..." I trailed off, allowing the unspoken threat to linger in the air. "You're going to be fucking sorry. Now keep that ass right there until I get back." I pivoted on my heel and slammed the door behind me.

"The Lombardis landed about an hour ago," Diego said when I rounded the corner, and my jaw clenched. "We lost them at the airport." He took a step back, waiting for my rage to boil over.

"Let 'em come."

"Your father told them why you're here," he said when I moved to walk past him, and I froze as what he was really telling me sank in.

They wanted a bride. If they couldn't have Eva, they'd come for my little doll instead.

I'd love to see them fucking try.

CHAPTER 18

OCTAVIA AGOSTINO

This new person I'd become was a force, one they kept doubting. When AJ brought me upstairs, he was kind. Warning me to stay put or he'd have to tie me down.

I'd needed to get Peiro to the hospital and I prayed he'd tell my family. Tell them what? I had no clue. I didn't know what I wanted anymore. What was real…

The compound—my childhood home—was just another prison. One made of gold, the other pure muscle. A caged bird often had their wings clipped, a way to ensure they never got too far if they escaped. That's what my family had done to me. While, in some ways, Carmine let me fly. Even if he was never too far behind me.

I'd stolen his car, freed his captive, made him bleed, and yet he still protected me. Watching him tear those men apart showed me the monster—the animal—I always knew was there. But seeing it was something else. He petrified me to my core. And the thing was… my core was dripping for him. His punishments were something I craved, and while I knew this one would test my limits, I wanted it.

I couldn't hear anything over my own frantic heartbeat. My legs shook as I kept them spread wide, terrified he'd know the instant I disobeyed.

"Good girl." Carmine walked back into the room. "Are you sorry for what you did?" His brow danced with the question. Dried blood was smeared across his face. His hands were torn open, the bone on his knuckles visible. I nodded. "Liar."

He undid his belt, popped open his pants, and undid the buttons on his shirt. Those tattoos wrapped around his strong neck, stretched across his toned stomach, and disappeared into his jeans. I wanted to count them. To trace them with my tongue.

"Do you want to beg for forgiveness? How will you do it?"

"Sir, may I close my legs?" I asked, and he nodded. "May I crawl to you?"

He crooked a finger, silent approval. His posture tense. Distrusting.

I dropped to my knees, my ass swaying as I crawled on all fours, stopping to rest at his feet. Grabbing his jeans, I pulled them down his thighs. His dick sprang free and I swirled my tongue around the head.

"Look at me," he grunted and I obliged. "No sharp knives?"

I lifted my palms, showing him they were empty.

"Lean forward and lift that perky ass so I can see it while you suck my cock. Hands locked on your lower back."

I followed Carmine's every command and not because he was telling me to do it. It was because I wanted to. He didn't hesitate to force himself deeper, making me gag. His grip on my hair held me in place. I fell forward when he tugged, my body now twisted at an odd angle. He bent down, pushing until my nose hit his belly, and my breath stalled in my lungs.

"Good girl," he repeated the compliment before pulling free from my mouth. He ripped his shirt, wrapping a piece around my arms and tying them together. "Open."

Alight with need, he pushed himself to the back of my throat and settled deep. His smile turned vicious and I immediately realized my error. Once more, I'd trusted him with my body as the hate between us burned bright. I fought against him, struggling to breathe. Tears poured from my eyes and spit flew from the sides of my mouth.

His voice was cold. "The Lombardis followed us here," Carmine grunted and my eyes rounded as I moaned around his dick. "Eva or you, they don't give a fuck who it is. They want what belongs to me. And like a stupid, immature little girl, you ran off. Why? For some chump who can't do shit to protect you?" He lifted his arm, and when I saw the belt in his hand, I tried twisting my head. But he walked me forward, forcing me to scramble after him. The bastard was enjoying himself. "Lift your ass, Octavia."

I winced at the mention of my name. It sounded wrong coming from him.

"You will keep me in your mouth and count each strike. Now breathe deep, baby."

I inhaled right before he pushed my nose to his stomach. I couldn't count. I couldn't think. All I could do was cry, moan, and scream around his dick as it stole my breath. Then pain seared across my ass. I could feel my pussy dripping, and I hated myself for it.

Was it five strikes? Ten?

He pulled completely out of my mouth, spit clinging to my lips as I whimpered through the pain. "You didn't count. Ten more."

"Carmine, please," I pleaded with him, my skin on fire and my throat raw. "Please, I won't run again." My thighs shook, struggling to hold me upright, while his hand in my hair was tight and the restraints on my arms burned my flesh.

"Oh, little doll." He stroked my face and I leaned into his touch. "You're a dirty fucking liar. Now. Open."

All the way down he went as fire lapped at my ass. My counts were off, and my words were unintelligible grunts, but I did my best to comply. My entire body thrummed to life, needing him. In one move, he pulled out of my mouth, freed my hands, and carried me to the bedroom. My broken cries followed us as I buried my face in his chest. He kissed my forehead, told me how well I'd done. And I was so fucking broken—so fucking pathetic—that I loved it. I needed his praise.

"Shit, babe." He placed me on the bed and ran a finger through my folds. "Ya fuckin' drippin' on my sheets." There he was. The relaxed Carmine. The version of the beast that I'd only seen in front of his family. The man who dropped his walls, the mafia titles, and just *was*.

First, I came from his fingers. Then his mouth. Then his fingers again. Then, finally, on his dick. Over and over until I was sated and half-awake.

Turning onto my side, I asked, "Why would your father trade with the Lombardis? They're nobodies. Doesn't seem like a smart alliance."

"Sold property and stole a shipment of guns that belonged to the *Bratva*."

I leaned up on my elbow to stare at him.

"Yep. I think it's time I let them know who they fucked with and make a call to a *friend*."

Holy. Fuck. The west was already at war with the east. Now we had to worry about the Russians. What the hell was going on and what did that mean for an Agostino sleeping with a Ragetti in the center of the madness?

Sleeping with or being held captive?

Good point. Because I wasn't even sure anymore…

"What if he sees me in the car?"

I'd met the Russian Wolf once, by accident. With a father like mine, I'd seen plenty of dangerous men come and go in my childhood home. So hosting the leader of the *Bratva* was nothing out of the ordinary.

Nikolai Volkov was covered in Russian tattoos with a pair of cold, crystal-blue eyes. That man terrified me. He was attractive but his smile was eerie. Dead. I'd just come down the stairs and he was turning on his polished shoes, headed towards the front door, when he pinned me with a glare. It was as if the man could see right through me. I'd been unable to move, my legs paralyzed by fear. And that was him being kind.

Now we were on our way to make a deal with the Russian Wolf. Carmine had called the oldest Lombardi, offering to hand me over to free Eva from JP's contract. The asshole was all too eager to make the exchange. I was here to keep up appearances, and maybe because Carmine didn't trust me enough to leave me behind again.

Semantics.

"Breathe, little doll. And stay in the car," he whispered as we pulled up to an empty lot, where several Mercedes formed a half circle.

Carmine got out at the same time Nikolai appeared. And an unwanted shiver traveled up my spine. I rubbed my arms to soothe the chill. Somehow, even at a distance, the Wolf's eyes seemed to glow. They talked for a few minutes, then shook hands before everyone returned to their respective vehicles. Everyone except Nikolai. His eyes were focused on me as if he could sense my presence. I ducked down in the back seat and AJ laughed.

When I looked up again, Carmine was standing by the car and The Wolf was approaching. "Your father," Nikolai said.

"I'll deal with him." Carmine opened the door. "Finishing up a few things, then I'm heading back west."

Nikolai and I made eye contact. If he was surprised to see me, he didn't show it. He just stared at me in silence. Then he shook his head and barked out an odd laugh.

"*Ty sumasshedshiy.*" He patted Carmine on the back. "Batshit crazy. All right, *moy drug.* Let's do this. Afterwards, you can tell me what I owe you."

"Want to get square now?" Carmine pulled a few folded papers from his pocket. "I know you have American connections that could help." When Nikolai didn't deny it, Carmine continued. "This can't come back to me. Not yet anyway. Can you deliver?"

Nikolai opened the papers, recognition crossing his face for a moment, then he locked it down. He glanced at me, inspecting my every feature as if to see if I were damaged. If I were bruised and bleeding…

Would it make a difference? Would it have The Russian Wolf swooping in to save me?

I doubted it.

"Give me two days." And then he walked off as Carmine slid into the back with me.

"Shit. Shit!" I started hyperventilating as I dropped my head between my knees. "He's going to tell my father—"

Dread settled heavily as I thought of what my father would think. Nikolai could tell him what he saw… a willing participant in the clutches of our enemy. My siblings had moved on, but I know my parents hadn't. They couldn't. But I deserved to be the one to tell them… everything.

Carmine's laugh cut me off. "No, he ain't. You're not the *Bratva's* problem." He pulled me across the leather seat, wrapping me in his arms. "Now repeat the plan."

"I stay by your side as we approach. The moment you give me the signal, I run back to the car and stay down."

"Good girl."

The drive to the next meetup spot was silent and filled with tension. And it wasn't just me who seemed nervous. Carmine would never admit it, but I'd been watching him over the last few weeks. When he was serious and concentrating, he clenched his jaw. Like now. I watched his lip dance with the motion. We came to a stop and a dozen men milled about in the distance. Their cars weren't nearly as nice and they seemed to circle a large cargo van.

Carmine motioned for me to stay as he got out. Then he and Diego met them halfway. A few words were exchanged before Carmine gestured to AJ at the same time two men went to the back of the van. AJ got out but waited at the door. Once the boxes were placed—unopened—in front of them, he moved.

"Make it Oscar-worthy, princess." AJ laughed, his tone far kinder than I deserved after what I'd done to him, and his hand around my bicep as he pulled me from the car. I fought against his hold while Carmine smirked, clearly enjoying the show.

"You weren't lying!" The portly creep with far too much hair gel laughed as he eyed me like a cow at market. "Holy shit. How'd ya get an Agostino?"

Carmine didn't bother to answer, motioning a hand at the boxes.

"All right, all right. All business. Forgot how you worked, Carmine."

The Ragetti men moved to open all the boxes to reveal the guns. After the third box was inspected, Carmine pointed a finger at the ground and AJ released my arm. I'd just turned and started to run when the gunfire erupted behind me. I dove into the car, through the open door, and took cover.

Carmine was enthralled by the chaos. In the center of all of it. And I couldn't take my eyes off him. He was flourishing in the mayhem, firing two guns rapidly. And it was so damn hot. Within minutes, it was done.

Slowly, my head rose and my heartbeat evened out. Carmine and Nikolai were shaking hands, appearing unfazed by the carnage in their midst. The Russian guns were being placed into the van, before being driven off by one of Nikolai's men. Once the handoff was complete, Carmine, Diego, and AJ walked back to the car.

"Probably got a couple of days till it gets back to JP." Diego went back to his phone.

Carmine wrapped his arm around my shoulders and absently stroked my head.

When did I start to crave his comfort?

"I think you should call your family," he said out of nowhere, causing everyone in the car to turn and look at him. "You want to go home, don't you?"

We'd just pulled into the warehouse. I refused to answer Carmine's question as I followed him up to the apartment while the weight of the world seemed to sit on my chest.

Why wasn't I jumping at the chance to call home?

I knew why. It wasn't complicated. Even as Carmine's prisoner, I'd felt freer with him than I had in years. He managed to set me free from my own demons and I felt invigorated. As Carmine disappeared into the shower, I sat at the kitchen island, my guilt eating away at me. Yes, I needed to call them. But, no, I didn't want to tell them I was coming home.

I didn't want to go home.

Hopping off the stool, I ran into the bathroom, stalling for a moment as I watched Carmine's large body through the glass. He was covered in soap and suddenly I wanted my hands on him.

"Little doll?" He turned, eyeing me up and down.

"I don't want to go back." I shook my head, surprised by how

loud my voice sounded. "I... They won't understand... They—"
How was I supposed to explain this to them? "I don't want to suffer.
I want to live. And if I go back..."

Carmine opened the door and motioned for me to step inside.
"Nothing has changed, Octavia," he said, and air escaped my lungs.
Was he sending me back? "This. You. She's been there all along.
Someone just needed to let you out of your box, little doll."

My heart ached at what this man had given me. Yes, he'd taken
plenty *from* me, but did it really matter? I'd already lost so much
before him. I was unraveling. And now I'd been found. I was
centered.

I stepped into the shower, fully clothed, getting lost in the feel
of the warm water, of his rough touch. He stripped me down and I
showed him just how thankful I was that he'd set a part of me free.
Once he returned the favor, we stepped out of the stall, and I went
to sit on the end of the bed. Carmine disappeared in the living room
before returning with his cell phone. He dialed and put his finger to
my lips to silence me. I could hear my father on the other end of the
line, demanding to know who was calling.

"She tastes so good. Her tears are sweeter than any candy. Her
cries are a soft symphony. And her blood, it's like a drug—giving
me the best high with every drop I take."

I couldn't hear my father's response, but I could tell he was
yelling. *Why was I letting him hurt my father? Why wasn't I saying
anything?*

A sick, fucked-up part of me realized... I wanted him to suffer.
It had been my choice to keep my secret. But that secret was formed
in the bowels of hell, designed to kill my father. Kill my family. I'd
protected them, but a little hurt was okay.

"I am going to take New York. I've already started to siphon
your power without you even knowing it. I didn't need to take your
daughter to conquer your city. I took her because I wanted her. Your
city under my control, your demise at my fingertips... it's not

enough. I want it all. I want to watch you fall apart knowing she's mine."

There was more shouting and a whimper escaped my lips before I could stop it. I didn't want to go home, but I didn't want my family to suffer either. They wouldn't understand, but I had to do this.

"Octavia, sweetheart. Do you have something to tell Daddy?"

"Daddy." I could hear my father breathing heavily on the other end.

"Octavia, baby. Are you okay? What has he done to you?" He wouldn't give me a second to answer him. "I will kill him for hurting you. I know it's a lot, but you can survive this. I'm coming for you, Octavia."

"You can't." My tone was rough, strong. Something I'd never used on my family before. "You can't save me, Daddy. Octavia is dead."

It was the truth. Octavia had bled to death on her sheets, thanks to her father's best friend.

"Don't say that, baby girl."

"Say what? The truth? If it wasn't this time, there would be another. I know, Daddy." My anger for every slight they'd dished out was rising to the surface and I couldn't hold it back anymore. "You were going to pass me off, hand me over to someone else because I was a problem you didn't want to deal with anymore."

"No, baby girl. No. It wasn't like that. I wanted to protect you. I wanted to save you from this life."

"Because I was the weakest child. You wanted to hand me over, to a stranger, because I was too weak to handle the life you built."

"No... I—"

"I'm not coming home, Daddy. He will never let me go." I looked at Carmine as some part of me hoped that what I was saying was true. That he'd never let me go.

"Octavia, don't say that."

I could hear glass shattering in the background as my father likely took out his rage on whatever was near. "It's the truth. Tell the family I love them and that I will be fine. But, Daddy, I need you to let me go."

He started shouting my name, calling out to Carmine. But I didn't answer. I'd had enough and my heart was breaking. He didn't understand why I needed to do this.

"But this is so much more fun. Octavia, say bye to Daddy."

"Tell Sienna I love her and to stop looking for me. Tell them all I'm okay, Daddy. Because I am. I love you."

The phone went dead and I was captivated by my own actions. Carmine stared at me, waiting on the breakdown. Instead, I swallowed roughly, wiped away a tear, and stood taller.

That was so much harder than I expected. But in the end, I finally felt free. No longer did my inner beast beg for me to let *her* loose, because she was already running wild and dangerous.

After the phone call with Mario, I held Octavia in my arms. When she'd come to me in the shower, I was shocked—if not fucking elated—by her declaration. *I'd fucking won.* My little doll had fallen into a peaceful routine of warming my dick while I set out to dismantle the Agostinos.

I'd had men on the inside—watching. Her father was falling apart. His businesses were suffering. His children were pulling away from him. Sienna had taken off, so now he'd lost two daughters. And I fucking reveled in each message of his pain.

She'd needed to say goodbye to her old life. Her old self. The scars were a thing of the past and she wore them with a sense of pride. Her award for survival. And it was goddamn sexy.

My phone rang and I answered it. "*Moy drug,* we're even now. Warehouse, in ten." The call clicking up and I motioned for Diego to move.

Exactly ten minutes later, Nikolai's crew dragged in a bound man with a hood over his head. They must've knocked him out because he hung limp, the tan fabric soaked in blood. Diego and AJ made quick work of tying him to the chair in the center of the room

—directly over the drain. Then Nikolai and I shook hands as he prepared to leave.

"I heard Mario got a call. A certain little girl didn't want to go home," Nikolai called over a shoulder, and I shrugged. "Innocent get hurt and *bred sivoy kobyly.*" He laughed. "War has costs. People die."

It was a momentary glance as the Russian Wolf stepped forward from the darkness within the man in front of me. Something broken flashed over his face before he locked it down. Even though it was only seconds, I felt a sense of foreboding. Nikolai's story was depraved and filled with personal grievances. The brief crack in his exterior told me as much.

And then he was gone.

Diego stood to my right. "You know I'll die for you, brother. Follow you through hell. But her… that girl has already been through hell. When is it going to be enough? You won."

"It's almost time for my little doll to go home."

There, between us, a silent agreement was made.

"JP isn't going to accept that."

I couldn't give a fuck about my father. Blood had been flowing in the streets back west. JP was creating a lot of problems that I needed to deal with. He was losing favor with people who were all turning to me now. I was ready to send Octavia home to complete my plan. Only then would I ultimately win this charade.

"Too fucking bad for JP then." Diego shook his head, clearly not believing Octavia would get out of this unscathed. To be fair, I never said she would. "AJ!" I shouted. "Bring her here."

A moment later, my little doll appeared in my favorite room. "Carmine, what's—" Her nose twitched with the fresh stench of bleach. "Who?" she asked, her eyes focused on the man presently bound to the chair between us.

"Come here," I barked, watching her bare feet slap against the tile as she stepped into my embrace. "I have a gift for you."

Diego ripped off our captive's hood and Octavia's *Uncle* Rick startled awake. I held onto her tightly, refusing to let her flee. She was going to sit and watch this. His mouth was sealed with duct tape, his words unintelligible as he fought against his binds.

Rick glared at Octavia and she flinched. "Don't you fucking look at her. You look at me, you piece of shit," I hissed.

He glanced at her again and AJ punched him across the face.

"You used her love for her family to keep her quiet. He was your best fucking friend. And you hurt his daughter?" I guided Octavia to a chair next to Diego. "She told me you had a son? Give me his fucking name."

He shook his head.

"Okay, you had your chance." I positioned a small table with devices on it in front of him. I'd heard stories about Apollo Deluca and his love for anatomy. His proclivity for getting up close and personal with different organs.

Not me. I just liked to make 'em fucking bleed.

My eyes flickered over to Octavia, who was staring at the ground with her hands over her ears. "Octavia," I barked, and she glanced up at me. "You begged and he didn't stop. I won't either." I ripped the tape from his mouth and leaned into his face. "Now I want to hear you scream."

"She's fucking lying, the little bitch!" he shouted. I punched him in the jaw. "Fuck! Ow! Shit!"

The old man thought his friend would protect him. That he was untouchable. He wanted something he didn't work for. That false sense of security showed he couldn't even take a punch. He was a sniveling mess. Fuck, Octavia had more fight when coming toe-to-toe with me.

Grabbing a scalpel—how fitting—I jammed it into his legs, his shoulders, and his hands repeatedly. His blood trickled towards the drain, and Octavia suddenly came alive, watching with rapt attention.

"Anything you'd like to say?" I motioned her closer, surprised when she moved. "He'll pass out soon. Now's your chance, little doll."

Instead of speaking, she stared at him blankly for a moment. Then she spit directly in his face, before landing a solid punch to his nose, and he screamed in agony. I was impressed. The girl had good form and I could hear the bone crack. She stared at him in silence for what seemed like forever. Then suddenly, in one swoop, she removed her shirt and Rick's eyes immediately fell to her scars. In a room full of men, she stood strong with the pain he'd inflicted on display.

AJ and Diego glanced at me, having seen the marks for the first time. I refused to acknowledge them. My attention focused on the beautiful creature in front of me. If I hadn't been watching her so closely, I would've missed the slight tremor in her hand.

"Tell me," she demanded, her voice strong. "I said. Tell. Me," she repeated, louder, and the coward started whimpering. "It's okay. Just tell me." She stroked his hair off his sweaty forehead, smiling at the battered man.

When he started mumbling in her ear, she went still. I couldn't hear what he was saying, but it was clear it rattled her. Then she patted his head like you would a dog and turned to me, offering a palm as she nodded, wanting the scalpel.

"Brucia all'inferno." The small blade carved a line straight across the fucker's throat before a fresh stream of blood coated Octavia's skin.

"What did he say?" I asked while prying the scalpel from her hand.

"Nothing, kept begging," she replied a little too quickly.

"Try that again." I lowered my hand, allowing the metal to clatter against the floor. "And this time, don't fucking lie to me."

She stared at his corpse a moment longer. "He. Begged." Her defiance was worthy of a beating. "And just like he did to me, I ignored it." She slowly turned to face me, and the blank expression gave me pause. "I won."

"Out," I shouted the command, and Diego and AJ immediately exited the room. "Not. You." I caught Octavia's arm when she tried to follow them. "What did I say about lying?"

"Do it." Her breasts rose to match her labored breaths. "Punish me, Carmine."

"Oh, you'd like that, wouldn't you?" She started squirming as I circled her. "Why should I give you what you want?" I pressed.

"Because."

"Because what?" She remained silent. "What!" I barked, making her jump.

"I'm dirty. Carmine, I'm so fucking dirty." Her blue eyes turned clear as drops of pain dripped over the edge. "I'll never be able to wash it all away. But when I bleed, my soul feels lighter."

Dipping my thumb into a tiny tear, I sucked the tip into my mouth. "Look at him." I turned her towards the dead man in the chair, holding her back to my chest with my grip on her chin. "He's fucking dirty. You were freed the moment you sliced his fucking throat." My fingers traced the lines on her exposed stomach.

"I'm—"

My grip on her neck stalled her pleas. "You're not. Not because of him. But for me, you're fucking filthy." She whimpered, her ass pressing tight against my cock. "That's your revenge. That's your nightmare. And it'll be washed down the drain because *you* killed him."

"I need to go home," she said suddenly and my hands shook, a silent threat to choke her.

"That's not your home anymore. They've moved on without you. They don't care," I reminded her. Octavia shook her head, fighting me. "And who is the girl returning? They'll hate her. They'll want the weak, sad girl I stole."

She spun in my arms, her hands to my face as she pulled me

down to kiss her. It was harsh and demanding, our teeth gnashing against each other. I lifted her by the ass and her legs wrapped around my waist as I slammed her into the wall. Her nails scratched at my skin, anywhere she could get purchase.

I bit her lip and she moaned as her blood filled both our mouths. What should've been metallic tasted sweet. Like a fine wine. And I'd fucking savor it until I sent her packing. I'd barely gotten my dick out of my pants when she squirmed against me. Her pussy was throbbing, her arousal smothering my length. I slammed into her, not stopping for a single second as I pumped forward. Punishing. Demanding. And fucking lethal.

For one moment, everything around us drifted away. Fuck our families. Fuck the names and duties we were bound to. She was just a girl with demons that matched my own and, fuck, was the sex incredible.

Octavia-fucking-Agostino wasn't dirty. She was downright filthy. And I fucking loved it.

"Come for me, little doll," I grunted, and her core clenched around me as I chased my own desire. "Fuck, you're so tight."

She trembled in my arms, succumbing to the aftershock of her orgasm while I pinned her to my chest as I came. I set her back down on shaky limbs and watched my seed drip down her thighs. Covering her with my shirt, I pulled her out of the room. My men were lurking about the vast warehouse as Octavia and I emerged covered in blood. Diego did little to hide his amusement, but AJ had the good sense to look away.

"I didn't want to interrupt." My eyes were drawn towards the sound of the familiar voice, landing on Nikolai presently leaning against a Mercedes. "May I speak freely?" When I nodded, The Wolf continued. "You've got some problems on your hands." He stared pointedly at Octavia. "Word has gotten back to the west. About the Lombardis."

"Oh. No." I shrugged and Nikolai chuckled at my obvious lack of concern.

"You may want to call your father. And. Someone knows where *she* is hiding," he added, and that made me stand taller. "Little blonde is relentless."

Fucking Persephone.

"I'll handle her," I ground out. "She should know better than to cross me."

Octavia went rigid in my arms before shrugging herself loose and darting up the stairs.

Was my little doll jealous?

"Now, *she* has me curious." Nikolai watched Octavia go with rapt attention, and I cleared my throat, forcing his focus back on me. "I hope this remains a silent arrangement as I finish my business with her brother."

I nodded and extended a hand. The *Bratva* was not an enemy you wanted to have. Where the Italians were a little more rule-bound, the Russians were brutal.

"Till next time, *moy drug.*" Nikolai dipped his chin towards his men. They all piled into waiting cars and left.

"Not gonna lie. That motherfucker scares the shit out of me." Diego shook his head as the caravan of SUVs pulled out of the warehouse.

"Pussy." AJ laughed.

"Your father's been blowing me up." Diego glanced at his ringing phone.

"I'll call him from my office."

The shower was running when I entered the apartment, and instead of calling my father like I knew I needed to, I followed her scent. Her lithe body moved around the stall as she hummed and washed herself. I stripped off my clothes and stepped inside with her. Octavia stared at me for a second, her expression blank and haunted, before she finally caved and launched herself into my arms.

"Thank you," she whispered against my neck, trailing kisses to my face. "They stopped."

"What?" Whatever it was, I'd do it again just to see this look on her again.

"The voices. The constant noise in my head. It stopped. Because of you." She pulled away with a smile on her lips, then tugged me into another kiss.

"No, little doll. You did it. I just brought the motherfucker to you."

My dick hardened against her soft, pliant body. And it wasn't long before we were fucking like wild animals against the tiled wall, the bathroom counter, and once more in the kitchen. I was insatiable when it came to this woman. She broke apart underneath me, time and again, but it wasn't enough.

I carried her into the bedroom, and then I did something I've never done before. I took her slow and sweet. I enjoyed every small piece of her and committed the feeling to memory. The way she became so lost to her need for me.

Sated. Spent. Sprawled across my bed like a dark angel, my broken little doll was put back together. I shifted slightly, sliding out from under her body before covering her with a blanket.

Gifted with a sleep-cloaked whisper, I waited as my little doll made her confession. "Love. You."

Two words, breathed into the silent room, echoed in my head like a gunshot. They were soft. Sweet. And the pull of a trigger that would end the game.

CHAPTER 20

CARMINE RAGETTI

"What's your problem?" Diego glanced up as I walked into the office. "You got a weird-ass look on your face."

"First, fuck you. It's called a goddamn smile."

He visibly flinched when I smiled again.

"Fucking asshole. And it's because I just put a bullet in Mario-fucking-Agostino's head." I sat in my chair, staring at the ceiling as I let the feeling sink in.

Octavia was the catalyst to her father's ruin. She'd fallen for my lies and sweet declarations. The time had come, I was sure of it. The more I saw who I was sending back, the more eager I was to wait to watch my destruction continue. Her telling him she didn't want to go home was debilitant. But being in love with the enemy was me putting the last of the dominos in ruin.

Diego opened his mouth to speak when my phone interrupted him. I picked it up and held it to my ear. "You stupid, good for nothing little fucker. You rat out the fucking Lombardis! Tell me, Carmine. Do you know what happened to them?"

"Don't play dumb. It doesn't suit you." I turned in my chair, staring out the window. "Did you honestly think I'd let you hand over my sister? Well, I kept her and got the guns. Sounds exactly like what you've taught me to do since I was a kid."

"Eva was going to be fine. I'd never let them keep my daughter. You dumb motherfucker, if you'd stop for one second to think—"

"Watch your mouth, old man. You're crossing a line and you're painfully unprepared for what you'll find on the other side. I don't give a fuck what you wanted—"

His mocking laughter had me gritting my teeth. "Eva. Or that Agostino pussy you have holed up in my warehouse. Which of them hurts worse, Carmine?" When I didn't answer, his laughter continued. "You're fucking weak. Just like your uncle. God knows he died chasing pussy. Are you next?"

John Paul Ragetti wasn't a man you could trust on a good day. Even less when he was plotting.

"I've got Mario right where I want him. His little girl is disgraced, ruined, and believes every fucking lie I've told her. Daddy is going to hate the *girl* I drop on his doorstep." My voice sounded fake even to me.

Movement at the door got my attention, but no one was there. Rising to my feet, I kept the phone to my ear and wandered to the open space. The living room was empty, but I could have sworn I heard the click of a door.

Are you eavesdropping, little doll?

"Oh, really?" JP pressed, and I rambled off my plans. What I was willing to tell him anyway. "That's my boy. Dump the bitch in a shallow grave and get your ass back here," he added before the sound of gunfire erupted in the background. And I sat up, confused. "Your little stunt with the Lombardis isn't going away. They're gonna want payment and I'm not gonna be the one to do it. You are." Then he hung up.

I hit dial on my phone, and one of my men back in Cali

answered on the first ring. "Sir, can't talk right now. I have no idea who the fuck your old man just blew up, but there's fucking—"

The line went dead. I'd planted one of my guys in my father's crew to keep an eye on him, and from the sounds of it, things were only escalating.

"Crazy motherfucker."

"Her family is going to fucking disown her," Diego muttered, earning him a smirk. "You're fucking sick."

"They say an eye for an eye… tooth for a tooth. Well, fuck that. Eyes for only me and teeth she shields when she sucks my cock."

Thunder boomed in the distance and a steady stream of rain pelted against the rooftop a few seconds later. Almost like a sign from God. Or the devil. Take your pick.

Diego laughed along with me, but it seemed forced. He was growing soft for the girl, which was just another reason I needed her gone. "Storm's picking up." He walked to the window, staring out for a moment before calling my name.

I jumped to my feet and glanced down, my eyes landing on the small figure in the middle of the road, lying on her back with her arms spread wide.

"What the fuck?" I darted towards the bedroom, already knowing I'd find it empty. "I'm going to beat her black and blue."

Flying down the stairs, I could hear the pounding of boots that told me Diego was right behind me as we darted through the open garage doors. Sure enough, half a mile away, Octavia was sprawled out on the concrete. My heart thumped at the thought of what I might find as I approached her.

"Hold up." Diego grabbed my arm and pointed. "She's got a nine, right hand."

"Little doll?" I questioned while taking in the eerie scene before me.

"Don't call me that," she replied, and I didn't recognize the disconnected, soulless voice I was certain was coming from her lips. "I'm not your little doll anymore. Maybe I never was."

"The fuck is she doing?" Diego whispered.

"Octavia, get up," I grunted as the rain continued to pelt us, but she just lay still with her eyes closed. "Now."

"Why do you care? 'Cause you'll lose your leverage?" So, she *was* listening. "Yet again, someone *hurt me* because of my father. Well, fuck all of you." She sounded so fucking sad.

I didn't know how to respond. Not with a nine in her hand. She could easily pull the trigger if she didn't like what she was hearing. Because no matter how I painted the picture, she'd kill me for the truth.

She waved the gun in the air, pointing towards the sky as if reading my mind. "You don't need a gun or knife to slowly kill someone, you know?"

"Little—"

She quickly cut me off. "Don't call me that!"

"Octavia, come inside."

She dropped the weapon back to her hip. "I was raped. Tortured. All because of a fucking name. A fucking name I didn't have a choice in selecting." Lightning flashed above us, illuminating the streets. "And then a *Ragetti* fucked me." She spit out my name like dirt in her mouth.

"Get out of the road before you get yourself killed."

She sat up straight and took aim again. "Would that fuck up your plans?" She shook with laughter, but the gun never wavered. "Neither of us is going to win this. No one in this life wins."

A pair of headlights blinded me as a truck turned the corner, coming right at her. She sensed it, plopped back down, and gave me one last look of *that* sweet smile. I charged for her, yelling at her to move. The truck wasn't slowing down. Diego and I were dressed in black and the rain was coming down heavier now. Octavia practically melted into the concrete as the oncoming traffic headed our way. I rushed forward, thunder echoing in the background, until I realized it wasn't thunder at all. It was gunfire.

"Fuck." Diego grabbed my arm and pulled me down behind a parked car. "She's fucking shooting at us."

"Crazy little bitch!"

She had a damn death wish. If the truck didn't kill her, I sure as fuck would. Chancing a look, I peered around the car and saw her staring right at me. She was still flat on her back, the gun aimed in our direction.

There were actions and reactions in life. And her present action caused my reaction. One that would kill us both. Ignoring the hail of bullets, I ran and dove on top of her. Searing pain struck my shoulder and my fists as the road bit into my skin and I curled and tugged her onto the grass. All while Octavia fought me with everything she had. Nails scratched down my face, teeth went for my arms, and limbs struck out at flesh. Hell-bent on attacking my nuts, she twisted and rammed her knee into my kidneys. The pain was all-consuming but my grip held tight. Then her thumbs turned towards my eyes, ripping open my cheek instead when I was quick enough to turn.

"I was finishing the job for you," she seethed.

Yep, she'd definitely heard.

Good. She needed to know that she'd fucked up. That she was a hot piece of ass, but she'd always be an Agostino and I'd always be a Ragetti. I was her enemy and her father was a fucking snake. No one was innocent in the mafia; we all had a price to pay for the life.

It wasn't my fault if burying my cock in her gave her a false fairy tale. She was my leverage and my need for it had expired.

"Poor little Octavia." My smirk was cruel. "No family. No loyalty. And no fucking brains in that pretty little head of yours."

"Get off me."

I rubbed my throbbing dick against her stomach. "Get you off?" She fought harder. "Maybe later. If you're my good little doll."

Pushing to my feet, I dragged her limp body up with me. When she didn't fight, shutting down instead, I threw her over a shoulder. She wasn't going to ruin my good mood.

A few minutes later, I was shoving back through the apartment door and throwing her onto the bed. She stared back at me, soaking wet and shivering. She'd yet to give me the satisfaction of breaking into a million pieces. Octavia was stronger than anyone gave her credit for. But this might just be her tipping point. I'd deceived her and there was no going back from that.

"No kiss goodnight?" I taunted, watching as she climbed down from the bed and peeled her wet clothes from her body until she was completely naked.

"Your turn." When I didn't respond, she climbed onto the bed, lying on her stomach with her hands at the headboard. "Your turn," she repeated. She was telling me to rape her. To cross a line that I'd never even thought of crossing. Her uncle and I weren't the same.

I rolled her onto her back. "Don't you ever compare me to that fucking trash again. Everything that's happened between us, you fucking begged for. Don't put that shit on me." I pushed off her as I shoved that little word back in her face. "Do you think you *love* a rapist?"

"I…"

Here came the lies.

"Love is cruel, little doll. Think. You loved your family, and they turned their backs on you. Now you're in love with a beast. My claws coated in your blood, your heart in my hands. While you sit and wait."

"Wait for what?"

"To see what I plan to do with it." I stepped towards the door, pausing at the threshold. "Time to go home."

"And then?"

"And then you'll be my good little doll and do every-fucking-thing I tell you to do."

I was sending Mario his precious little doll, my newly committed spy. She was going to give me every detail about them. All while pushing them away as she fought to figure out who the fuck she was now. And if she didn't… I'd hit her where it hurt. She had her issues with them, but Octavia would always protect her family. Even now.

"Or?"

"Or… you know what. As much as you hate them right now, you'll protect them. You obey or they suffer."

Moving fast, she grabbed the bedside lamp and threw it at me. The door slammed shut and the glass erupted on the other side. Her screams filtered through the wooden barrier as I rested my head against the vibrating panel. A minute or a month later, who really knew at this point, I snapped the locks into place. On the door. As well as on this girl's effect on me.

But monsters came alive in the dark, and I'd officially buried her in my shadow…

CHAPTER 21

OCTAVIA AGOSTINO

For as strong as I'd pretended to be, it didn't last very long, did it? Carmine had ripped down the walls that hid the steel bars of my cage. The place where I kept my rage and who I was under layer after layer of lies, to protect *them*.

Now that she was loose, and I was free, my power was pulled out from under my feet. A red mist—an eerie haze—had settled over me for years. I remained submissive to the role they'd given me, until I was finally freed from their chains.

He was right. I was their little doll just as much as I was his. They put me in the prettiest dresses, gave me rosy cheeks, and positioned me where I was wanted. The face of innocence they hid behind. If only they'd have realized I'd surpassed *il diavolo*…

I didn't burn in the flames. Within the fire and pain. No, I came alive. And I'd handed myself over to a beast because I loved the scratch of his claws and the depths of his bite.

As I drifted off to sleep, the usual nightmares had vanished and were replaced by terrifying growls…

Carmine was gone and I had barely left the bedroom. Whatever fairy tale I'd made up in my mind was clearly over. His absence only solidified the fact that I would be returning. The question was: what would he demand of me afterwards?

The beast thought his *little doll* was made of glass. Instead, blood and organs would be plastered across the pavement. People would pay to see an Agostino corpse, murdered at the hands of a Ragetti.

Sudden footsteps echoed in the distance and then he called my name, but I ignored him. If he wanted me, he could come and get me himself. The game was done. It was time to go home.

You couldn't kill what was already dead. And Carmine-fucking-Ragetti pierced his jagged fangs through my heart. All that remained were flesh, bones, and nothingness.

"I called you." He stood in the doorway.

"And I ignored you," I fired back.

He smirked but the expression wasn't playful. It wasn't even malicious. It was triumphant. A look of pure joy.

Fucker.

"Time to go home to Daddy." He tossed a bag onto the bed, and my curiosity got the better of me as I unzipped it to see what was inside.

"Seriously?" My eyes dropped to the dress. Like one of the hundreds I'd complemented with a pair of sensible shoes, a pretty smile, and unquestionable obedience over the years.

"Your family wants you back, polished and pretty. But…" Carmine ran a hand down his sharp jaw. "The new you ain't gonna please 'em."

The asshole was back. And I broke.

I hated the tears. And even more, I hated the way I slowly walked into his embrace.

Why did he have to be such a brute? A monster? A fucking beast? How could he be the same man who helped me kill the phantom of my nightmares in one breath? Then the next, he was the animal that chewed through my heart, breaking me down at just the thought of leaving.

His tongue traced the trail of salt along my face. "You don't have to do this," I whispered into his chest.

Carmine held me for a moment longer before I felt the rumble of laughter. Pushing me out to arm's length, he pinned me with a glare. And I hated it. There was a semblance of pity, but worst of all, there was amusement. My demise and disgrace—it was all so entertaining to him.

"Oh, Octavia," he barked out, and I winced. "Once I realized you loved me, I won. You're a fucking Agostino. I got what I wanted and now I'm done with you. Simple as that. I can't wait till your father smells me on your skin." Carmine rubbed his erection against me. "One last round before I send you back?" He laughed when I shoved him off.

"Fuck. You."

"No time. Now listen closely, little doll. You'll be my fucking eyes and ears in that house. Every closed-door conversation. Every underhanded deal. All of it. If someone takes a shit, I want to know about it."

"Not a chance in hell."

"Hell? Funny you should say that. Because I could very easily make your life a living hell. You think a little bit of starvation, a lack of clothes… was hell? Try being locked in that basement with just your thoughts. Around-the-clock beatings to remind you who owns you."

"You wouldn't," I gasped. Though his smile told me he would. "I won't do it. You might as well kill me now. I'm not a rat."

"You will. Or I'll kill everyone you love. Starting with your little nephew—Nico, I believe that's the kid's name, right? Just look at how easy it was for me to take you… You know I can and will do it. Now, do we have a deal? Your life, your family's… for a little intel."

"I fucking hate you."

"Not as much as your family is going to hate you." He stalked closer. "Think about it. We never used protection. Not once." His eyes dropped to my stomach before flicking back up to me. "I hope I knocked your ass up. That your parents won't be able to bear the sight of you with a little Ragetti in that womb of yours. Now stay the fuck out of my way until it's time to leave."

"I hate you!" I screamed at his back. It was the only thing I could think of in the haze of my growing rage.

"Make sure you're nice and pretty for Daddy." He grinned, then slammed the door behind him.

The harsh sound did little to comfort me. A barrier between us, and yet he still held my heart in his claws. All it took was a flex of his hands, and I would crumble.

Maybe death *was* better. A hand to my stomach, I prayed he was lying while knowing it didn't matter if it was true or not. He'd won. Everything my stupid mind made up about *us* was a painful reminder that I was gullible.

I'd created a fantasy and now I was going back to a very different reality…

CHAPTER 22
CARMINE RAGETTI

Killer. Degenerate. Ruthless. *Heartless.*

So many attributes, so little time.

My little doll had no idea the plans that I had for her. She assumed her tears would protect her from my destruction. They wouldn't. Nothing and no one could save her from the road I was forcing her down.

"She's gonna run," Diego said, leaning against the wall.

"Yup." I stepped to the bar, pouring myself two fingers. "I love it when she fights me."

"You're sick." He shook his head before quickly changing the subject. "Alessandro called. Shit is getting worse back west."

Bodies were piling up and JP was doing little to hide his rage. Local gangs, rival families, and civilians—no one was safe from his bullshit. Octavia leaving was finally a step in the right direction. I needed to get back to Tacoma, focus on my reign. One that no longer needed JP alive.

"I don't fucking have time for this." I tossed back my drink, immediately needing another. "It's like handling a temperamental toddler with a loaded gun."

"What's the plan?"

I motioned for him to sit, leaving the office door open to watch for her. "I got what I wanted and now she'll go back. Then we can head home—" Movement caught my attention. "Yes, little doll?"

Octavia was dressed in a pair of leggings and one of my shirts. She walked past with her nose in the air, the same stuck-up behavior I loathed from her sister.

Did she really think she'd get away with ignoring me?

"Octavia!" I barked, and she froze. "Come."

Fiery blue eyes rounded in my direction. I smirked and patted my knee. A moment of indecision passed over her face before she gave me the finger and kept walking towards the door. She opened it as Diego and I glanced at each other. Her hesitation was noted. It probably hurt that I didn't jump to stop her.

"Told ya." Diego turned his chair towards the door.

We remained in our spots, listening to her footfalls down the stairs. The garage was wide open and the weather was still shitty. A few more minutes and then the sounds of a struggle traveled across the space.

"Put. Me. Down!" she yelled as heavy steps marched back up the stairs.

"Sir?" AJ walked into my office with Octavia slung over one shoulder.

"Chair." I pointed and he dropped her. Once her ass touched the leather surface, she tried shooting up again. Diego held her shoulders down and I grabbed her thighs, leaning into her face.

Fuck, was she hot when she was mad.

"Don't you fucking move from that chair." My glare was challenging her to do it. "Good girl." Those eyes would haunt me— angry and cold. I opened my mouth to speak when she spit in my face. My lips snarled and I shoved at her shoulders, forcing her back into the seat. She shook me loose and slapped me across the face. My head whipped to the side and I stared at the wall for a moment

—a second—to save her life. "Do it again." I slowly turned to look at her. "I fucking dare you."

"Kill me. I. Dare. You."

Oh, that's how she wanted to play?

"Don't fuck with me, *little girl*." No matter how much she claimed to hate it, her expression always dropped when I called her anything other than *little doll*. "Nobody here will save you. Not from me."

"You're sending me away, so why can't I just leave now?"

"Because," I grunted, and she waited. "You leave when I tell you to leave."

Sure, Octavia was different from the rest. At first, she stood out to me because of her innocence—her submission. Then, when I saw the flare of her fire, I wanted her even more. And it became much more appetizing to bend her to a heel than command her to her knees. Until that smart mouth sealed her fate.

"Okay, Daddy." She gave me a fake smile. "Whatever you say, Dad—"

Very quickly she'd realized her mistake as I grabbed her wrists in one hand, forced them onto her lap, and got in her face. My body shook with unspent joy as I met her hate head-on.

"Call me Daddy again," I urged. Her mouth remained sealed. "Looks like you got the Daddy you need now." I leaned forward, tracing my tongue across her lips. "The one you wanted." My tongue floated along her jaw, to her ear, as I whispered, "And another Daddy who doesn't fucking want you."

Of course, I'd expected her to fight me. To hit me. To lash out. But my little doll had to prove she wasn't broken at all. As I sat back, expecting rage or tears—maybe both—I saw detachment staring back at me instead. Her breathing was calm and even, not a single tremble. She was ready for my game to end.

And then…

"Fuck!" My hand shot to my bleeding nose as I threw myself back against the seat. "Oh, you, little—"

"I know. I know." She hopped up from the chair, my blood smeared across her forehead. "I'll pay for that."

Diego started to laugh but quickly turned it into a spluttering cough when Octavia's fingers jammed into his throat to silence him. A few seconds later, AJ dropped to his knees after a swift kick to his balls. She made it to the door, running so fast her long hair blew behind her. Allowing me to grab a chunk and pull her back. Her lithe body bounced off my toned chest before she turned to fight me. I wrapped her silky strands around my fist, so tight her neck pitched awkwardly. A bruising hold on her hip kept her in place in front of me.

"So. Beautiful." I nipped at her shoulder. "And so. Dumb." Using my grip on her hair, I dragged her along to the bedroom. Slamming the door and shielding her only exit. "Get on your knees and fucking *pray* for forgiveness."

Her coy smile should've made me cringe, not harden my dick. "You want my teeth again?" She bared the white daggers. "You know, I think they got it wrong."

"What's that, little doll?"

She slowly sank to her knees. "When they tell our story, they'll name *you* as the beast…" She pulled her hair into a high ponytail. "But it's my bite they should be worried about."

At first, my plan had been to force her to give in to her more base desires. I'd wanted her to bend to my will. But I didn't have to force her to do anything. Octavia glared at me as she roughly grabbed my dick, licking the length before taking it deep in her throat. Her eyes flared with the challenge. She wanted to be in control.

For now, I'd let her think she was.

Back and forth, she sucked my dick like her life depended on it. And let's be real. It did. She'd pushed the limits of my patience far beyond anyone else. My nose dripped onto her face, my blood evidence of her misbehavior.

I combed my fingers through her dark locks, taking over. Quickening her pace as her saliva flew from the sides of her mouth and her nails clawed at my legs hard enough to bleed. The noises that filled the room were primal. Animalistic.

"I don't want to come in your mouth." I tugged Octavia up from her knees, throwing her across the room and onto the bed. "Put that ass in the air. Palms flat on the mattress."

For as angry as she was, how much she claimed she hated me, she didn't fight. Not even as my hand struck her ass, over and over again, until the red glow glistening off her cheeks matched the blood on my face.

"Shut up and fuck me," she *commanded*. I didn't hesitate before entering her in one rough thrust.

Without relenting, without allowing her a moment to breathe, my dick assaulted her pussy. She screamed through one orgasm after another. I could never give her, or any other woman for that matter, more than this. More than sex. She'd never survive in my world. My men, my family, would never accept her. While hers would never allow her to leave the east coast. I had no doubt that she'd become a bored politician's wife the moment I sent her home.

I flipped Octavia onto her back, her legs pressing into her chest as I gripped her neck and continued to fuck her. Squeezing tighter and tighter as I thrusted forward. This was my goodbye to her. The last thing I could give her before we had to part ways for good.

Her fight dwindled, those blue oceans became a stormy abyss, and her mouth parted. Her eyes rolled into the back of her head and I let her go, fucking the breath back into her lungs. Her body went limp and I came, pumping my seed deep inside her.

"Fuck, little doll." I pulled out, and she slumped to the side. "Octavia." I reached out a hand to twist her onto her back and shook her pliant body. "Fuck!" Leaning over her, I started giving her mouth to mouth, my hands pumping on her chest. My cursing became louder—frantic—as I ordered her to fucking breathe. The door slammed open and Diego came in with AJ at his heels.

"Shit," Diego muttered at my side while AJ paced at the end of the bed.

"Octavia." I slapped her across the face. "Fucking breathe." My mouth went to hers once more, and right as I went to continue with chest compressions, she gasped.

I yanked her up by the back of the neck, as her hands shot to my arms. Those once-emblazoned eyes were now frightened, unfocused. She panted aggressively, tears pouring down her face as she fought to get her bearings.

"I'm calling the doc." Diego had his phone to his ear and was already stalking out of the room with AJ in tow.

"Carm—what?" she started to ask. I shushed her, pulling her under the covers and tugging her into my side. "What happened?"

"You thought you could leave me," was all I said as I held her tight to my chest.

"You're making me leave." Her voice was raspy, bruises already forming on her neck.

"It's what's best."

She tried to push me away from her, and I refused to let her go. "Best for whom?"

"I don't fucking know," I said honestly.

Not once. Ever. In my entire fucking life had I felt fear like I did a second ago. Cutting her open, her blood coating my hands, made my dick hard. Hearing her little gasps when I choked the breath from her lungs was so fucking hot. But when she went limp beneath me, unresponsive, it unsettled something in my gut. Something I refused to acknowledge.

My little doll didn't deserve a bastard like me in her life. Sending her home *was* what was best. This was proof I wasn't good enough to hold on to something—someone—so precious. Even if the thought of her *under* someone else infuriated me. The fact of the matter was there was too much on my plate to add an Agostino to the mix.

After all, I'd already gotten what I wanted. Her love, her affection, and the betrayal left in her wake. Daddy wouldn't know what to do with her now.

"Don't do this," she whispered, suddenly pulling me closer.

Before I could answer her, the door opened and Diego ushered the doctor inside. He pushed me out of the way and gave Octavia a full look-over. Once he confirmed there was no permanent damage, he left with a disgusted parting glance in my direction and the promise of a hefty bill. He had a daughter Octavia's age.

Tucking her back under the sheets, I watched as her eyes drifted closed. Within a few minutes, she was out cold.

I'd almost killed her. Again.

I closed the door and headed to my office. Diego and AJ refused to look at me. And part of me didn't blame them for it. I couldn't look at myself at the moment.

Grabbing my cell, I sat behind my desk and made the call I'd been avoiding.

The familiar voice started cursing me to hell and back the moment the call connected. "Perse," I barked, interrupting her tirade. "Arrange the pickup."

Persephone knew I had Octavia, even if she didn't have evidence to prove it. The girl knew me and my motives far too well. It only took her a second to put it together, especially knowing she was the catalyst that stoked the fire.

I'd refused every one of her calls until now. Until I was ready to send Octavia back. And because Nikolai called to let me know Perse was gunning for me. The little shit always got what she wanted, so it shouldn't have surprised me that she'd gotten the *Bratva* involved.

"The hell were you thinking, Carmine!" a woman's voice had my eyes shooting open.

Inhaling deep, I froze at the pain the ripped through my neck. "Motherfucker." It came out strained and raspy. I grabbed my throat, wincing at the slight touch, before tossing the covers back and slipping into his shirt. Combing my fingers through my hair, I opened the bedroom door and froze. Anger, pain, and sadness consumed me. Threatened to drown me.

A thin, gorgeous blonde was in Carmine's arms, her back to me as he held her close. I don't know why I was surprised that he'd called in his whores already. The moment he saw me, he dropped his arms and she struck out at him.

"I cannot believe you fucking did this! After everything you know I went through. After all of it! You took an innocent!" She slapped him across the face, but his eyes remained on me. "How dare you hurt her! These games, this bullshit is between you and Mario! Not her!"

Who the hell was this girl? And why was she so damn upset? Especially about me?

"Little doll," Carmine said, making the blonde spin around to look at me.

Her pained blue eyes inspected every inch of my skin, as if expecting a limb to be missing. Her shoulders relaxed when she realized I was in one piece.

She was gorgeous. And I hated her for it.

Then another person in the room caught my attention. "Dominic?" I froze, staring at the only Moretti I could tolerate besides my sister-in-law.

"Octavia." He stepped forward, but Carmine checked him with a shoulder.

"Don't you fucking touch him!" The blonde was back in Carmine's face, and Dom used the distraction to approach me.

"Are you okay? We're going to get you out—" His eyes focused on the bruising on my neck. "You son of a bitch."

The girl glanced back to us again and Dom motioned towards my neck.

"You bastard!" She landed one more solid punch before Carmine gripped her wrists and shoved her onto the sofa.

Dom pulled the girl against him. "What the fuck is wrong with you? You had more right to kill me for my father's actions than to hurt her for Mario's."

"Like you don't choke her? Force her to submit?" Carmine gestured to the blonde before storming past them to pull me into his arms. "She's going home. Make the arrangements," he grunted, then turned and stalked into his office.

"Octavia," the girl whispered, approaching me like you would a wounded animal. I hated her look of pity; it agitated me. "That's right. Give me your anger. Be proud of it." She laughed, crossing her arms over her chest. "Stronger than your sister. Sienna never would've survived him." She glanced at Dominic while hitching a thumb towards Carmine.

"I'll call Nikolai. Tell him to set up a drop," Dom said, stepping into Carmine's office with Diego and AJ following close behind.

"Your family, especially your sister, has been worried sick about you."

I scoffed. "Yeah, right."

"They are. They all deal in different ways. Your goddamn phone call didn't help either."

"I saw their *concern*. Family dinners, trips around the city. Broken, sad, clearly missing me. Whatever. Make the arrangements and I'll get ready." I turned to walk back into the room when her cold fingers wrapped around my arm.

"Don't. You. Dare." Her blue eyes lit with rage. "You called your father to stab him in the heart and made your sister question your love for them. She's dealing with her own issues, but never stopped looking for you."

"I watched them you know." I sat down on the bed, pulling my knees to my chest. "For years, they thought they were protecting me, but they never really *knew* me. I was hurt under their own watch. Scarred in more ways than one. Long before Carmine sunk his teeth into me."

The blonde glared at me for several minutes until realization settled over her features. "You're sitting here alive and breathing. He—whoever he was—didn't ruin shit. And if Carmine saw something in you, don't take that shit for granted." She got up from the bed, going to the door before I could ask her more. "There was a time when I thought I was damaged. And Carmine pulled me out of it, helped me get my revenge on everyone that hurt me. I've healed. And you will too."

"One down, one to go," I muttered under my breath.

She turned to look at me from where she stood in the doorway. It seemed like forever before she spoke again. "But you know who he is." It wasn't a question. "Good for you." She laughed, flipping her hair and shouting over her shoulder, "Let me know if you need help with the body."

"What body?" Dominic asked, walking past her and entering the room as the blonde left. "Octavia… I'm sorry."

I waved him off. "You can't be blamed for your father just like I shouldn't be blamed for mine." He went to speak but I raised a hand to stop him. "I'm fine. I'm going *home*." I paused. *For now.*

This time, he didn't say anything. No one could help me. I'd go home, see the *devastation* my absence caused with my own eyes. Then, once things calmed down a bit, I'd leave again. No longer would I be the face of my family. It was time I made my own way.

"Who is she?" I motioned towards the blonde arguing with Carmine in the next room.

"Your savior. And maybe mine." Dom smiled when something shattered in the distance. "It wasn't pity she gave you; it was understanding. If you knew what she went through because of *my brother,* you'd know why she looked at you like that."

"What did Gio do?"

Dom shook his head, telling me that's all I'd get from him.

"Sienna killed Gio." The blonde reappeared at Dom's side. "You want your revenge, go get it. But just know it doesn't stop the pain. It's up to you to make sure it doesn't drown you." Dom pulled her into his embrace, and she quickly added, "And don't hesitate. Just pull the trigger. You'll be okay."

"I want to know why he did this to me."

She shook her head. "The why doesn't matter because, in his fucked-up brain, his actions were justified. All the *why* will give you is a knot in your stomach and more unanswered questions." She nodded, a signal for them to leave. "Your sister killed my demon, but the nightmares got worse. So I had to save myself from drowning and it wasn't easy. But, Octavia, you're stronger than I am. You got this."

"How do you know?" I asked her.

She laughed while glancing at Carmine. "You slaughtered one of your rapists and brought that bastard to his knees." Her eyes lit up. "Yet something tells me all of us have constantly underestimated you." She *knew*, saw me for the monster I was.

And for some reason that made me really happy.

"Look me up when you get home." She flipped Carmine off as she finally turned to leave. "I feel as if our kindred souls could cause a lot of fuckery." Dominic pulled her towards the door as she called out over his shoulder, "Remember: don't think! Just pull the trigger!"

When the door closed, it felt as if the air had been stolen from the room along with them. Carmine and I stared at each other, neither giving the other anything. This man had broken me, ripped me apart, and then seemingly put me back together. He was tearing at my heart sending me back, but it would always have come to this.

"Planning to shoot me?" he asked, and I let my silence do the talking. "Better be fast and precise. One shot is all you'd get."

It was either send me back or kill me. Although there wasn't much difference between the two.

I spun on my heel, opening the bag with the dress, and started getting ready. At first, I thought it was like the outfits I used to wear back home, but then I realized the material was tighter and more revealing than what my family would expect me to wear. I loved it. And I hated him. I'd survived a Ragetti and was coming home a new woman. The *real* Octavia Agostino was coming home. They'd have to learn to accept me or they'd lose me altogether.

Glancing one last time in the mirror, I loved what I saw. My blue-steel seemed different. More steel than blue. My long hair had dried with its natural wild curl—something I used to attempt to tame. My makeup was soft, natural, and the dress hugged me nicely. Once I'd slipped on the pointed Louboutins, I walked into the living room. Carmine's back was to me, but he stopped barking orders when his men glanced my way. Diego didn't hide his approval, while AJ looked bored.

Carmine—realizing their lack of focus—turned towards me. His hungry gaze traveled up and down. The future Don was back in place, a crisp suit and his long hair oiled back. I stepped up to him and immediately hated how powerful we looked together, how well we fit.

I'd be one hell of a queen, but if he didn't want me, well, then fuck him. No one else would compare. No one else would contain his crazy. Because no one else… was me.

I tapped his nose, the damage doing little to tarnish his strong features. His chiseled jawline popped out even amongst the bruises.

"Make me one promise," I said and his teeth clenched. "Don't hurt them. Just let me go."

His responding smirk was taunting, cruel, and demeaning.

"I mean it, Carmine. You got what you wanted. I broke them with my absence. And I'll break them all over again when I return as their little girl gone."

Because she was. A stranger was coming home.

Diego stood next to my desk, his scowl expressing his clear displeasure. He'd settled up with the doctor, but he'd want to speak his mind on the matter. On my actions with Octavia. Diego was loyal to a fault, but I could tell my little doll was starting to pull my men into her corner. He looked at her the way he looked at Eva. Which told me if I were anyone else, I'd have a slug between my eyes.

I sat at my desk, wanting to drown my soul in a good bottle of Scotch. "She's fine."

"She wasn't breathing. You've fucking lost it." Diego glanced to AJ, who remained mute. "Send her home."

"I am!" The glass shattered in my hand, drops of red dripping across my desk. "I am," I said, a little calmer, smearing the blood across the surface.

"I don't know what—" I stopped speaking when my phone rang.

Eva's name flashed across the screen, her whispered voice coming through the line a second later. My jaw clenched as I grabbed the remote and tuned into the news station like she'd told me.

"Skyview shows the armed man waving a gun at anyone who gets close. As of right now, we can see what appear to be bodies in the center of the road. Police have set up a perimeter, containing the threat, but the man is out of control. Let's see if we can get some sound bites for our viewers."

It wasn't some man, like the news anchor claimed. No, it was my father. The chopper flew lower and I could see that same crazy look that I'd known too well. He had officially lost it, shouting out delusional mentions while referencing God and the devil. I watched as the chopper pivoted in the sky when JP started shooting at it.

"He's fucking lost it. And I mean worse than normal," Eva repeated what I was already thinking. "And, Carmine, watch yourself. He thinks you're turning on him… for her."

"Then he's an idiot. We'll see you soon.," I said and hung up. Then I walked into the living room and I went over the plan once more with my men. Persephone and Nikolai had informed us of the drop location. Sienna Agostino would meet us there.

I could feel her at my back long before my men started eye-fucking her. Once they saw my glare, they were smart enough to disperse. The dress fit her perfectly. Bruises littered her neck and arms. But through it all, she was a goddamn dark angel, her wild hair loose around her face.

"You don't demand anything of me, little doll," I replied when she asked me to make her a promise I wouldn't keep. Then I tugged her against my body. Hard to soft. The way she melted in my embrace was doing little to help me maintain control. To stay focused on my plan.

"Please." Her eyes softened. "Don't hurt my sister."

I didn't say a word, just beckoned her down the stairs behind me. My men along with a handful of Russians were waiting at the bottom.

Nikolai was heading with us to the meeting point, acting as a silent peacekeeper. As I approached with an outstretched hand, another car pulled into the warehouse. Romano and Romeo stepping out to meet us.

"I heard you were returning her," Romano said, and Octavia scowled at him. "Pity." He looked her up and down.

"I can't believe Sienna ever once thought you were *nice*. You're disgusting and fucking dead when—" Octavia went to step forward, but I pulled her back.

Romano smirked at her. "The little one has fire. Who knew?" He laughed, tapping on the glass. "Since you're sending her back with a message, I'd like to send one of my own."

Octavia stiffened in my grasp, as the car door opened, and he reached out an arm. He pulled Kennedy from the car as she stood submissively at his side, her eyes focused on the ground. Octavia stared at the girl in horror. If she thought this was bad, she was about to be in for another shock.

"I feel horrible for her, being with such an asshole. Did he abduct her?" Octavia whispered, glaring at Romano's arm around Kennedy. Between her and Persephone, I needed to watch my back. Their protective nature when it came to damaged women was palpable.

"Does she look like she's being kept against her will, little doll?" I asked, and Octavia glanced back at Kennedy, who was holding onto Romano for dear life. "Remind you of someone?"

My laughter caught Kennedy's attention and her head snapped up. Both girls gasped as they stared at each other. The similarities were there: height, weight, shape. Octavia was a little shorter and her hair was almost black versus Kennedy's lighter hue. But there was no denying their matching blue-steel eyes.

"What the fuck?" Octavia muttered under her breath while staring at Kennedy, who didn't appear nearly as shocked by the resemblance. When Octavia went to step forward, I held her back a second time. And Romano laughed, shuffling Kennedy inside the car again.

"Please. Give your old man that message," he said. Octavia started cursing, fighting against my hold, as Romano climbed into the car and pulled away.

"What the fuck! Why didn't you do something?"

"I have enough issues with you right now. *That...*" I motioned to the exiting vehicle. "...isn't my problem."

Her bottom lip trembled for a moment before she stood tall and locked down her expression. Ignoring me and Nikolai, she climbed into the back of the SUV. AJ closed the door and slid into the driver's seat.

"How is that possible?" Nikolai asked, and I shrugged as we shook hands and returned to our respective vehicles. I had no idea who or how Kennedy came to be. Nor how Romano found her. But, again, that wasn't my problem.

"You sure about this?" Diego asked while tapping away on his phone. "What's the worst that could happen? She and Eva become best friends and lay out on the California beaches all day long. Pissing all of us off with their bitchy-ass attitudes?"

"Funny," I grunted in reply.

"Think about it. I'm sure the girl could whip your crew into shape while you deal with—"

I gripped his shirt, slamming him into Octavia's door.

"All right! All right!" The bastard smirked, raising his hands in surrender.

"This was always the plan, Diego," I reminded him.

He shook his head at me. "Plans can change, Carmine. We all see it." He glanced at the tinted window. "She doesn't wanna go back any more than you want her to leave."

I lit a cigarette, taking a drag while relishing the burn in my lungs. "It was all a game, her tears a sweet prize. When she gets back, they won't be able to stand the sight of her. My little doll will kill them with her need for me." Blowing smoke in his face, I opened the door and slid inside next to her.

Diego waited a moment, motioning for the other cars to pull out ahead of us. Then he climbed inside and gave AJ the signal to move. Octavia barely waited a second before tossing questions in my direction.

"Did you know?" Her tone pissed me off. "Who the hell is she?"

"Her name is Kennedy. That's all I know. And before you ask, I have no idea how, who, or where. Romano brought her with him to our last meeting and I don't care enough to ask for more."

"Carmine, she—" Octavia spluttered as I gripped her throat.

"Enough! I said I don't give a fuck! Tell Daddy and let him deal with it."

She sat tight-lipped for the rest of the car ride. Matteo called me twice, but I didn't have the energy to answer him. I'd be back west to deal with JP as soon as I could. Then my text went off.

JP fucked us. Club N beach house torched. Coming for you.

Octavia kept fidgeting beside me as we pulled into the meeting spot. The car was silent, heavy, as we waited for her sister. She shifted closer to me and I opened my arms, tugging her against me. If we had more time, I'd send her back to her daddy with her clothes mussed and her mascara running down her cheeks.

She stiffened, as the car pulling up in front of us sent everyone on high alert. I grabbed her hand before she could run away. Then we watched as the door slowly opened and her sister stepped out. It was uncanny how different the two girls were.

Sienna was sexy, confident, and demanding. But she was also emotional and rash. It made her sloppy and susceptible to manipulation.

Octavia, on the other hand, played submissive but only to the untrained eye. Now that I'd seen the rage, I was shocked I had missed it in the first place. Her silence was taken for willing submission. When—in reality—it was to hold back the monster lurking deep. The one who sucked my dick before trying to bite it off. The one who spit, stabbed, and cut at me. The one who almost broke my nose and taunted me every chance she got.

Never. Not once. Did I ever think I'd love someone fighting me the way she did. Anyone else would've been six feet under that first time she bared those white teeth around my cock. But her fight made my dick hard.

"Ready?" I glanced at Octavia as another text sounded off.

JP knows about the drop!

Fuck.

I pulled Octavia back once more, texting Diego the same message, and she sat straighter in her seat.

Motherfucker had something up his sleeve. Only time would tell what it was.

Octavia stared at where I held onto her wrist, practically begging me to keep her. The fact that she thought there was a chance showed how much I'd fucked her up. I opened my mouth when Matteo's name popped up again.

Before opening the text, I kissed her roughly one last time. There was no love *and* hate in our world. It was one or the other. And Octavia was a problem I needed to remove from my life. I motioned her out of the car with the flip of my middle finger.

As she closed the door to my taunting laughter, I lifted my phone and scanned the text thread. Clenching my fist, I watched my little doll slowly walk out of my life. I read it twice before I slid over to the door and took a deep breath, then opened it. With my gun at my side, I stepped into the sunlight.

Octavia turned around and looked at me with pure loathing written on her face. She'd wanted me to make her promises I never planned to keep. While the message on my screen told me exactly what I had to do…

Without a thought. Without a hint of hesitation. I did just that. I lifted an arm, stared down the end of my barrel, honed in on Octavia, and pulled the trigger.

CHAPTER 25
OCTAVIA AGOSTINO

My heart raced as I thought about seeing my family once again. I wasn't the same girl who was taken from them. If they only knew who I was now and why I was coming back, they'd hate me for it. Hate me for my deceit.

I was beyond thankful to see them but also didn't want them sullied by me. I was damaged, no longer their *prezioso piccolo bambino*. Their daughter had been slayed by the beast. He'd stitched me up like a little doll, concocting a plot to enact his revenge from behind my family's walls. And I hated that I had to follow his demands. I hated him. Most of all, I hated myself.

A part of me longed for his touch, for the tenderness he rarely showed me. The other part was disgusted that I allowed myself to believe any of his lies.

I looked up. The car was getting closer and closer.

This was it. Here was where I'd die, betraying my family as I prepared to bury myself six feet under. I used to think they were untouchable, that our followers and strength were unmatched. I was so wrong, my bubble popping years before I was taken. Since I woke up in my nightmare, a piece of my soul was removed with each passing second.

I swallowed roughly and opened the door, the wind kicking up and forcing me to shiver. My sister stood in the distance, looking as gorgeous as ever. She seemed happier, a glow about her that had me questioning several things.

I glanced over my shoulder once more, staring into the eyes of the man who both ruined and saved me. A growl from the back seat gave me pause, but his flip of a finger sent me on my way. I slammed the door in his face, the metal doing little to diminish the sound of his booming laughter.

With each step closer to my sister, I felt myself lighten. The door opened behind me and my steps faltered, knowing all hell was going to break loose. My brother, Al, and Apollo stormed from the car, charging towards Sienna. Then a gun was cocked at my back. I turned to look at my captor and the bastard was smiling at me.

My words, my thoughts, and time itself seemed to cut off after being rattled by a loud discharge of a gun, and my body throttled with the force.

Pain. That was all I felt. My family returned fire as figures emerged from the trees and I was dragged to the car. He'd told me time and time again that he wanted to ruin me and my last name. I just didn't believe he could be so cruel after… everything.

He broke my heart as one last punishment. Before he killed me.

"He fucking shot her!"

My sister's panicked voice pulled me from my shocked stupor. I shifted uncomfortably on the floor of the car. That son of a bitch shot me. My sister continued to scream, as Apollo and Lucky fired out the window and Al sped away. It was like a red-hot poker was stabbing at my arm.

What the fuck just happened?

"Let me up." It was barely a damn scratch!

"It's not safe! He fucking shot you!" Sienna pushed on my shoulder. "Stay down!"

Was she always this extra? My sister was something else. No matter who or where we were, Sienna was Sienna. But right now, that fact was pissing me off.

"Let. Me. Up." I glared at her. "I'm not dying. It's barely bleeding."

Apollo nudged Sienna aside and helped me to sit upright. My sister looked at me like she'd seen a ghost. Like she didn't recognize me. *Good.* They needed to learn I wasn't the same girl anymore. Apollo inspected my arm and recommended a few stitches.

"Oh my god." Sienna looked sick, focusing on my neck.

The pained expression and heavy tears told me how wrong I'd been. I rubbed at the bruised flesh, knowing they could see the scars of the man I'd fallen for. Her devastation made me hate myself. I never should've believed him when it came to their love for me—their concern.

When Carmine took me into the city, I saw what he wanted me to see. And I fell for his bullshit like an idiot.

Carmine had played me. And I'd let him.

Now that I was in front of them, I could clearly see the pain they were in. Sienna continued to cry and Lucky leaned around the seat, holding my hand. The three of us stayed locked together the entire ride. As we pulled up outside the compound, a moment of peace settled over me. I hadn't realized how much I missed them. Missed this place.

Apollo pulled me into the kitchen. "Doc will be here soon to numb you up first."

"Just do it."

Both he and Lucky glanced at each other.

"Just. Do. It," I repeated, and Apollo made quick work of stitching me up.

I went to wash the blood from my hands and watched my sister step into his arms. He held her close as she wiped at her eyes, their smiles lighting up their faces.

"You two finally figure your shit out?"

Sienna nodded, and Apollo gave me a little smirk. A loud and bright blur shrieked in the distance as she darted towards me. My mom was on me the next second, sobbing, while my father lurked in the distance. The pain and indecision on his face hurt my heart. I was so mad at his choices, but I also missed him.

"Dad." I broke first, running into his arms.

Mario Agostino was a powerful *capo* and a loving father. I hated how I was so sheltered and yet still suffered through a life within these tainted walls. Also, I hated that I'd never regretted my silence until right now. I squeezed my father tight, telling him I was sorry. He hushed me and held me close. I'd been so angry at everyone else for so long when I should've been angry at myself for hiding.

A squeal unlike anything I'd heard before echoed in the small room, and Bella walked in. In her arms was an exact replica of my older brother. My nephew. *Nico.*

I stepped up to my sister-in-law, and her son reached out a hand and tugged on one of my curls. He smiled happily, with the same eyes that matched the rest of the family's. He was huge, Bella's tiny body having to tilt sideways to hold him on her hip. My brother proudly tugged his wife and son into his arms. Lucky seemed different, as if fatherhood turned him into someone tolerable.

"Nico, meet your Aunt Octavia," he said, holding the infant in my direction.

Then there was another squeal. I glanced at Nico and realized it wasn't him. I peered around Bella and saw Al walking in with another child in his arms. I stared, shocked for a moment, while wondering who the hell my brother's enforcer had knocked up…

But the moment the little boy turned to look at me, I froze in disbelief. He watched me with the same brown eyes as his father. There was no doubt he was Apollo's son. My sister grabbed him and moved to stand in Apollo's arms again.

"You. You?" I raised a brow, motioning between the two of them. "You?" I was stunned.

"Yeah." Sienna laughed at the same time Apollo said, "Salvatore, meet your aunt."

How long had I been gone…?

They'd had children, fixed their relationships, and lived their lives. I couldn't even be mad. For once, my sister didn't look haunted by the man at her side. He embraced her and his son, finally claiming her like he always should have. They'd found each other while I fought to find myself.

"Are you hungry?" my mother asked, and I nodded. She immediately ran to the oven and pulled out an entire tray of lasagna.

I sat at the island as everyone talked all at once. They filled the uncomfortable silence with updates on their businesses, the family, anything other than asking me the million questions I could see in their eyes. They did their best to avoid looking at the bruises across my skin. My dad would flinch when my voice rasped or I broke out in a coughing fit. Their pain was evident in their uncomfortable chatter, their forced smiles, and their shared glances whenever they thought I wasn't paying attention.

My dad broke the sudden silence. "We never stopped looking for you. Even after your call."

"I'm sorry I hurt you. But…" How would I explain the why

behind my decision? "You needed to understand your little girl is long gone. I—"

He squeezed my hand, interrupting me. "It doesn't matter what he did to you. What he made you do… I never stopped—"

My fork clattered aggressively on my plate. "Don't do that. I was broken long *before* Carmine took me." He snarled at the name. I ignored him and kept talking. "You're not listening. Today has been too much. Let's just enjoy our company."

Tomorrow I would tell them everything. About Rick. About his son. About my new mission to find the guy and make him suffer. I'd tell them everything that happened and why I had to stay away. Tomorrow I would get my head on straight and figure out what this new life of mine was going to entail.

My father's reply was cut off by the front door opening. Several men entered the room, nodding at my father and glancing at me. And then I saw *him*.

"Sorry, sir." I tensed at the sound of Peiro's voice. "Riccardo is nowhere to be found. It's like he disappeared."

Motherfucker.

Even when he'd given me the name, I didn't want to believe Rick. Didn't want to—but immediately knew it was the truth. Now, everything was coming full circle as the sting of his betrayal threatened to drown me.

"Octavia, are you okay?" Sienna glanced at me, concern filling her eyes.

I gripped the edges of the island, desperate to breathe. Until Persephone's voice spoke up in my head.

Listen to your gut.

And for the first time in my life, I did just that. *He* needed to be removed from all our lives. To be punished for what he did to me.

"Tell me," I hissed in Riccardo's ear, his life slowly draining from his eyes.

"Your father didn't deserve your silence. Should've told him... then maybe I would've had the balls to finally kill." He spit up blood. "My son... the bastard loves you."

"Give me his name."

"So damn strong. You never broke." He was coughing harder. "We fucked up think-thinking you would."

"You did fuck up. Now tell me his name so I can give you peace."

He sighed, uttering the final answer I needed before I slit his throat.

My brother pulled me from my memories. "Octavia?" He and Apollo stepped closer to me.

"Get. The kids. Out of here," I gritted the order between clenched teeth.

My mother and sister-in-law moved fast, whisking the boys out of the room. My heartbeat echoed in my ears and my jowls salivated. Flexing my fists, I hated that I wished Carmine was here. To encourage me. To demand that I get my own justice. To celebrate me taking my life back.

When Rick told me his name, I wanted it to be a lie. But it wasn't. His cologne, the feel of his calloused hands, his whispered words…

How had I not put it all together before?

I turned in my chair and the bastard smiled at me. *My son loves you.* I'd known for some time that the man felt something for me, but it was always one sided. Even now, the warmth that radiated from him was so real. Tangible.

How could he do that to me?

I held everyone's attention as I approached him. Catalogued him. My stomach turned as it all came crashing down around me. The ring that bruised my flesh. The whisper of my name. The cold, empty eyes. I was so fucking dumb because I didn't see it until now.

Rick had told me the truth. Peiro was his fucking son… and my rapist.

Men I didn't recognize stood at his back. They tensed at the glare I gave them. He must've gotten the crew my brother promised him. A loyal cluster of bastards just like him. My smile was cold, creepy, and I enjoyed the way his eyes widened.

But the crunch of nasal bones against my knuckles was damn amazing. "You fucking asshole!"

Peiro tripped over the edge of the table, falling onto his back, while chaos and shouting broke out around us. I jumped on him, punching him repeatedly. My dress tore and blood erupted as he fought against my attack.

"How could you! How?" I pulled his face closer. "How could you do that to me?"

"Because I love—"

"Octavia!" Lucky ripped me off his enforcer, shoving me to the side. "The hell has gotten into you?"

"Me? What's gotten into me?" I screamed all my pain into his face. Apollo's arm wrapped around my midsection to hold me back. "We trusted you! I trusted you!"

Rough hands gripped my waist, his fingers skimming over my scars. Apollo turned to glare at me, shocked. He glanced at my brother, motioning towards my torn skin. I wouldn't hide anymore. They needed to see it. To hear it. To avenge it.

"The fuck is going on here?" My dad stepped to my side.

"This motherfucker is a liar. A cheat. He's Rick's son," I hissed as my father shook his head. "Yeah. They lied to all of us. Did you know he resented you?"

"Your uncle—" My father's words died on his tongue as his brows knitted together.

"I have no idea how I didn't see it. How I didn't realize it was you. Your disgusting, piece-of-shit father told me the truth right before I. Slit. His. Throat." I ignored the collective gasps that followed my confession. "But not before he told me all about *you*. His bastard son who took what didn't belong to him. You both thought you could break me."

"Octavia." Peiro looked at my father. "I have no idea—"

"You fucking raped me." This time, the oxygen was sucked from the room. "Because your sick daddy told you to."

"What? What did you do?" My father and Lucky stepped closer, angry as hell.

"They wanted to take over *il famiglia*." I turned back to Peiro. "Was it worth it in the end? Because you turned your back on the only family that gave a fuck about you. And now… you'll die for it."

He stepped towards me, his palms raised as more lies spilled from his mouth.

Don't think. Just pull the trigger.

He moved quickly, drawing his gun and raising it at me. If the memories hadn't already torn me apart, the look on his broken face would've hurt. But he didn't deserve my mercy.

"You're sure?" my father asked, and I nodded.

"Carmine gave me a priceless gift once I told him what happened," I said, watching on as Peiro froze. "Your fucking father ratted you out after a few measly punches. Right before I slit his fucking throat."

"You're lying."

"If I knew where he was buried, I'd dig him up and pray to the devil to let me kill him all over again. In the end, your father thought I'd save you." A deep, guttural, and cathartic growl filled the room. This time, I knew where it was coming from. It was me.

Let her loose.

He glanced around, noticing the way my family was closing in on him. The hot end of his barrel bounced from one person to the next. That pained expression was gone, and in its place was the devious fuck who raped me. The bastard I'd never noticed under all the kind words and sweet gestures.

"You. Deserved. It," he sneered at my father. "Your reign was over. Is over." Lucky was next. "And you… what a fucking joke, forcing me to be at your side for all these years. Watching. Waiting."

My brother paused before spitting at him. The two men shouted back and forth at each other, their voices turning to white noise as the monster inside me finally broke loose.

"Wanna know the last words I said to your father?" My palms itched as I spoke. *"Marcire all'inferno, maiale."* I pulled Apollo's nine from under his jacket, raised my arm, and pressed down on the trigger.

Unfortunately, it was at the same moment his men made their moves and his own weapon fired. Chaos ensued in the room and I was shoved behind Apollo. The gunshots lasted for only a few seconds before the front door slammed.

"No!"

The shouting behind me faded into white noise as I stared at the empty, blood-soaked floor. The very spot where that man's body should've been lying.

I'd done it. I'd attempted to take my revenge and it was almost bittersweet. He should've collapsed onto that floor. A bullet between the eyes sending him to those pits of hell where his father was waiting. The silence drifted me into oblivion as I felt my limbs collide with the tile. Even as the world closed in around me, I grinned.

But it wasn't over yet. There was so much more blood to spill.

"When we land, I want you to take a crew to grab Eva," I instructed, and Diego nodded as the plane powered up.

The moment my bullet hit Octavia, we peeled away from the meeting point and boarded my private jet. JP had started a war out west and I'd had the east nipping at my heels. Without a backwards glance, I'd left my little doll with her family to return to *where I belonged*.

My father couldn't know she was home safe. Not yet. We let the news spread that she was dead, killed by my hand. My bullet. At the moment, the west thought we'd won. Thought that my uncle could rest in peace, having earned our revenge.

My mole inside the Agostini family would report back to me. His orders were to update me on every move she made. This wasn't the end of us. She played right into my hand and I'd make sure she knew I still owned her.

Had she told them? How she'd fallen in love with the beast—the enemy?

The answer was simple. No. She hadn't said a word. She'd kept secrets from her family for years. Spared the man who'd hurt her to protect them. She'd never tell them the truth about me. Which was a shame. Because I'd pay to see the look on Mario's face.

My eyes flicked over to Diego. "Keep my family safe. No fuckups." My phone sounded with an incoming message. "The fuck?" I glanced at the text, reading it once, then twice more.

Gunshots. Octavia taken to hospital.

"What is it?" Diego looked to me. "Boss?"

"Hospital. Now." I dropped my phone into my pocket. "Fucking now!" My men followed me from the plane to our SUV, and AJ jumped behind the wheel.

"The fuck is going on?"

Breathe.

"I don't know." I remained silent for a moment.

"Hey. It was a clean shot to the arm." Diego was trying to calm me, but my chest was tight.

A man like me didn't miss. It hadn't been my intention to kill or wound her seriously. She'd only been back home for a few short hours.

What had happened? And then it clicked.

"Unless my little doll had been lying all along." I smirked, just thinking about the monster I'd created. "Her *uncle* gave her a name."

In life, there were a lot of moments where you were left questioning your actions. Abducting Octavia wasn't one of those moments. To watch the Agostinos' *weakest link* flourish and show her true colors was downright fucking addictive.

My dick hardened at the memories. Of her lips around my cock and a scalpel in her hand. The damn crazy look that consumed her when she was dead set on making me bleed. It had always been about revenge. But in the process, I'd created a little beast.

The devil ensured her wings were clipped to keep his hold on her. Claiming family above all else. Yet, without her wings, she was drowning and no one noticed. I'd wanted to teach them all a lesson, and like a desperate man, I revealed too much and she turned the tables on me. I'd become addicted to her fire, to her bite, and that crazy attitude.

"Boss?"

The car had stopped in front of the hospital. I motioned for AJ to wait while I allowed Diego to follow me inside. The nurse stared at me in horror when I tapped the desk and demanded Octavia's room number. Diego's charm did little to soothe the woman's panic and her silence was pissing me off. This bitch was trying to bait me into ruining a six-thousand-dollar suit. When there was someone much more deserving of my attention just waiting for me somewhere within these walls.

If her family caught me, I had no doubt they'd put a slug between my eyes. That didn't slow me down. We'd go toe-to-toe, no matter whose blood was spilled in the process. I kept telling myself that once I saw her, knew that she was okay, I'd leave. She was never supposed to come to Cali with me. The plan was always to leave her behind.

Her crying about me to her daddy was my revenge. I'd taken something so sweet and damaged and returned a wild animal. I had no doubt that if my little doll was okay, she'd hunt me down for her own revenge. Mario had no clue what I'd returned home to him.

Once the receptionist snapped out of her stupor, she gave me the information and Diego charged to the stairs with me. I threw the door open on her floor and Diego stopped me in my tracks, motioning towards the devil himself and his psycho right hand headed in the opposite direction.

But the Ragettis didn't hide.

Quickening my pace, I stalled outside her room. Most of the lights were out except for the one over her bed. She was so fucking small. How in the hell did that little girl make me bleed? And more than once? She had more balls, more fight, than some of the men in my crew. Though as she sat in the oversized hospital bed, it suddenly struck me how innocent she was. An observation that had nothing to do with a thin membrane protecting a tight pussy.

Stepping inside, I ached to touch her. She played in the darkness because that asshole had forced her there with the expectation she'd drown. But my little doll was a goddamn force to be reckoned with. Even as she lay alone, her mouth slightly parted as she slept, I knew she wasn't done with me. The wires and equipment surrounding her wouldn't keep her down. A sinister grin pulled at my lips, my jowls quaking with the desire to see what tricks she had up her sleeve. Because Octavia fucking Agostino wasn't the weakest link, she was a fucking fighter.

The door opened, but I didn't move. "I should fucking kill you. Right now," I muttered, my hand itching to pull my gun.

"You won't." Mario paused before sighing. "Because she'd never forgive you. And she'd make it hurt."

"What do you want?" I grunted.

"I want to tell you why I covered up your uncle's murder," he said, and my fists clenched at my sides. "It was because your father was the one who ordered the hit. Your grandfather and I came to an agreement for peace because he didn't want to lose his only remaining son."

"JP wouldn't do that." Even as I said the words aloud, I knew Mario was telling the truth.

He shook his head. "He did. He wanted your grandfather to destroy my city. And when he wouldn't… your father showed up in New York. Threatened me, my wife and my unborn son. But I got a leg up on him and was able to put him back in his place. My silence in exchange for him staying out west."

I pivoted and walked into the hall, watching Octavia through the windows. "Why didn't you turn on him? It would've started a war that you would have won, hands down. All the families would've turned on him."

"Because of you," Mario said, and I scowled at him. The same eyes that matched his daughter's seemed tired. "Your uncle and I were close. He knew Serafina and I were in love, but breaking my marriage proposal to Isabella wasn't an option. So, he promised to take care of her for me."

We stood in silence as I digested his words. *Could it be true?*

"We did a lot of business together over the years. He'd wished you were his son. Told me all about you. How you were the right future for the family." Mario smiled at his daughter as she twitched in her sleep. "Your father was jealous of your relationship with Sal. Yet the fucker didn't have the balls to step up for you or to do the dirty work himself. Anthony was greedy—the fucker got the cash and the girl. And all it cost him was a single bullet."

"Again. Why didn't you tell the families?" Every made man would've gunned for my father. That type of shit would've had repercussions. My uncle was too respected and too high up in *il famiglia*.

"Like I said. Because of you. Your brothers. Eva." Mario motioned for me to follow him down the hallway. "Even if I tried to protect you, the other families would've wanted you kids dead. They'd come for you, no matter how old you all were. Your uncle and I wanted peace between the coasts, always did. We'd both done a lot of fucked-up shit to get to the top, and we didn't want the next generation tainted by it."

"Why're you telling me all this now?"

"I know you'll hate me no matter what I say and I accept that. But your father needs to be dealt with. And then..." Mario glanced at his daughter through the door, and I followed his line of sight. "And then you need to take over... just the way your uncle taught you to do."

I didn't care for the fact that he was right. JP's reign was done. Octavia's return home was step one. Cali was calling and I needed to handle it.

"Keep your nose out of my business," I grunted and Mario nodded as I turned to walk away.

"We have a common enemy." This had me stalling one more time. Diego and I pivoted back around. "I don't know all of it, but I know I've failed her more than once," Mario admitted.

She'd told him.

"Did she tell you who the other one was?" I asked, unable to stop myself.

He shook his head. "She didn't *say* anything."

I nodded while stabbing at the button for the elevator.

"But he got away."

"Who the fuck was it?" I rolled my neck, ready for another fight.

"My men are out looking for him as we speak. Peiro made it out alive, but he won't be able to hide for long. I will find him."

He wouldn't have to because the little motherfucker was dead. I snarled while conjuring up all the painful ways I'd make him suffer. I'd hated the bastard before. But now, he was in for a world of hell for touching my little doll.

"Handle your father. I've got this. For once, I will do what is right for my daughter," Mario added.

"How do you know I won't come back for you?" I asked him.

"You carried the same pained look my daughter did when you handed her over." He paused. "I know you're more than willing to kill me the next chance you get, but not at the cost of losing her."

If what Mario said checked out, then I'd let him live. He was right. His daughter would cut my dick off if I hurt him. And just the reminder of her teeth on my cock made me smile. At the end of the day, my plan had worked. Mario was a shell of the man he once was. The guilt. The pain. All of it deepened the lines on his face.

Octavia didn't have to tell him… Because he saw it for himself. His daughter was in love with the enemy. And I was fuckin' elated to see that a bullet didn't need to be the damage I inflicted. This weakened man before me was a hell of a lot better of a prize than a corpse.

The time had come for me to return to Cali. JP had a lot to fucking answer for. Then I'd send him to fucking hell where he belonged. Mario and I would never be friends, but once this shit checked out, we'd be even. JP was going to die, and I knew I'd have a truce with the east when I took over.

Diego and I stepped into the elevator. And just as the doors were about to close on us, I gave Mario the final punch to the gut. "Give my regards to Philly."

His brows pinched in confusion.

"I hear congratulations are in order—a new husband for your *other* daughter."

The doors started closing when we heard his reply. "You found her?"

He knew?

Mario Agostino might have been innocent enough when it came to my uncle's death, but he was still guilty as fuck about a lot of other shit. Romano was going to teach him another lesson about family. All the while, I'd wait back home in Cali for my little doll to show her face… or her Glock.

"I want that little fuck Peiro found. Now." I commanded Diego.

My uncle raised me to do my own dirty work, claiming it kept life from being boring. And a lot of hard work was going to meet me in Cali. JP wouldn't step down on his own. He'd only give up his throne over his dead body… and I already had his grave dug. While my mother was just as much to blame in how she supported her husband blindly. It was time for the next generation to make a clean sweep on their rise to power in Cali.

The car pulled back up to my private plane, and a few minutes later, my crew was storming inside. Once I reached the top step, I turned back for one last glance at New York. A little burst of sunlight was streaming through several dark clouds.

Buttoning my jacket, I chuckled to myself. "Come and find me, little doll. This shit ain't over."

And she would. Goddamn Octavia Agostino was going to make the west coast a hell of a lot more fun.

To be continued...

EPILOGUE

KENNEDY

"You promised," I whispered, even though internally I was screaming.

My jaw shook and my fingers twitched while the high I craved raced through my veins. It could never be filled; the pain of that primal need would never be satiated. Romano told me he'd never do it. He'd never allow me the satisfaction of jumping into the deep end and letting the darkness devour me. But each new day I remained clean, it still burned bright.

His harsh fingers gripped my jaw and forced me to look at him. My lip bounced and my teeth clattered together as I fought to maintain control. There were far too many moments when this man made me so goddamn angry. Glancing at him now, I had images of cutting his throat just so I could be free. From him. From reality.

"I promise a lot of things to a lot of people, Kennedy. What did I promise you?"

"That I could—" I stopped, watching the warehouse disappear behind us. "I want to get to know *her*."

"Did she look like she gave a fuck about you?" He lifted a questioning brow, and I winced, closing my eyes when he wouldn't let go of my face. "Kennedy, look at me."

"*They* don't know about—"

He cut me off, shaking my jaw. "They. Will." Romano leaned in close, staring me straight in the eye. "You're not ready."

I slapped his hand off my face, flopping back in the SUV to look out at the storm we were driving through. New York wasn't much different from Philly. The same lingering smell of trash, homeless people on street corners, and the ignorance of the hustle and bustle.

Except Philly didn't make my skin crawl quite as much. There was something calming about the *City of Brotherly Love*. I had no family, so I had no idea what that meant, even though I lived in squalor in a city that turned its back on me. The streets were my home.

Being this far away from them… I hated it. I thought it would be okay if I were with Romano, but I was wrong. That hunger only increased and my desire to turn into another person was all-consuming. My hands shook as I scratched down my arm.

"You. Promised." A single tear dripped down my cheek.

"Romeo, dinner," Romano barked, and the car made a sudden left turn, following his command. "I think it's time I treated you to a nice meal before we head home."

"I want to go home now."

He ignored me, returning his attention to his phone.

"*You promised,*" I whispered against the glass.

A moment later, we pulled up outside an Italian restaurant and Romano's crew ushered us inside. It was a small family-owned pizzeria, empty, but it smelled like heaven. Romeo pulled out a chair for me at one of the linen-covered tables off to one side of the room.

"*Ciao, amico*. How's the family?" Romano asked while pulling an elderly man in for a hug and kissing each of his cheeks. They carried on in Italian, ignoring me as I watched them.

My left hand dipped between my thighs, my right scratching my nails from elbow to wrist. Over and over, each stroke harsher than the last. I was crawling out of my skin and the repetitive action helped ease the ache. I rocked slightly, my teeth clattering as I faded out, no longer paying attention to whatever was going on around me. Focusing only on that need pulsing through my veins. The wildfire of urges that came straight from hell and burned me up from the inside out.

"Kennedy." Romeo squeezed my shoulder, pulling me back to reality.

Everyone was smiling at me. Expectant. Waiting. I stood from the chair, realizing Romano was motioning for me to come to him. He introduced me to the old man, who praised Romano on such a beautiful bride.

Beautiful?

I scoffed at the thought. If only they could see the true ugliness that blossomed beneath this painted veneer. I'd been told I was pretty all my life, but beauty was only skin deep. And that skin wanted to melt off my bones.

"She's shy! My, *che premio!*" The old man laughed, slapping Romano's back. "Sit. I get you the special!"

"Sit, Kennedy," Romano repeated, his patience with me clearly dwindling.

And I use the word *patience* sparsely. The man had patience for nothing. He didn't like to wait. He wanted things done his way or you bled. And you better not cross him. Romano was a possessive man. So much so that once I was in his sights, *free* was no longer in my vocabulary. I'd seen firsthand just what happened to people who displeased him.

The three men shared a meal together, chatting like old friends, laughing and rambling on in Italian—dissociating me. It was amusing how Romano was head of the Italian mob in Philly… but he wasn't even full-blooded Italian. Which just went to show you the man refused to let anything stand in his way. If he wanted something, he got it.

I finished my meal—it was damn good too—but well after my stomach bulged from overconsumption, the hunger was still there.

It never went away.

We said our goodbyes and Romano opened the car door for me. A moment later, we pulled away from the curb and disappeared into traffic.

"Now where?" I asked, only to be met by silence.

I wasn't an idiot. The man wanted me for one thing. And, sadly, it wasn't for what sat tight and wet between my thighs. Yes, he indulged in it, often, but that wasn't why I was here.

He could give me as many pleasantries as he could afford. But it wasn't pussy that kept a man like Romano Bianchi locked down. It was power. And I was the key to that power. The ring on my finger was the sign of my ownership, and Romano would never let me go until he bled me dry.

The car ride was silent, something I preferred. Kennedy often got lost in her head, which kept her mute. It worked for me. I didn't need idle chitchat to fill the void.

Now, don't get me wrong. Kennedy was far from dumb. She was smart enough to know her place and her purpose. On my arm, as the bullet I was loading into my chamber.

We were getting ready to leave New York, the first part of my plan going off without a hitch. The look on Octavia's face told me she'd squeal to her family about her little run-in with me.

It wouldn't be long before Carmine was going to release her and set the rest into motion. The girl was a damaged little bird, like his precious sister. He needed to watch his back, because when I learned he was fucking with my plans to go after Mario, Eva was next on my list. Instead, I stumbled upon Kennedy, and as they say, that story told itself. I wanted Mario on the edge of the plank I was forcing him to walk across. At first, my sights were set on the eldest Agostino daughter but then Sienna had to go and fuck with that idea too.

Honestly, I never saw Apollo's kid coming. For all I knew, the bastard was celibate. I mean, you didn't usually have a harem of women waiting around for you when you were that fucked up in the head. Real life wasn't nothing like that dark romance, chic-lit shit. He really would kill a bitch on her knees, just 'cause.

"Stop it." I snatched up Kennedy's wrist and inspected her arm, my eyes following the trail of scars and marks. "Look at what you're doing to yourself. Enough," I grunted before tossing her hand aside.

"Where are we going?" she asked again, and I ignored her, tapping away on my cell phone. "Romano." Her tone was harsh, yet still sweet. My little submissive.

"I have a present for you." I watched her eyes light up before adding, "But you have to stay in the car." They quickly dimmed.

Like I said, she wasn't dumb.

The car entered the parking lot for the hospital right as Carmine and Diego walked through the front door. Pulling around the side, we idled by the rear entrance. I motioned Kennedy to come closer and she leaned over my lap as I pointed towards the window.

"What?" I shushed her, telling her to be patient.

As the minutes ticked by, Kennedy's body tensed as she leaned over my lap. She was growing impatient, wondering what the big surprise was. Then, just as she was about to give up, two men came walking out from the rear exit.

"Look, Kennedy," I said. "The man in all black is your adopted brother, Apollo." She gulped, her eyes wide. "And the one in the white shirt? He's your blood brother, Lucky."

"My brothers?" Her questioning tone told me she didn't believe me. As the odd pairing drew closer, I rolled up the window to keep us hidden. Lucky quickly glanced in our direction as he passed. He couldn't see inside, but Kennedy's gasp told me she'd seen him all right. More specifically, she'd seen the blue-steel eyes that matched her own.

Mario Agostino was a piece of shit, the kind of man who used people until he didn't need them anymore. Something I should have been pleased to say we had in common. Because I sure as fuck wouldn't lose sleep over the truth I was about to reveal.

Family was everything to him or so he claimed.

My mother was all I had and she'd been dead for over a decade. Something told me he wouldn't remember her, but I'd remembered enough for the both of us. Whether he admitted it or not, her death was on his hands while his long-lost daughter would be the means I'd used to remind him.

Kennedy wasn't just my wife anymore. The girl would be my rifle and I was a fully trained sniper. I'd put the fucker in my sights, and when the moment was right, my bullet would send him six-feet under.

Mario, you're already in range of my scope.

It didn't matter if whatever happened next drew his attention, because I had one hand on the trigger. And I couldn't wait to see his brains explode. He was my soon-to-be father-in-law and I wanted to show him the same courtesy that he'd shown my family.

Don't you worry, Mario. I'll lick the sweet tears off your daughter's face right before I fuck her next to your corpse.

Gioco finito, Papà.

About the Author

Corporate sales by day, closet romance novelist at night—Dahlia Reign has always had an unparalleled taste for dreamy alpha-men. In her youth, Dahlia had journals by the stacks that she used to jot down her innermost thoughts; subsequently, turning them into romantic stories. Now, years later and with her picturesque alpha-man at her side, she's taken the literary world by storm. Her man, her pittie and an overactive imagination mixed with her bleeding heart—she's set off to tell the world her stories. Buck up and grab a bandaid, shit's about to get heavy.

www.TheDahliaReign.com

facebook.com/authordahliareign

instagram.com/authordahliareign

tiktok.com/@authordahliareign

ALSO BY DAHLIA REIGN

<u>Agostino Crime Family Series</u>

Contracted to the Devil: Book One

Clever as the Devil: Book Two

Beautiful Deception: Book Three

And Twice as Twisted: Book Four

Bittersweet Revenge: Book Five

<u>La Reina de Escorpiones Duet</u>

Infinite Sorrow: Book One

Endless Deceit: Book Two

<u>Standalones</u>

The Sins of Our Father

www.TheDahliaReign.com